Those Jordan Girls

Also by Joan M. Drury

The Other Side of Silence
Silent Words
Closed in Silence

Those Jordan Girls

Joan M. Drury

Spinsters Ink

Duluth, Minnesota

USA

First edition published June 2000
10-9-8-7-6-5-4-3-2

Spinsters Ink
32 E. First St., #330
Duluth, MN 55802-2002
USA

Cover art and photography by Kathy Kruger, Whistling Mouse Illustration & Design

Production:

Liz Brissett	Claire Kirch
Charlene Brown	Jean Nygaard
Helen Dooley	Kim Riordan
Joan Drury	Amy Strasheim
Tracy Gilsvik	Liz Tufte
Marian Hunstiger	Nancy Walker
Kelly Kager	

Library of Congress Cataloging-in-Publication Data
Drury, Joan M., 1945–
   Those Jordan Girls / by Joan M. Drury — 1st ed.
   p.   cm.
   ISBN 1-883523-36-2 (alk.paper)
     1. Mothers and daughters—Fiction. 2. Women political activists—Fiction. 3.
Minnesota—Fiction. 4. Feminists—Fiction. I. Title.

PS3554.R827 T48 2000
813'.54—dc21   00-026516

Printed in Canada on recycled paper

Acknowledgements

E ndless gratitude to all the good people in my life who make my work possible: my editor, Kelly Kager, who did an extraordinary job of "midwifing" (in her own words) this book, leading me to those final stretches; my copyeditor, Charlene Brown, who did the final scrutiny, catching all that everyone else missed; everyone at Spinsters Ink, who not only did a fine job of producing this book but always make it possible for me to find time to write—Zad Walker, Claire Kirch, Marian Hunstiger, and Liz Tufte; the women who maintain Norcroft: A Writing Retreat for Women and also buy me time—Tracy Gilsvik, Kay Grindland, and Willie Williamson; my assistant, Jean Nygaard, who helped with the research, as did Tracy Gilsvik; Roberta Cole, Virginia Henrikson, and Karen Blackburn who take care of the myriad financial details of my complex life; Paul Eckhardt (who is NOT the butler-who-did-it) and Ria Reis, who both keep the clutter and distraction to a minimum (doing an admirable job of keeping me from cleaning instead of writing); Deb & Ron and the rest of their crew; Irving and crew; plus all the volunteers and interns and contract workers and sometime-workers at Spinsters and Norcroft and Drury Enterprises.

I also have to thank my co-conspirators/co-residents at Norcroft—women who listened to my work, my problems, my hopes, and were unfailingly sympathetic, encouraging, and pushy: Sibyl Johnson, Ting Ting Cheng, Maria Fire, Lisa Groshong, Dory Lynch, Shirley Bostrom, Rosalva Hernandez, Clare Hanrahan. And resident Jackie Mimranek, who gave me a phrase that shows up in this book.

My life and work wouldn't be possible without my *family*— blood and otherwise—who give me ideas, challenge me, and just plain sustain me with constant support, laughter, touch, love: Allie, Mirranda, Kevin, Scooter, Karie, Kelly, Marilyn, Rita and Diane, P.J., Deb and Tom, Arlinda, Barb and Lynn, Sue and Ellen, Jill and John, Miriam and Emmie, Therese, Tim and Leslie, Katherine, Shevy and Ruth, Rosalie, Doug, Kim and Pam, Tom and Marcia, Libby, Nancy and Joe, Betsy, Prudy, Marcia and Hazel, Ruth and Judith, Nancy and Roger, Karen and Ellen, Mary Lou and Bev, Margot, the book club women, the Center for Family Crisis women, and all the others I'm overlooking or forgetting.

A special thanks to the four friends who let me read this book to them as it was being written, waiting impatiently during the long hiatuses between some chapters (when I was finishing another book, for instance), and also to my first readers, invariably thorough, helpful, and annoying (*you want me to what?*)— Pamela Mittlefehldt, Marilyn Crawford, Arlinda Keeley, Nancy Gruver, Paula Barish, Mimi Wheatwind—as well as some others.

I am indebted to a handful of books responsible for "putting me in the place" as well as enlarging my knowledge: *A Prairie Populist:*

The Memoirs of Luna Kellie, edited by Jane Taylor Nelson; *Crusaders: The Radical Legacy of Marian and Arthur Le Sueur* by Meridel Le Sueur; *Eyes on the Prize* by Juan Williams; *Jailed for Freedom: American Women Win the Vote* by Doris Stevens, edited by Carol O'Hare; *Labor and Desire: Women's Revolutionary Fiction in Depression America* by Paula Rabinowitz; *Minnesota in a Century of Change: The State and Its People since 1900,* edited by Clifford E. Clark, Jr.; *Open Country, Iowa: Rural Women, Tradition and Change* by Deborah Fink; *The Political Career of Floyd B. Olson* by George Mayer; *The Progressive Era in Minnesota: 1899-1918* by Carl H. Chrislock; and *Visible Women: New Essays on American Activism,* edited by Nancy A. Hewitt and Suzanne Lebsock.

Boundless appreciation to my grandmother, Bertha Kamrar Houghtaling, who died before I was born, but whose stories, passed down to me, inspired so much of this book. And to my other grandmother, Luella Blamton Drury, whom I did know a little and whose strength of character and determination also inspired this book.

I can't leave out Kaye Gibbons and Marleen Gorris. Kaye's lovely book, *Charms for the Easy Life,* got me started down this road, and Gorris's astounding film, *Antonia's Line,* kept me moving. If you've not read or seen these two fine works, I exhort you to do so!

Thanks also to my characters who feverishly took hold of me and would not let go until I got it right.

And finally, thanks to my readers—those of you who return and return to my books and those of you who are coming for the first time: you make it all possible! And remember, even though this is a work of fiction—**every word is true.**

To
my grandmothers:
Bertha Kamrar Houghtaling
whose stories inspired this novel
and Luella Blamton Drury
whose indomitable spirit resides in this novel
and
to
my granddaughters:
Mirranda Lynn and Allie Marie
who bestowed upon me
the wondrous gift of
grandmotherhood.

1

Those Jordan Girls
Never Did Want
Anything to Do with Sex

The story about Gummie that always got the most attention was the one about her never having had sex with her husband. Of course, everyone always wanted to know then, how I—her great-granddaughter—had come about, but actually, that was the easy part. The hard part was: was it true? My grandmother was adopted, so it was possible, you see, to have subsequent generations without sex. Was it possible, however, to be married—and what appeared to be happily married—for fifty-five years without sex? Or could it be, I wondered as I grew older and wiser, they were happy *because* there was no sex?

I was about ten when I first heard the story. It wasn't meant for my ears. I accidentally overheard the man who had fathered me—a man I hardly knew because my mother had never married him

1

and he rarely had anything to do with me even though we lived in the same small town and consequently ran into one another on occasion—telling another man it was amazing I'd ever been born at all because "you know, those Jordan girls never did want anything to do with sex."

"That so?" the other man inquired back.

My father, deep in his cups (as they used to say) even though it was no more than 10:30 in the morning, nodded solemnly and said, "You know, that old Iris never did have sex with her Hubert. Everyone knows that. Her kids were adopted." Iris was my great-grandmother, *Gummie* to me and my mother. "Then her daughter, Hester? She only had the one kid," that one kid being my mother, "so who knows how much sex she ever allowed?"

The two men were sitting on the rear steps of the liquor store, and I was lingering in the bushes by the back of the property, scratching my dog Jack's ears so she wouldn't get restless. I hadn't planned to eavesdrop. We had just been gamboling along the alley when I heard that first statement drifting over the hedge and it, naturally, piqued my interest—my *being* one of "those Jordan girls."

"I fathered that puny kid, Maddie . . ." my father puffed out at this statement as though it were some sort of amazing accomplishment while I bristled. I definitely did *not* like being called puny, and many boys in the fourth grade rued the day they referred to me in such a manner. ". . . and as far as I know, Jane has never had sex with any man since me."

The other man leaned over and said something low in the ear of the man who was my father, and both of them guffawed as I crept away, turning this information over and over in my head. I knew all about sex. It was 1962, after all, and most ten-year-olds knew something about sex. What I mean to say is I *really* knew about sex because my mother was very "modern" and thought children should know they could count on their mothers to discuss anything with them. I also knew Gramma—the woman he called Hester—had been adopted. So, I guessed it was possible.

That evening after supper, when Mom and I went for our usual walk in the slightly cooler air of coming dusk—Minnesota summers being unbearably hot and humid—I asked her about what I'd heard.

She laughed. "Oh, that Roman, he just likes to talk."

"So it's not true?" I asked. "About Gummie, I mean?"

She hummed a little, the way she did when she was thinking about how to tell me something, a habit she'd picked up from Gummie.

"Well, Maddie, I don't know for certain. That part might be true. Even though it's pretty hard to believe, I *have* heard it before. My mother once told me Gummie'd had a hysterectomy before she and Guppie were married. She insisted that, in those days, they just sewed you right up, so you couldn't have sex."

I pondered this for a few minutes as the swish-swish of sprinklers sliced through the hot night air and screen doors slammed while kids ran out for one more jaunt before bedtime. "Sewed you up?" I ventured. "You mean . . ." Of course, you'd get sewed up after surgery, I thought, so this must mean something else. "You mean they sewed her vagina up?"

Mom shrugged. "Something like that. I think it's the vaginal walls, actually, but Maddie, I don't really know if that's true. Except your grandmother was a nurse, so she *should* know."

We walked in silence for a few minutes as a dark, moist heat enveloped us. The occasional bark of a neighbor dog—causing my dog Jack to prick up her ears—joined the increasingly loud cacophony of the night critters: the tree frogs and crickets and hungry mosquitoes. Bats whooshed overhead, and moths batted themselves against lit window screens, joined by the random plonking of June bugs.

"And the rest?" I didn't feel quite comfortable asking her directly about her own sex life. The truth is, I'd not thought about it before I'd heard Roman's words. It had not occurred to me that my mother never did seem to date anyone. It wasn't like she was an old dried-up prune or something. Even though, at nearly thirty, she seemed pretty old to me, I knew she wasn't *really* old, especially compared to Gramma, who was fifty-two and Gummie, who was eighty-nine that summer.

Mom hummed some more before answering. "I don't know about my mother and father. She wasn't very old when he left." She paused. "I just don't know, Maddie. I doubt there's any reason to believe she and he didn't have a fully enjoyable married life." I knew she meant "sex" by that odd phrase. "After he left, there never was anyone else for her. No one I knew of, anyway. George broke her heart—partly because he didn't confine his loving to home and partly because he left her. And there were me and the boarders and her nursing. She never took time, or risk maybe, for other relationships. I guess she just concentrated her loving on me. And then you."

I wondered if that was true for her, too. I knew the circumstances were different—Roman had not left Mom like Gramma's husband had, and her heart was not broken in the least. I knew Mom had chosen him in order to get me—and no more.

"As for me . . ." More humming before she continued, as her feet beat a steady rhythm on the ground. "I enjoy sex, Maddie, and I just don't think there's much more that needs to be said. I'm not certain I think it entirely appropriate a mother and daughter—until such daughter is fully grown—converse about such things."

I knew that was all she was going to say on the subject because she always used this formal and almost archaic language when she didn't want to talk about something but also didn't want me to feel like I couldn't ask her anything. However, I was very aware of the way she'd said, "I enjoy sex," definitely in the present tense. Making it sound like, maybe, she was having some. Such a thought shocked me and then embarrassed me because I felt the daughter of my mother and the great-granddaughter of Iris Jordan—both rather shocking women—shouldn't be shocked by such a revelation. I was, nonetheless. I mean, really, how was she getting sex? Sneaking around, meeting men away from the house? I finally decided I had heard that statement wrong and attempted to dismiss it. I didn't really forget it, though.

These nightly promenades began earlier than my memory, but the routine apparently remained the same. Mom always washed the dinner dishes, then went for a walk—regardless of weather. When I was a baby, Mom would put me in the buggy that had been hers when she was an infant, piling on—or peeling off—whatever layers the temperatures demanded. She would push me down the sidewalk, cooing and humming, singing and talking to me. Unless it was winter, in which case she would maneuver the buggy onto the street, the sidewalks being unreliably cleared, and her verbal soothings, being blunted by the amount of clothing between us, were replaced with a certain amount of jiggling and swaying of the buggy itself.

As soon as I was old enough to object to the pram, we both walked. Although these walks were initially shorter, they eventually stretched out as my legs stretched out.

I did not know, in those early years, that our nightly ritual was something of a forced march. Gramma did, though, and voiced objections in a variety of situations, most of them involving inclement weather conditions.

"That child's gonna catch her death! You can skip your walk once in a while, Jane!"

Mom would attempt to deflect Gramma's criticisms with responses such as, "A little fresh air never hurt anyone, Mom. Madelaine and I are perfectly healthy," or "I know it's raining, Mom. What are we? Sugar cubes? We're not going to melt, you know," or "I sit at a desk all day, Mother, my body needs to be able to count on a little exercise at the end of the day."

I was never certain, as I grew older, if our walks were more about Mom being a precursor of the fitness movement or simply her way of assuring a little uninterrupted time alone between the two of us each day. Either way, I was pleased and eager to join her. I do remember the time she tartly told Gramma, at the end of one of Gramma's tirades against our walks, "Mom, I like our living arrangements very much, but—you know—Madelaine and I could just go and live by ourselves somewhere, if it's too difficult for you to allow me to make my own decisions about her welfare." I remember this statement so well because I felt a stab of anxiety, hearing it. Gramma apparently felt the same way, as all protests regarding our evening constitutional immediately ceased and were never voiced again, to my memory.

And so we walked, no matter what the climatological condition. If it were a warm rain, we strolled through it unprotected—and I was allowed to stomp delightedly through puddles. If it were a cold rain, we dressed warmer and—when we got home—stripped off our soaked clothing, vigorously toweling ourselves down, gladly accepting the mugs of hot chocolate Gramma had prepared for us, and gratefully climbing into a steaming hot tub. Cold never deterred us, just demanded more layers and less talk. The only exigencies I remember ever being an excuse for abandoning our nightly ritual were if one of us were truly sick (sniffles didn't count) or if there were a thunderstorm or a blizzard, obviously curtailing our safety.

Otherwise, we walked every night. I had no idea our saunters

were mandatory—so eager was I to join my mother each night—
until I was older and tried to squirm out of them occasionally.

"I don't think I'll go tonight, Mom, I've got too much homework."

She'd just say, "I'm waiting, Maddie."

"Did you hear me, Mom? I've got to work on my science project."

"I heard you, Maddie, and I'm still waiting. You'll have time."

Later, I might try, "I don't feel well, Mom. I just got my period.
You go without me tonight."

"I'm waiting, Maddie."

"Mom!"

"Best thing for cramps is exercise. Get your sweater, Maddie."

It eventually became something of a challenge for me, to find a
way to weasel out of our walks. Mom never *ordered* me to go, she
never *told* me I had no choice. She would just stand by the front
door and wait, of course informing me that she was waiting, and
I always gave in.

Except for the coldest months when the sound of our voices was
too muffled by layers of wrapped scarving, we generally talked on
these walks—sharing the events, or lack thereof, of our day and
exploring the varied mysteries of life—"Why do mosquitoes want
our blood? How many stars are there? How come Mrs. Ostrander
looks the other way when you say 'good evening' to her? Where
do babies come from? How come you don't have any more?"—
such questions growing increasingly complex as my understanding broadened.

Usually on warm summer evenings, Gummie and Gramma
would be on the porch waiting for our return, unless it was
Gramma's Sewing Circle night—she met with the other ladies
every Wednesday night. Mom called it her Stitch and Bitch
Circle, and Gramma sternly admonished her not to use such
language in her house, not without a twinkle in her eye.

Gummie might be in bed already. As she approached ninety, she was generally worn out by the end of her demanding days at the newspaper office, especially in the summer when the heat lay like smothering quilts over our town, making you want to kick them off and feel stifled when you couldn't.

I was born in 1952 and was the fourth generation of those Jordan girls. My great-grandmother, Iris Jordan, had been born in 1873. When I was born, she was seventy-nine years old and still living with her husband, Hubert, the man who gave us our last name and whom my mother and I called *Guppie*. They'd been married for fifty-five years when Hubert died in 1960.

"He was a good man," Gummie said, "good" being the highest praise she'd bestow on anyone, "a bit quiet, but a good man. A man of rare and immense integrity." I grew up knowing "integrity" and "good" were two of the most important words in the English language.

Then Gummie moved in with us: my grandmother, Hester Emma Jordan Thoreson; my mother, Jane Ann Jordan; and myself, Madelaine Iris Jordan. Hester'd been named thusly because one of Gummie's favorite books was *The Scarlet Letter* by Nathaniel Hawthorne. Gummie, as was her way, interpreted the book somewhat differently than most people and named her daughter Hester in the hopes she would grow up to be a free thinker, as brave and unconventional as Hester Prynne. Her middle name, Emma, was after Emma Goldman, a free thinker—anarchist, champion of birth control, suffragist, publisher—who Gummie'd met once and admired greatly because she wasn't afraid to be imprisoned for her beliefs. Gramma was determined to fulfill her own destiny, however, which was to be *nothing* like Hester Prynne or Emma Goldman, and lived a life quite the opposite of her rather wild and original mother's life and expectations of her.

Although her mother had insisted she get an education, Gramma got married the minute she graduated from nursing school. "To an absolutely gorgeous and utterly useless man," Gummie always intoned unemotionally.

"He wasn't *entirely* useless," my mother would slyly remonstrate at Gummie's statement. "Don't forget, he did have *something* to do with producing me."

"Humph," Gummie would snort, a quirky smile tugging at the corners of her mouth. "Precious little, I would think; still, you do have a point, Jane." This gorgeous-but-useless man, "that odious man," Gummie usually called him, left my grandmother by the time she was thirty, and Gummie would say, perhaps a little too often, "Aren't you glad I made you get your education?"

Hester got a nursing job to support herself and her seven-year-old daughter rather than move back in with her mother. Gummie would always laugh when she got to this part of the story, saying, "That girl never did understand! It's supposed to be mothers disapproving of daughters, not the other way around."

Oddly enough, even though Gramma clearly didn't fulfill the promise and hope implicit in her name, she named her own daughter with the same kind of intentions: *Jane Ann* was chosen with the vision of a quiet, well-behaved, obedient daughter. Naturally, Gramma had as much luck with her daughter as Gummie had had with hers. Although my mother was decidedly quiet and well-behaved, she broke the biggest rule of all: get married or don't have children.

So I was born, *out of wedlock,* when my mother was just nineteen. "Nineteen going on thirty-nine," Gummie always insisted. "Jane was *born* an adult."

Gummie applauded Mom's independence and courage. I was named Madelaine—"Just because I liked it," Mom said—

Madelaine Iris Jordan. Mom changed her own last name to Jordan at that point, too.

"Why are you doing this?" Hester wailed, horrified her only daughter was doing everything she could to make the neighbors talk, as if it hadn't been bad enough having been raised by a mother like hers and then having been the recipient, she was quite certain, of pity for the years during which her husband had openly run about with other women, finally abandoning her.

"Mom," Jane shook her head, "why should I use the name Thoreson when that man deserted you and me? I'm certainly not going to give his name to Madelaine, so I might as well change mine, also. You should, too. Why would you want to continue using his name?"

"I never," Hester declared and refused to comply, though she might as well have, since *everyone* thought of us as *those Jordan girls* anyway, practically forgetting Gramma had ever been married at all.

As soon as I was born, Mom got a loan from Gummie, left me with Gummie's day helper, Sylvie, and went to college. Even though Hester was mortified and uncomfortable that my mother would have a baby without the benefit of marriage—"Like the *benefit* of marriage did *you* so much good, Mother," Jane would point out—they actually liked each other a lot, and we continued to live with Gramma.

When Mom graduated from college and got a job at the library, Gramma quit her job and became what she'd always wanted to be: a full-time homemaker. Then, in 1960, our household opened up to include Gummie, and our fate was forever sealed as *those Jordan girls*.

2

An Uncommon Woman

It wasn't common for girls to attend college in 1890, but then Iris—at seventeen—was already an uncommon woman. And, as she made clear to me over the years, there always have been plenty of women who choose uncommon lives. I've seen the picture of her taken on the day she left for college. She was wearing a high-collared white blouse with a barely noticeable ruffle at her throat and a long, plain, inky skirt, flared slightly at the hem. Her dark hair was piled on her head, something like a Gibson-girl style, only firmer, more severe. She was not smiling. "It was not the vogue to smile in photos in those days," she told me once when I asked her why she looked so solemn. Her head was held high; her eyes had something of a fire in them; she was regal and imposing, formidable actually, and very beautiful in an austere manner.

She was one of four daughters born to Jon and Hannah

Herrington. This great-great-grandfather of mine lost his farm in the volatile economy of the 1870s. He always blamed it on the banking/railroad monopolies, which led him to focus his attention on the swelling agrarian activism of the times. He became a leading organizer of the Populist Party, an outgrowth of the earlier Farmers' Alliance. After losing the farm, he and Hannah moved to town—a village in southern Minnesota—and got jobs at a newly built hotel. At first, Hannah worked in the kitchen while Jon did maintenance.

"He was not really inclined toward working," Gummie would say. "My father probably did not lose his farm because of banking or railroad monopolies, although unfair practices certainly existed. He more than likely lost it because he was not much of a farmer. He was a dreamer who preferred complaining to hard work. Most of his attention went toward meetings and organizing. Even though that's honorable and necessary work, it's not always responsible if one has a family." Then she would sigh and press her lips together while shaking her head slightly from side to side.

"What it meant was, Mama had to take up the slack; she had to make certain the family was housed, fed, and clothed. Luckily, she was capable of doing such. In very little time, Papa was no longer working at the hotel while Mama was put in charge of the kitchen and, eventually, the whole hotel. She wasn't actually called the manager or anything. She was, after all, a mere woman. Still, the owner could clearly see how smart and competent she was, what fine organizational abilities she had, and so he leaned heavily on her skills without giving her an actual title to go with the work she was doing.

"Nor did she get paid what she should have been paid. She did, however, threaten to leave if the owner didn't provide housing for the family, and there was no question about her employer risking losing her. So, Papa was able to attend to his *much-more-important* political activities while Mama stayed in the background, making the living quietly so Papa wouldn't be humiliated by her being the breadwinner."

"Didn't this make her mad?" I'd inquire. I always thought it would make me furious, especially later, when I was an adult and more fully understood the implications of Mama and Papa's story.

Gummie would tilt her head back, gazing up at the fully leafed elm trees in our front yard and sigh again before answering. "Not much, I guess. I think she was angry sometimes, but she also just accepted her lot in life. She did agree with him politically, and she knew *he* could be more productive as a reformer—few being willing to accept a woman as a leader—so she accepted her role as the behind-the-scenes supporter. I've known lots of marriages like this, over the years."

I would wrinkle my nose and scrunch my brow up, thinking I wouldn't much like my great-great-grandfather, and Gummie would laugh at my expression. "Yes, Maddie, it was unjust, and Papa was, at best, annoying. On the other hand, his self-centeredness ended up providing me with an incredible role model: my mother's life made it clear to me that women can do anything."

"You and Guppie didn't have a marriage like that, did you?"

She would shake her head and smile merrily, the way she usually did when talking of her husband. "Oh no! We were both ambitious and committed to causes and work. Neither of us was a shirker."

Hannah moved her husband and three remaining daughters— the eldest, Violet, had already married and moved to Minneapolis—into the hotel. The girls were all expected to help in the summer months but not while attending school. Hannah had been a schoolteacher before she married, and she valued education above everything. She wanted her daughters to nurture and expand their intelligence.

There were four Herrington girls, their ages spread out over a twenty-year period. Violet was born the year Jon returned from the Civil War, 1865; Iris was next in 1873; Dahlia—always called Dolly—arrived in 1880; and the youngest, Pansy, brought up the rear in 1885. There had been a half dozen miscarriages, stillbirths, and early deaths between the girls. Violet had been married a full two years when Pansy was born.

There was also a portrait of the family, including all except Violet, taken that year Iris left for college. Iris was wearing the same clothing she had worn in her own picture; perhaps the two portraits were even taken the same day. In the center, Papa was standing behind Mama, who was sitting on a chair. He was tall and serious, a large, droopy moustache obscuring his mouth. His hand rested on Mama's shoulder. Her clothing was similar to Iris's, but her body was stouter and shorter than those of her tall daughters, and there was a resigned tiredness about her eyes (or else I imagined it, who knows?), which made me feel sorry for her.

Iris was on one side of them with a book clasped to her bosom, an affectation I'm sure she decided upon herself, and Dolly stood on the other side of them. Her demeanor was as serious at ten as her big sister's at seventeen, but one could already discern the beauty intended for her. Heavily lashed eyes, too big for her petite face, would be arresting, no doubt, later in her life. Five-year-old Pansy sat on her mother's lap, two fingers in her mouth, seeming to hold back the smile that struggled to escape.

"Can you imagine?" Gummie would bellow, reciting these stories, over and over. "Naming a child *Pansy*? I swear, it made her one. She was the weakest, the silliest of us all! A complete ninny! *Violet* and *Iris* and *Dahlia* were bad enough but at least had some strength, some passion."

"Dahlia was never called by her full name, was she?" I'd ask, as I knew I was supposed to.

"Oh no, she was Dolly almost from the beginning. I didn't like the name Dahlia, so I just called her Dolly, and it stuck. Mother's desires were rarely equal to mine."

I would smile at this statement. Even as a small child, I couldn't imagine *anyone's* desires being equal to Gummie's. She was so sure of herself and so fiercely forthright, I was—as most people seemed to be—quite terrified of her until I became more cognizant of her equally fierce affection for me. "It seems to me Dolly could've been kind of a lightweight, too, with a name like that, couldn't she?" I, of course, knew she wasn't.

"Dolly wasn't quite the silly name in the 1800s as one might view it now," Gummie would explain to me. "*Our* Dolly was definitely not a lightweight."

Both Violet and Dolly were dead before I was born, but I was thirteen when Pansy died, at the age of eighty. Gummie was ninety-two the year Pansy died, still going to work every day, although she'd cut down to shorter days by then. At least, *some* days were shorter.

Aunt Dolly—"the most beautiful, the most talented, the most intelligent of us all"—was also the most mysterious. She died at fifty-three, and I could never find out why or how.

"Gummie, why did Dolly die so young? Was she ill? Did she have an accident? What?"

This remarkable great-grandmother, who always thoroughly answered my questions with candor, who talked to me about subjects generally thought of as inappropriate for children, would never answer this question. "She just died, Maddie. People do, you know."

"But Gummie, was she sick?"

Gummie would press her lips together and repeat, with a little emphasis on each word, clearly indicating finality, "She just died."

I bothered both my mother and grandmother about Dolly's demise, but neither of them had any information or wouldn't give it to me if they did. Honestly, I didn't think they knew. My mom was so scrupulously honest with me, I was sure she would've told me if she knew anything.

Gramma would say, "Why do you want to know about all that old stuff, Maddie? It's ancient history."

"Gramma," I would object, "it's *our* family. I just want to know everything."

She'd shrug. "Well, maybe I'm not so interested as you because I was adopted." She'd pause in her sweeping or baking or dusting and stare out the window, thinking about this for a moment or two before continuing her activity.

"Gramma! You were around when Dolly died. Surely you must know what happened." I had already calculated the years. Dolly had died in 1933; Gramma was twenty-three.

"I was busy with my own life," she'd respond. "I got married and had Jane that year. I don't remember anything about it. She just died," she echoed Gummie's words.

I was momentarily sidetracked. "You got married and had a baby the same year?"

Gramma's eyes narrowed at me, and she said, "Don't get fresh with me, young lady. We were married in January, and Jane was born in November. There was no funny business about any of it."

I nodded, almost disappointed. Gramma's life seemed so circumspect, the most exciting part of it was the husband who ditched her. "Weren't you curious about how Dolly died, Gramma? You were a nurse, after all."

She shrugged, resuming her chores. "You are a pest, you know that, Maddie? No, I wasn't curious. She was dead, that was all there was to it." Her face softened a moment. "I was crazy about George. Then Jane came . . ." She stopped, gazing into the past for a minute or two again. "Plus, Gummie was not particularly happy with me that year, so I . . ." she faltered a moment, then said quietly, "I was just concentrating on my own little family, I guess."

After a moment's silence, Gramma added, "First Jordie died. Then I got married. Mom wasn't happy. About anything. She didn't like George, and she thought we should've waited longer. But I'd waited long enough." There was an unfamiliar spark of anger in her eyes. "We exchanged words . . ."

When she didn't continue, I filled in, "You and Gummie had a fight?"

She nodded somberly, then her face eased into a grin. "Oh yes, a real doozy. We didn't talk for months."

"You didn't?" I was astounded, not being able to imagine members of this highly verbal family not talking to one another.

She shook her head. "Nope. It was a relief, actually. We needed a break from each other."

"What happened to get you talking again? Dolly's death?"

"No, we still weren't talking during that time. I went to the funeral, of course, and talked to Dad, but your gummie and I did not say a word to each other. No, not Dolly's death. What changed everything was Jane's arrival. Babies tend to heal most things."

"When you did start talking again, didn't you ask what had happened to Dolly? Or ask Guppie?"

"No, we just sort of picked up like new. Like the previous year or so hadn't actually happened."

I couldn't imagine her lack of curiosity. Even though, at ten or eleven, I thought fiftyish was rather old, I was still smart enough to know it was too young to die, especially in a family in which almost everyone lived to venerable old ages.

Then I would natter at my mother. She, at least, shared my

inquisitiveness. "I don't know, Maddie. No one ever talked about it. I always wondered, too, when I was younger, but could never get anyone to tell me anything."

Once I even asked Aunt Pansy. She looked alarmed and shouted—she was increasingly deaf and so assumed no one could hear her because she couldn't hear herself—"Who?"

"Dolly!" I shouted back. "Your sister! Dolly! How did she die?"

"Is she dead?" Pansy responded. "Are you sure she's dead? Wasn't she just here?"

"That was Iris! I'm asking about Dolly! The one who died during the depression! Remember? The one who never got married!" I was talking fast because Gummie'd just gone to the bathroom, and I sensed she wouldn't appreciate my questioning Pansy like this.

Pansy drew back from me like I was crazy and said, "Dolly was married! What are you talking about? Who are you, anyway?" She was always a little vague the last years of her life, and I gave up.

When I next had a chance, I asked Gummie if Dolly had ever been married. I thought she'd never married, had spent her life pining for Hubert, who chose Gummie over her.

"Why would you ask me that?" Gummie responded. I was startled. This was highly unusual of her, to be evasive in any way.

"Because Pansy told me Dolly was married. Was she?"

"Oh Pansy." She dismissed her sister. "She doesn't make much sense these days. She thought I was Violet the other day."

I stared at Gummie in growing astonishment. She was clearly avoiding answering me, and I couldn't ever remember this happening before. "Gummie, what's going on? Why aren't you answering me?"

She frowned, then said, "You're just a little too sharp, do you know that?" I smiled because I knew she liked it that I was a "little too sharp," and she smiled back. "Okay. Yes. Dolly was married. Supposedly. Are you satisfied now?"

"No," I answered. "Aren't you going to tell me about it? What do you mean—'supposedly?' And while you're at it," I added rather tartly, "you might tell me about her death, too."

Then, Gummie did something I'd almost never seen her do before—she got truly angry at me. She didn't shout or strike me or anything similar. Instead, she pressed her mouth together in such a thin line her lips almost disappeared, and the frown that was perpetually between her eyes—"my thinking frown," she always called it—deepened, and she said in a hard and tight voice I don't think I'd ever heard before, "The so-called marriage was brief and didn't really count. If you remember, young lady, I already told you: *Dolly just died.* Enough, Madelaine Iris Jordan. I want to hear no more of this."

That anger so startled me, I complied completely, not mentioning Dolly's marriage or death again to Gummie. It did not, however, stop me from wondering about it. In fact, it exacerbated my interest. I would turn it over and over in my head, talking about it endlessly with my best friend, Annie Rees, until she'd insist, "Stop! You're boring me to pieces!"

What could possibly have happened to Dolly that would result in this big secret? Why would Gummie refer to her marriage with words like "supposedly" and "so-called?" I made up stories about Dolly. I had her throwing herself in front of the 4:38 train, distraught with the pain of losing the only man she'd ever loved, Hubert Jordan, to her older sister. I had her addicted to heroin, finally OD'ing. I had her still alive, running off with the mystery man she'd married, whom the sisters found so unacceptable they treated her as if she'd died. Who would be so unacceptable, though, that Iris would do this? I tried on Negro and Chinese in my mind, but such imaginings collapsed, knowing Gummie would probably applaud such flaunting of convention. What then? A Republican, maybe. Or, probably the most unacceptable to Iris, an awfully stupid man. Still, I couldn't truly imagine Iris cutting her beloved Dolly out of her life, for any reason.

3

Something of an Oddity

Violet Herrington, the oldest sister, married at eighteen and left home to live with her husband in his family's mansion in southeast Minneapolis. Judging from everything I've ever heard about Violet, she must've been a lot like Gummie—strong, resilient, and full of self-confidence. She was—by city standards—nothing but a "hick farm girl." I imagine it would have been easy for her in-laws to believe they could intimidate her. Violet was probably a surprise to them.

It was clear to her, immediately, that even though her fancy in-laws had money and a posh lifestyle, she was far more educated than they were. She figured her erudition just about cancelled out their sophistication, making them all equal. So, she never took any guff and tried not to give too much, either.

While Violet was starting her family and establishing herself in the city, Iris was helping Mama with her younger sisters. Then she left home for college. In 1894, after graduation, Iris moved back to Blue Earth, her hometown. Her parents encouraged her to move to the big city where she could use her education, and Violet offered her a place in her home—it not being proper for a single woman to live alone. However, Gummie said, "I wanted to live with my folks and my baby sisters in the sweet little town I loved so. I didn't get an education to 'use' it! I got an education because I wanted it."

She went to work for the town attorney as his assistant and secretary. Mostly, the only jobs young women took in those days, at least with Iris's farm and working class background, were scullery jobs in hotels and boarding houses, or domestic work in someone else's home, or—if you were educated—nursing or teaching.

So Iris was something of an oddity, but she didn't mind. In fact, she probably reveled in it, always pointing out to me, "If you're odd enough, people either avoid you—mostly the kind of people you want nothing to do with anyway—or admire you—mostly the kind of people you do want something to do with. In fact, the odder you are, the more freedom you have."

Sometimes, after I was an adult, it seemed to me she had more freedom than most of the women I knew seventy years later. She went to work in her prim white blouses and dark skirts and big, floppy hats. She went to council meetings in the same clothing, getting up frequently to argue with what she thought were "absurd motions." She talked throughout the county against "demon rum," eventually becoming President of the Blue Earth County Ladies' Temperance Union. Whenever she talked about temperance, she also threw in a few well-chosen phrases about women's suffrage and birth control. She was on the hospital board and the orphans' board. She wrote letters to the editor, arguing with every conservative stance the local weekly took.

She also began what was to become a lifelong habit with her:

she wrote to every newly elected governor and senator and congressman of the state of Minnesota and every newly elected president of the United States, advising them in precise and stern language of their many responsibilities and of the needs of the "ordinary" people, from whom she believed most politicians were unnaturally estranged. Many of these dignitaries wrote back to her, sometimes resulting in correspondences stretching over decades.

At home, Iris donned the horrifying and much-scorned bloomers that were the closest thing ladies had to pants in those days. She continued her education by reading widely and fervently, discussing and arguing with anyone who had any opinions at all. When she wasn't at work or reading, she took her younger sisters, Dolly and Pansy, on "field trips" to streams and meadows and woods, gathering specimens of the insect world as well as the flora in these various locations. It was her duty, she felt, to teach her sisters all she could about the natural world.

"I'd gotten science in college, but not much was taught to girls in the younger grades. I knew Mama would take care of their literary education. She'd done a superb job with Violet and me. Mama'd also teach them about numbers, something at which she was particularly adept. And Papa would teach them about history and politics. Consequently, I saw science as my responsibility. Dolly took to it right away, but I can't say Pansy ever warmed up to it. She had a problem with bugs and birds and just about anything alive, from a tree to a squirrel. God, she was such a pansy." Then she'd laugh at her own joke, a wonderful deep rumbling, always reminding me of summer thunder.

I'd heard all these stories about education and found them a little tedious. I loved school myself, but I wanted to find out more about important matters—like her sex life. I'd try to change the subject. "Did you go out with boys? Did you have lots of dates?"

Gummie'd shake her head. "No, Maddie, I sure didn't. That's one of the things I mean about the correlation between 'odd' and 'freedom.' I was a little too odd for most of the boys in my town, which gave me the freedom not to hurry up getting married and the freedom to just plain do what I wanted to do. A man who was interested in someone as independent and different as I was, I realized, would be worthy."

"So you didn't go out at all?"

"I went out occasionally, but I think I mostly scared the bejesus out of those boys." She'd laugh loudly again. "Maddie, you listen carefully now, because this is an important lesson: having a boyfriend, having dates, even getting married—that's not everything in life. There's plenty of other things a woman can do and should do than just sit around waiting for a man to show up. Don't you forget this."

"Oh, Gummie," I'd retort, "I know! Don't you think Mom's told me all that stuff already?"

Gummie'd nod, saying, "I bet she has, indeed."

In 1900, Dolly decided she wanted to go to the University of Minnesota in Minneapolis. Violet was thirty-five by then and had children almost as old as Dolly. Because she lived near the campus, she offered her home to Dolly. Mama and Papa decided, however, that Dolly needed her family around her. They also thought Pansy, who was fifteen and showing inclination for nothing more than marriage, needed to have a wider range of choices in men.

So, they moved to Minneapolis, only a couple of blocks away from Violet and her family. Mama had saved money carefully, mostly hiding it from Papa, who would've squandered it. Consequently, they were able to buy a dilapidated three-story

Victorian, which they fixed up to operate as a boarding house for students, since they were near the University.

"How come they didn't move to town when you went to college, Gummie?"

"Oh, Carleton was in a small town like Blue Earth, so it didn't seem like much of a change. Anyway, they knew I could take care of myself."

"Couldn't Dolly take care of herself?"

"Sure she could, but she wasn't quite as brazen as I, a bit quieter. Besides which, I suspect Mama and Papa were just ready for a change themselves. Especially Papa."

Iris thought it might be time to change her life, too, so she quit her job and moved to Minneapolis with the family. The three girls were given the third floor, while the five bedrooms on the second floor were rented out to students, and Mama and Papa took a small room in the back on the first floor. Papa did some maintenance and a little gardening around the house but was mostly off at his meetings or at the local working man's bar, where he engaged in shouting matches with other men. In the meantime, Mama—with the help of Pansy—did the cooking, cleaning, and laundry for her family as well as the boarders.

Papa would bring home reformers to share dinner with the family. These men were politicians and organizers and philosophers and cut across class and party lines—Republicans like Charles Lindbergh, Sr. and Bob La Follette and socialists like Eugene Debs and Bill Haywood. Even Mary Elizabeth Lease joined them, once. Debs was the undisputed leader of the Socialist Party while Haywood became one of the founders of the Industrial Workers of the World, the Wobblies. La Follete was a Wisconsin senator whose name would become synonymous with radical progressivism while Congressman Lindbergh championed justice for farmers and laborers everywhere. Lease was one of the founders of the

Populist Party and was much appreciated for her acerbic pronouncements, such as, "What you farmers need to do is raise less corn, and more hell!" Their meals would hum with heated discussions and arguments about politics.

"Stimulating as all of that promised to be," Gummie told me, "I decided it was time for me to go on a trip. I was between jobs and had never been anywhere except a few towns in southern Minnesota. I had a good friend, Bertha—one of the other women who was at Carleton with me—who lived in San Francisco. I got on the Great Northern Railroad and traveled across the western plains and mountains—through North Dakota and Montana, Idaho and Washington—then down the coast to visit her. It was a grand adventure."

Iris had a sleeping car because it was considered disreputable for a lady to be sitting up for four days and nights with strangers surrounding her. The porter would bring meals to her room because it also wasn't acceptable for a lady to enter a dining room without an escort.

"That arrangement lasted for one meal only. I realized I would be completely isolated—a horrific prospect, totally undermining the whole point of travel. I settled for 'odd' once more and proceeded to sit in the lounge and dine in the dining room, affording me the possibility of meeting other people."

I would picture my gummie in her proper, early century clothing, trying to maintain decorum while also reaching out to connect with others. She met a couple who'd been in vaudeville and were moving to Oregon.

"He was a magician, and she'd been his assistant; you know, the one who climbs in the box to get sawed in two. They shared many amusing stories with me, had traveled all over the U.S. and Europe. They were retiring and wanted to live by the Pacific in Oregon. They described the area to me—created mind pictures of sand dunes towering above trees, and rocky obelisks embedded in the middle of sandy beaches, and wild waves pummeling cliff faces, arches, and caves. It sounded like a gorgeous place to me."

She also met a group of circus people who regaled her with their stories of lives so radically different from her own that they were almost unimaginable—trapeze artists, tightrope walkers, clowns, a lion tamer, and behind-the-scene's folks who set up and took down the tents, handled the costumes, fed the animals.

"Did it make you want to run off and join the circus?" I had only been to a circus once, but I thought it would be a super life—having every eye focused on me as I did death-defying things way up in the air, traveling from town to town across the country, making people laugh and gasp and gaze in awe and delight.

Gummie frowned a little, then smiled indulgently. "No, Maddie, I can't say I ever entertained such an idea. I was more interested in serious work, but they were a colorful bunch, and their work was honorable, too. All work is. It would be easy to understand why people—especially women who had limited choices—would be attracted to that kind of life."

Iris's favorite person on the train was a woman whose mother had been at the 1848 women's convention in Seneca Falls, New York. "That's when women first, publicly and officially, demanded the vote. In 1848, Maddie. And we still haven't gotten it." She'd pause, then shake her head, like she was waking herself up, and say, "I mean—we still hadn't gotten it then, when I met this woman. Her mother had spent her life fighting to gain the vote for women. And died before we got the vote."

"You fought for women's rights, too, didn't you?" I knew she had because, by ten, I knew most of her stories.

Gummie removed her glasses and held them up to the light, then breathed on them and polished them slowly and thoroughly with a hankie—unused, I assumed, shuddering at the thought of the alternative. "Yes, I did what I could. 'We were but a handful . . .' Elizabeth Cady Stanton uttered those words back in 1848 at that first women's convention, Maddie. And in 1905, when your guppie and I were in New York, I met Harriet Stanton Blatch. She was Elizabeth's daughter and was organizing working women."

"How about Susan B. Anthony?"

"Did I meet her? No. She died in 1906, just after uttering her famous words, 'Failure is impossible.' Women's fight for suffrage is an important part of our history, Maddie, one you won't get in school. It's important you know all about it."

Eventually, she would come back to describing her trip out West, telling me of the paucity of trees or other impediments, resulting in skies "so big you'd get a sense of the vastness of our universe—ground and sky." Beyond the mostly treeless, arid plains, majestic snowy-peaked mountains reached into that big sky, vistas entirely foreign to someone who grew up in the gently rolling green and forested hills of southern Minnesota. Gummie would describe cowboys with leather chaps and misshapen hats on horseback, moving large herds of cattle. "I guess in search of fresh grassland or maybe on their way to market. I had no way of knowing."

Sometimes, Indians on ponies would gallop to the top of a rise swelling alongside the train tracks, pausing to stare at the "iron horse" thundering by. "Those Indians seemed very romantic, although the plight of the Red Man in this country is anything but romantic."

Later in the sixties, I was sometimes embarrassed by the way she talked. It was so "noblesse oblige." I tried to explain this to her, and to her credit, she listened carefully, asking many questions. She was, she always said, never too old to learn. Her newspaper published articles about the American Indian Movement, and she switched from using the word "Indians" to "American Indians" or "Native Americans," as did most of us during that decade.

"I would sit in my room after nightfall and stare out at the dark shapes moving past my window, the occasional faint light in the distance—someone's ranch, I would imagine, with kerosene lighting probably—and a smattering of lights in the small towns we rumbled through. I would think about all these other peoples' lives, people all over existing without knowing or caring about me. It made me feel small and insignificant in a way nothing ever had."

I would try, truly, but I couldn't imagine anything making Gummie feel small or insignificant. Sometimes, at this point, she'd pause in her story and rock a while. We were usually sitting on the front porch, unless it was winter. During those cold months, we'd sit in her bedroom, so as not to disturb Mom or Gramma if they were listening to the radio or reading. Gummie sat in a big upholstered rocking chair, her feet on a tiny little footstool with a bright pink flower crocheted onto a black background.

I would sit on the multicolored rag rug on the floor or lie on my tummy on her big brass bed. Gummie's room was the only place in our house where Jack, my dog, was not allowed. She learned this very young but never really reconciled herself to it. She would lie on the floor outside Gummie's room, her mournful eyes beseeching Gummie, who had no trouble ignoring her.

When I was very little, before she lived with us, I'd often snuggle into her lap while she talked, one or the other of my small hands patting her cheeks. Her ancient skin was buttery-soft and full of furrows, like a crumpled piece of wash-softened cloth. I loved the feel of it and would stroke it deliberately, like a baby with her favorite blankie, until Gummie would kiss my fingers and gently shift my hand away from her face.

When she moved to our house, she brought her favorite things with her—the chair, the footstool, the rug, the brass bed, a quilt one of her friends had made, a painting of willows along the bank of the Mississippi River another friend had done, her books. Her bedroom had been a sewing room before she moved in with us, but Gramma moved all the stuff out to other parts of the house so Gummie could have a first-floor room.

"I can take the extra room upstairs," Gummie'd insisted. "What do you think? I'm too old to do stairs?" She was eighty-seven at the time.

"No," Gramma answered calmly. "I think *I'm* too old to worry about you on those stairs." That was the end of the argument.

"How long did you stay in San Francisco?" I'd ask Gummie if her reverie stretched out too long. Sometimes when she paused, she'd take a little nap, and I would read or wander into the kitchen for a snack. When she woke, she would usually pick up right where she'd left off.

She had stayed out West for almost six months. Bertha's husband was wealthy, and they lived in a grand old house in Pacific Heights, where they could sit in the parlor and gaze at the ships coming in and out of the harbor below them and across the bay at the golden hills rising above the water.

"Bertha's husband's politics and mine were at opposite ends of the spectrum, and we got into awful rows about almost everything. Still, he was a jolly fellow who took nothing very seriously, enjoying the fights for the stimulation of it all, but mostly for the joy of poking fun at my intensity. At first, I took umbrage at this. Gradually, I realized he meant no harm, was simply a cheerful man who enjoyed life too much to be unpleasant. I learned to like him, in spite of his fuzzy thinking."

Bertha and Harold's three children were mostly taken care of by their nanny, leaving Bertha and Iris free to explore the city. "San Francisco was wild and exciting in those days, crowded with people with great amounts of money, yet very little education or knowing even. This was before the big earthquake and fire. The city was young and vibrant, wholly undisciplined. It seemed to me people were remarkably rude and crass, but it was thrilling, too.

"It was like looking at an exotic bird. I felt I'd gone to an entirely different country! The houses were painted in jelly-bean colors and built so they were touching one another, marching right up one hillside after another. Chinatown was most amazing to me, a girl from Minnesota who hadn't seen many people who weren't just like me. They talked in languages resembling nothing I'd ever heard, so I was bombarded by unfamiliar sounds and sights and surrounded by hordes of people who pushed and brushed up against you in ways I'd never experienced."

Bertha and Iris took cable cars everywhere—up and down hills that seemed too steep to build on, to the wharf, to restaurants specializing in seafood and Oriental food, dishes not available in Minnesota.

"All that money, mostly from the gold and silver mines. Hubert could have found plenty of labor work out there!"

"Would you have liked living there, Gummie?" I tried to imagine what my life would be like if we all lived in San Francisco instead of Minnesota. The biggest diference would be a lack of winter—no ice skating, no sledding, no mornings when every branch, twig, bush, electric line was shimmering in the sunlight from ice frosting. No giant icicles hanging off roofs for us kids to throw snowballs at, trying to dislodge them without impaling ourselves. No snowmen or snow angels. Also—no boots, mittens, leggings, heavy coats. No frostbite. No freezing in the winter, sweltering in the summer. After all, hadn't Mark Twain said the coldest winter he'd ever experienced was a summer in San Francisco?

"I don't think so. Oh, at the time, I fantasized about staying, getting a job there and an apartment. It was a delicious prospect, but—in the end—I knew I would just go home. These were places for me to visit, not live. We took a railcar out to Golden Gate Park. It was still being created but was clearly going to be wondrous. We went to the sand dunes at the end of the rail line. I stared out over the Pacific Ocean and realized I'd never even thought of what it would be like to stand on the edge of a continent and gape at water stretching beyond the eye's looking. You'll have to go to the ocean someday, Maddie. You'll have to go lots of places."

I nodded, going all dreamy inside myself. "I know. I intend to. I'm going to Europe. I want to go to all the places you and Guppie went on your honeymoon. I want to go to the moors where the Brontës lived and to Daphne du Maurier's Manderley. After that, I'll go to Africa, where I can steam up the Congo just like Mary Kingston did almost a hundred years ago. Then, I'll go to India where Rumer Godden grew up. And in Singapore, I shall take tea at the Raffles Hotel where Somerset Maugham always stayed." Some of these authors I'd read myself, others had been read to me.

"That sounds splendid," Gummie would agree. "Yes, just fine." We smiled fondly at each other for a couple of minutes, lost in our own mental journeys—hers into the past, mine into the future. I'd been putting together this dream trip, little by little, for years.

"And when you came back?" I'd prod her as she sat lost in contemplation for a minute or two.

"Yes, well, I came back to Minneapolis and got a job at the newspaper."

"And?" I shrilled, expectantly.

She'd smile and say what she knew I wanted to hear. "And Hubert Jordan had moved into Mama's boarding house while I was gone."

4

Life is Not Something That Just Happens to You

"If I had known Dolly was in love with Hubert, I wouldn't have encouraged him at all. If I had known they were even seeing one another . . . But Dolly and Hubert never said a thing; no one else said anything, either. At that point, I guess Dolly didn't quite know she was actually in love with Hubert. I think it became clearer to her when she realized she was going to lose him.

"I knew nothing of this. I only knew there was a nice young man staying at my parents' house. It was soon obvious, even to me who hardly ever noticed these things, that this nice young man was quite smitten with me."

Hubert Jordan was a small-town transplant also. He was tall—a good thing, too, since all the Jordan girls were tall—and good-looking in a "nice" way, which is to say he wasn't flashy at all. In the pictures taken during this period, he wore rimless glasses—like Gummie's—and had plenty of dark hair, all of which later disappeared. He was just beginning law school and was a year younger than Gummie. It was 1901; she was twenty-eight years old, pretty much making her a hopeless old maid, although I doubt she paid any attention to such conventions. "Hopeless" was not a word that would ever be part of her vocabulary, especially not as applied to herself.

Hubert had been out of school for a few years—he had a degree in English and had taught high school. He had decided to return because he wanted to dedicate his life to legally defending farmers and laborers against big business and moneyed interests. He was a serious man, looking very grave and determined in his pictures. I thought he looked perfect for Gummie.

Dolly was almost twenty-one, starting her college years a little late. She was studying biology and talking about the possibility of medical school. In those same pictures, she was smaller than Gummie—prettier, softer. One would think most men would fall head over heels in love with Dolly. Gummie, on the other hand, had enormous presence. It seemed to me, hearing all the different versions of the story when I was growing up, Hubert was dazzled by Gummie's awesome intelligence, her strong opinions, her fearless declarations. I guess Dolly just faded, in comparison.

"I went looking for a job. You know, being odd didn't make as much difference in a big city as it had in a village." I always wondered if that's why Gummie and Guppie eventually moved to this small town where Gummie, again, became noticeably larger than life. "There were so many odd people, you see. Odd or not—I was a woman, and that was still a liability. I went around to a lot of law offices; they all but snickered in my face. They only 'gave jobs to young gentlemen.' In the end, I went to the daily newspaper, the *Minneapolis Journal*, and applied as a legal reporter. You don't work in a law office for six years and not pick up a lot about the law itself." Not if you're Iris Jordan, anyway.

"Well," she said with a brittle archness to her voice, her anger having survived sixty-some years, "they *did* laugh at me. Then, to shame them a bit, I demonstrated my keen knowledge of the law by discussing in detail a couple of big cases occurring in Minnesota's Supreme Court at that time, including quoting pertinent precedents. They were impressed; I got a job, all right, but not as a legal reporter. Big surprise—I ended up on the society page. A euphemism for women's news."

"You must have hated that."

"I did, but I made the best of it."

No doubt, I thought, knowing she had written articles on suffrage, birth control, temperance, and politics in general, proving women were more interested in "real" news than newsmen had ever believed. For her, not being hired in a law office turned out to be the pot of gold at the end of the rainbow because her temperament and skills were particularly suited to newspaperwork. It led to a lifelong passion.

She also got involved in all her usual extracurricular activities. Violet was already on the boards of the Maternity Hospital for Unwed and Indigent Mothers and the adjacent Orphans' Home. She got Gummie on, too. This led to more direct work with birth education. "They never would use the phrase 'sex education' in those days," Gummie would laugh. "Most people were horrified by the term 'birth education' even."

"Why?"

"People wanted to pretend babies really did just come from a stork or were gifts from God who just sort of floated to the earth." She snorted. "Sex was just too awful, you see. Especially for the ladies. It was considered evil, a necessary evil if you were married, but still evil. So, if you were talking about birth education—

which was really birth control—another term no one used, everyone knew you were really talking about how to 'do it' without getting pregnant. In other words," and she would lower her voice to a stage whisper at this point, "s-e-x."

"That hasn't really changed much," I observed, thinking of the demonstrations around the country against sex education classes in public schools.

"Yes, I believe you're right, Maddie. Then, of course, there was the problem with the Romans."

"The Romans?" I asked. In my mind, I had a picture of Ben-Hur-like characters and wondered how those ancient people in their chariots or lying around on couches eating grapes could have had anything to do with sex education.

"The Roman Catholics, Maddie. They have this absolutely ridiculous notion married folk only have sex to have children. They also think the true believers—themselves—should have many, many children to make the Church—their church, obviously—strong and powerful. Their attitudes are so pervasive, people just blindly think using birth control is sinful, having sex for any reason other than procreation is sinful. With that in mind, it simply meant everyone who had sex was sinning because most folks do it for reasons other than getting pregnant."

It didn't sound to me, the way Gummie talked, that sex was something she never did. She seemed totally relaxed talking about it, even rather enthusiastic. Once, when I was feeling particularly brave or was lulled by her own matter-of-fact tone, I blurted out, "So did you and Guppie have an enjoyable married life, Gummie?"—using my mother's euphemism for married sex.

Gummie looked at me intently with no annoyance, but I felt as if she were looking right through my skin, right through my skull into the far recesses of my mind, discovering all my shameful questions and secret desires. It made me shiver. Then she said, in her usual calm voice, "Sex is a good thing, Maddie. It is not wicked, as so many have tried to portray it. However, what happens between two people is a private matter, and no one with good manners should ever attempt to intrude into that privacy."

I was mortified and disappointed: I was convinced I was never going to know, for sure, if they'd ever actually 'done it.' "I'm sorry," I mumbled.

"Don't mumble, Maddie, it's unbecoming and indicates lack of conviction. And don't worry about apologizing. It's quite all right. This is how you learn manners. Courtesy is the bedrock of social interchange. No matter what you're doing, even if you're fomenting revolution, you can still be courteous."

I did remember. In the late sixties and early seventies, when I was doing sit-ins and demonstrations and protests, I was dubbed "Maddie Manners." Half the time I participated in these activities, Gummie or Mom or both, sometimes even Gramma, were also there, but I like to think I would've been polite even without their watchful presence.

Gummie got involved in the National Woman's Party, more determined to force the issue of woman's suffrage, and she continued her temperance work by joining the local Women's Christian Temperance Union, even though she eschewed Christianity, because, as she said, "The WCTU was the most active organization working against the horrors alcohol inflicts on both family and society." Her own papa's forays into the local bar had become more frequent over the years.

Eventually, she started speaking on the Chautauqua Circuit around the Midwest on subjects as divergent as woman's suffrage, socialism, labor organizing, and birth control. The paper began encouraging her to do this because she'd write articles about the other speakers, about the great issues of the time, and also about the places she visited. Some of her articles even found themselves on "hard" news pages.

"I met Marian Le Sueur on the Circuit, an astounding woman of great intelligence who lectured primarily on women and economics—how women were forced into prostitution because of unlivable wages, on women's right to have control over their own bodies, and on women's right to not have children if they couldn't afford to feed them. We became great friends. I was delighted when, years later, she and her husband, Arthur, moved to the Twin Cities. Hubert and Arthur also knew each other and worked on many causes together."

When Gummie wasn't immersed in her work or going to her various meetings, she'd gather with the other young people in the house after dinner for an evening of passionate conversation and matching of wits.

Sometimes, Pansy would play the piano. They would listen if it were classical music or join in singing if she played popular tunes. She was talented, and it was a pleasant diversion. Mostly, however, they simply talked or—more often than not—argued. Except for Hubert, the men all thought it was absurd for women to get an education. Pansy would eagerly take their side, having no intention of cluttering what she believed to be her pretty little mind with useless facts and knowledge.

Gummie would shake her head in disgust. "That girl had all the opportunities the rest of us had. I don't know what made her so stupid. I declare, her name ruined her."

"Gummie," I would point out when I got older, "two of her three older sisters were 'old maids.' Maybe she was just *acting* stupid to ensure her a man because that's what she wanted most in the world."

Gummie would snort. "No doubt."

"Anyway, Gummie," I would add rather mischievously, picking up my mother's habit of pricking Gummie's pronouncements, "look at you and Gramma. Neither of you got exactly what you wanted in daughters by naming them carefully."

She would stare at me in her X-ray manner; as I got older, I mostly got over being intimidated by that look, so I would just gaze back. Eventually, she would start to chuckle, and then laugh uproariously as I joined her. When her mirth subsided, she'd agree. "I guess you're right, Maddie. Yes, I guess you're right, indeed."

The other women—Iris and Dolly and the sole female boarder, Inga Johnson—all objected vehemently to such Neanderthal ideas. Hubert, in his quiet way, would speak up and say something like, "Why shouldn't women have the same opportunities to learn as men?" The three women would cheer. "After all," he would continue, "they're just as intelligent as men." The men would boo. Then he'd add, "As far as that goes, why shouldn't women vote? They're people, aren't they?"

At such an audacious statement, pandemonium would break loose. Most of the men would be yelling about "What was the world coming to?" while most of the women were yelling, "Oh, you've done such a terrific job being in charge, haven't you?" It was lively and stimulating. Gummie loved these nights at home, almost as much as her job.

Other times, they talked of literature—the classics as well as current books. Other topics they covered included the wonders of science and its constantly shifting discoveries; technology and the industrial age—debating its merits versus the toll it was taking on human society; politics and current events; art; religion. They were atheists, agnostics, and Christians—all sure of their own opinions.

"Oh yes," Gummie would sigh luxuriously, "life was so good then. Actually, my life has always been pretty good. I've been lucky, and I've made careful choices. But those halcyon days, they were the best."

She would look far away, and I never interrupted her when she was so clearly floating in the warm seas of pleasant memories. Then she'd come back to me and say, "Now listen carefully, Maddie, because this is an important lesson: life is not something that just happens to you. It's something you choose. Every day, every hour, every minute. If you ever think your life is hell, you'd better look to yourself and the choices you've made."

I'd nod, but I'd also consider my own opinions. *Did black people have the same choices as white people? Or rich and poor people? What about their choices?* I'd think about it all—weighing her words against my own thoughts, wondering about Gummie's.

5

Know Yourself

The next couple of years passed swiftly. Boarders came and went, except for Hubert. In 1902, one of the boarders, Albert Melville, graduated from college and asked for Pansy's hand in marriage.

"It came as no surprise," Gummie said. "We all knew they were sweet on one another."

"How did you know?" I was eleven and trying to figure out how these things manifested, trying to determine if I wanted such things happening in my own life. I certainly couldn't imagine having—or even wanting—*sex* with a boy, and this worried me a little because I still remembered my father's words of the previous year. "Those Jordan girls never did want anything to do with sex." I *was* a Jordan girl, myself, so was it true? Was I just like the rest of them?

"Don't be dumb, Maddie," my friend Annie would counsel me.

"How *could* you imagine having sex when the boys our age are such ignoramuses! That must change when we get older. Don't you think?"

I devoutly hoped so. I could, sometimes, imagine wanting to kiss a boy. Not actually any of the boys I knew. They were all such dullards. It seemed like they were only interested in sports and guffawing with one another over dirty jokes and ribald comments. When Annie and I read books or went to the movies, we would get ideas about a different kind of man. I *did* want to be kissed by him—that perfect man in my head.

"Oh, mostly Albert and Pansy just gazed at each other with soulful eyes, like a couple of horses off their feed. Sometimes, one of us would speak to one of them, and they wouldn't even hear us or acknowledge our presence. It was a little sickening, actually."

"Weren't you and Guppie acting that way, too?" I knew what she was talking about because Annie's older sister, Robin, was in love, and Annie and I spied endlessly on her and her boyfriend. We witnessed this same kind of behavior and also found it to be a little sickening. It was fascinating, though, that lovers still acted the same way after—I had to count the decades on my fingers—sixty years.

Gummie would shake her head dismissively, her mouth pinched in distaste. "Certainly not!" she'd protest. "We were mature, rational beings who connected on a higher plane than the physical."

So high you didn't *have* sex, even after you got married? I didn't ask. "You said it was clear Guppie was smitten with you. How could you tell if he wasn't mooning over you?"

"Oh, it was obvious in other ways. He'd ask me more questions than anyone else. He'd say things I doubt he'd normally have said—just to side with me or maybe impress me."

"You mean they were lies?"

"No, no. Hubert would *never* lie. It was just . . ." She'd hesitate for a minute, remembering with soft, happy eyes, "he would not have stirred things up. It was not his way. He was secure in his opinions, didn't need to trot them out or test them against others' ideas, but, because *I* was so voluble, he put his oar in from time to time, to make certain I would know he agreed with me."

Actually, I liked what she was saying. It did sound much more important to me to have a man think like me than to have him making vapid eyes at me. Years later, I was to remember this conversation—and similar ones—and comprehend the wisdom in Gummie's words far more than I could at the time I orginally got this information.

"Anyway, Mama and Papa would not let Pansy get married. She was only seventeen. I suggested they might convince her to wait until after she'd gone to college—I had a great many ideas, as you can imagine, on how to raise that child." I suppressed a smile. Yes, I certainly could imagine. "Mama just laughed and told me it wouldn't do any good to *force* Pansy to go to college. No, she'd just have to wait until she was eighteen; then she could marry Mr. Melville or whomever she wanted.

"After all, they pointed out to me, Violet got married at eighteen. Violet, though, was far more intelligent than Pansy—or at least *used* her intelligence more—and continued to improve her mind after her marriage, even after her children started coming. Regardless, I had to concede because I wasn't the parent, and anyway, I knew they were right. Forcing Pansy to go to college wouldn't change her. If she wasn't dedicated to learning by seventeen, she wasn't going to be."

So, Pansy spent a year pouting and flouncing and planning. She and Albert got married on her eighteenth birthday. "Were they happy, Gummie? Was it a good marriage, do you think?"

"Oh, I don't know. I guess so. It wouldn't have made *me* happy, but then—different things make different people happy. Pansy wanted a devoted man, and she got that in Albie. He was steady, supportive, and responsible—a bit dull, maybe. That didn't matter to Pansy, though. She wanted someone who adored her, and she certainly got that. So . . . yes, I guess it was a reasonably good marriage."

I turned this information over in my head, more and more as I got older. "I take it Guppie wasn't dull?" I'd only been eight when he died, and he'd been in bed most of the last two years of his life so he seemed pretty dull to me.

"Hubert?" she'd almost shouted. "Oh no, Hubert was never dull. He wasn't dashing or irresponsible or anything—certainly not like that odious man," she meant Gramma's husband, "but he had an exciting mind. Intellectually, there were few who could compete with him. He loved to read and discuss things. He was far more radical than I was, although few who knew us both would've thought that, just because I was more combative. Hubert did great things to change the face of America. He was on the ground floor of the labor movement at the turn of the century. He defended and advised strikers and Wobblies all over the Midwest. He fought for the rights of the foreign born and individuals' rights to free speech. He worked with every firebrand and notable. Everyone respected him."

"Who were the Wobblies, Gummie?" I interrupted. I'd been hearing that name since my birth and could never remember who they were. I always remembered the word, though, because it was so evocative. It made me think of those little Russian nesting dolls, one after another smaller than the first and all fitting inside the original. Each of the dolls had rounded bottoms that made them wobble from side-to-side, back-to-front. So, every time Gummie used that word, this is what immediately leaped to my mind, erasing the actual meaning.

Gummie glanced sharply at me, a little irritated at the interruption, I imagined, as well as my lack of memory. "You know, Maddie. I've told you before."

"I know, but I forget."

"The Industrial Workers of the World, the IWW. It was far more radical than the A.F.L. or other succeeding unions, wanting not just a piece of the pie for the workers but a whole new pie, a different economic system."

I nodded, still flicking at the round-bottomed dolls with my mind's finger. "But why were they called the Wobblies?"

Gummie looked startled, then meditative for a moment, finally shrugging. "I don't know, Maddie. They just were. I guess I never thought about it. Or if I did, I don't remember any more. Something about a mispronunciation perhaps." She repeated her shrug.

Then, she continued her description of Guppie.

"Beyond that, Hubert was very modern. Not many husbands of his time were as supportive as he was of my work. He didn't just *tolerate* my activities, he truly believed they were fine. If I 'wanted to do something, then it must be done'—was his attitude."

Pansy once told me, in one of her semi-lucid moments, "Oh Hubert and Iris. Of course, they had a perfect marriage. She ruled the roost. Everyone knew that. Whatever Iris wanted to do, she got to do. Hubert never argued with her or differed from her, so she thought he was perfect. He was such a *wimp*. All the men thought so. Couldn't control his own wife, keep her in her place."

I had thought much of what she said made sense until she used the words 'wimp' and 'control.' That disturbed me, the idea of a husband controlling his wife, the result being he was a wimp if he didn't. I knew what Pansy said would make Gummie really angry, and I also thought Gramma would have to defend her beloved Daddy, so I asked Mom what she thought of Pansy's opinion because she probably had enough distance to be more objective than either Gummie or Gramma.

"I'd say Pansy was both right and wrong. Guppie was a brilliant man, Maddie. He was smart enough to realize arguing with Gummie would be a waste of time and smart enough to discern what was most important to him: peace. Don't forget, he'd lived in the same house with Gummie—the boarding house—for three years before they got married. He knew what he was getting, and he loved what he was getting. Calling him a wimp, however, was just the other men's way of bolstering their own egos and attempting to tear Guppie's down. It didn't work, though, because Guppie never cared about their opinions. Then Pansy, she always sided with her husband or other men. She was just that sort of woman. The kind who has no confidence in her own ability to form an opinion so lets someone else do it for her. That someone is almost always a man."

While Hubert went to law school, Iris built her career, ran the city as much as she could, and hung out with the gang at Mama's boarding house. In the winter, they would go skating or sledding or to indoor entertainments: lectures, concerts, plays. In the summer, they would play tennis or go for picnics at nearby state parks or go to outdoor concerts at Lake Harriet or go rowing at Loring Park. All year round, they would talk and argue and examine and critique. There was no conspicuous pairing off; they did everything as a group. It was understood by all, however, that Pansy and Albert were a couple and so were Iris and Hubert.

Then, when Hubert graduated from law school and passed the bar, he asked Iris to marry him. "Did you say yes immediately?"

Gummie smiled but shook her head. "Maddie, I worry a little about you. You seem a little obsessed with boys and marriage and such. Remember what I told you?"

"Yes, yes," I waved her off, then—to reassure her—I quoted her own lines. "'There are other things a girl can do and should do than be waiting for some man to come along.' I know, Gummie, but you and Guppie *did* get married, so I just want to know everything."

She shook her head again, then continued her story in her own way. "I'd been at the paper for three years. They gave me more and more to do all the time, but—naturally—I never got more money or a new title. I had more responsibility than anyone, except the editors. I knew I was trusted; still, I was a *girl*. Someone, they figured, who would just get married and leave them. I begged them to let me be an editor, just a page editor. I even volunteered to be editor of the abhorrent society pages, but no dice. The city editor didn't like me, actually. He thought I was too pushy, but the publisher loved me, recognizing how valuable I was to the paper. He told me he wished he could give me an editorship, that I deserved it, but his 'hands were tied.' Men, he insisted, would never agree to work under me. I just kept working harder and harder, hoping time would change their minds.

"In the meantime, I loved the job. I was a good interviewer, and I had what was known as a nose for news and the most valuable of all assets—perseverance. If it were a slow day, I knew who to call or where to go to get some kind of news. I was really sharp when it came to running down leads, and I gradually compiled a reliable bunch of sources.

"I was such an oddity, you see, people would talk to me out of curiosity at first, then forget soon enough I was a girl. In addition, I learned everything I could about the business. After hours, I would visit the other departments: advertising, accounting, the typesetters, the printers, the photographers. I even talked to the newsies—the boys who delivered the papers or sold them on the streets. I asked everyone countless questions. I was fascinated with the workings of the company and wanted to know everything. This, I think, was why the publisher loved me. He recognized and appreciated my passion, knew it matched his own."

"Gummie! What does all this have to do with Guppie's proposal? Did he get down on his knees to ask you to marry him?"

An indignant look leaped to her face. "He did not. Actually, he talked to Mama and Papa first, before he ever spoke up to me."

"He did?" I scrunched my face in distaste. "You were—what? Thirty by then?"

"Thirty-one. Didn't matter. I was a single woman who lived at home. Hubert was proper and knew it was best to talk to my parents first."

"That didn't bother you?" I was thinking how annoyed I'd be if some boy came hanging around and asked my mom if he could take me out.

"No. I knew he was just being polite and respectful of my parents. I've told you before, Maddie, manners are essential."

"Had you kissed each other by then?"

Gummie gave me that penetrating look of hers. I tried not to squirm. "Maddie, where are *your* manners right now?"

"Oh yeah, I'm sorry, but . . ." I thought fast. "I'm just interested, historically, whether or not boys and girls, you know, kissed before they were married. During their courting, you know." I figured that was a pretty good way to handle it, partially because it was true.

She frowned, looking at me skeptically, but I knew she was going to answer because a smile was tugging at the corners of her mouth. "Maddie, don't say 'you know' all the time. It makes you sound tentative and unsure of yourself." I nodded agreement, waiting silently. "I guess it's understandable you'd be curious about the mores of the time. Most couples, if they formally announced their engagement or if the man had asked her parents permission to come courting, were allowed some time alone. Almost all of them insisted they never kissed until their wedding night, except for the occasional chaste kiss on the cheek or hand. Almost all of them, I'm convinced, lied."

I should have known she'd find a way to answer me without giving me any personal information. I forgot myself for a minute and said, "You and Guppie, did you . . ." Her brows bunched like storm clouds; I abruptly dropped the rest of the sentence. Later, when I thought about her answer, I realized she probably *did* tell me they had, indeed, kissed each other. Otherwise, why would she believe most couples lied about kissing? To get her sidetracked from that dreaded look of hers, I asked, "So, did you say 'yes' when Guppie proposed?"

"I did not," she replied, her eyes resuming their normal intensity. "I was telling you, Maddie, all about my job, so you would understand how important it was to me. When Hubert asked me to marry him, I told him I would think it over. I was very fond of him . . ."

"Fond?" I interrupted. "Didn't you *love* him?"

"Oh yes, I did love him, but I loved a great many things. I loved my freedom, my independence, my job, all my causes. I knew Hubert probably expected me to give the job up and everything else to create a home for him. That's what women did in those days. At least women who were middle- or upper-class and were marrying men who made enough money to support them. Even when there wasn't enough money, most women stayed at home—cooking, cleaning, raising children. I was quite certain I couldn't bear that, even for the pleasure of making a life with Hubert Jordan."

"So, after thinking about it, you turned him down?"

"No. After thinking about it, I told him I 'would be honored to be his wife,' but I must keep my job and my other interests or I simply couldn't do it. I knew if I married him under any other circumstances, I would be miserable, and I would make him miserable, too."

"And?"

"He responded, in his usual quiet way. 'Why Iris! I would never expect you to change a hair on your head for me. I know you would not want to give up your job, and I would not want you to.' He was, you see, an extraordinary man. One in a million. I knew, the minute he responded that way, he was truly the man for me."

After a moment of silence, she added, "Now listen carefully, Maddie. You've got to know yourself and what you want in life before you attempt to choose a life partner. Our union was so successful because we both knew what we wanted, what was important to us."

Which wasn't sex? I wondered but had enough sense to not ask.

6

To Be of Use

Robin, Annie's big sister, got married the summer we were eleven; Annie was in the wedding, and I got to go. Afterward, I felt a little enamored of the idea of weddings, of the fairy-tale quality of a bride decked out in glorious raiment. Sometimes now, I wonder if that's what most girls dream of: princess-for-a-day. What an effective way to enslave us—convince us we must have a memorable wedding in which every eye is focused on our beauty, our grace, our special-ness. Never thinking much at all about what comes after the wedding.

"What was your wedding like, Gummie?"

I'd heard about Pansy's "ridiculously sumptuous" wedding, where she, in a gown with a snug bodice embedded with pearls (she'd stitched on those myriad pearls herself during the interminably long year she had to wait to marry her "true love") and a fluted-wine-glass-turned-upside-down skirt falling in cascades to tickle the floor, had floated down one side of the split staircase in her sister Violet's mansion while Albert, resplendent in coat and tails, bounded down the other half of the staircase, to be joined in matrimony in the enormous foyer. By the time I was born, this mansion had been torn down to make way for a parking lot. I considered it one of the tragedies of my young life that I never got to see it.

Once I made the mistake of voicing such musings to Gramma, who I thought might understand because she had attempted to choose a more conventional life for herself. She stared at me for a moment or two, then harrumphed (a noise we all made, I noticed, as I grew older), sounding ever so much like her mother. "Maddie, take my word for it. If not seeing Violet's mansion is a major tragedy in your life, you can be certain your life is almost free of tragedy." She said no more, but I felt properly chastised for my obvious shallowness.

I had better sense than to tell Gummie that Pansy's "absurd and ostentatious" wedding completely enthralled my imagination. I was sure Gummie's own wedding had been nothing like Pansy's.

"It was very practical," Gummie said. "We got married in Mama's parlor with just family and a couple of close friends. A justice of the peace performed the ceremony. Mama and the girls had prepared a delicious feast for us."

"Were you dressed in something rapturous?" I asked, momentarily forgetting to whom I was talking.

"Certainly not," Gummie'd answered, dismissing such a notion with a quick shake of her head. "We saved a lot of money having a simple wedding, money we needed for our very special honeymoon. Hubert wore his suit," her matter-of-fact statement making it clear to me there was only *one* suit, "and I wore a plain white blouse with a navy blue skirt and jacket. Right after the festivities, we caught a train to New York City.

"While in New York, I got to meet Emma Goldman, Harriet Stanton Blatch, and Helen Keller—three of my heroes. Hubert met with some of the reform leaders of the time—Eugene Debs and Alexander Berkman and others. It was a fitting beginning to a union such as ours. Then we got on a ship and sailed to Europe. We thought we should see a bit of the world while we could, before the demands of work and family tied us down."

"Tell me everything," I demanded reverentially, just as if I hadn't heard about this trip dozens of times. Push-come-to-shove, I think I would probably opt for the excitement of a trip abroad over the romance of a perfect wedding day that would, after all, only last one day.

She would share the details of her trip with me then, information sandwiched between her work and increasingly frequent naps and my forays into the rest of the world—such as hanging out with Annie or helping Gramma or going to school. She described London with its sooty but mysteriously rhapsodic fog, its flowers everywhere, its air of civilized gallantry. "Specious, mind you."

"Specious?" I would furrow my brow at this statement, searching my memory for its meaning and thinking of all the books I'd read about England with its afternoon teas and gracious gentility. "You don't think England *is* civilized?"

Gummie would let her thunderous laughter escape before answering. "Maddie, be careful of being seduced by literature. Don't forget the lessons of history, too. Great Britain has a monstrously bloody history, both internally and externally."

I wanted to contradict her words, but the thought of Henry the VIII's wives' heads rolling left and right sprung unbidden into my mind. And I thought of Cromwell and the London dungeons as well as the London Tower, Bloody Mary, and the constant and pernicious imperialism and colonialism (of which I learned more about at home than I ever did in school). I knew Gummie was right. Yet . . . I still longed for a stroll along the Thames, the sonorous tones of Big Ben nearby.

Then she'd speak of Paris with its wide boulevards, its sidewalk cafés, its passionate citizens—all seemingly orators; of Venice, a quixotic and poetic place, of gliding through its canals, being surrounded by people who seemed otherworldly in their dedication to the affairs of the heart; of the magnificent architecture of the German castles surrounded by sublime natural beauty and the bustling of Germany's dirty but humming cities.

I would be regaled with tales of train, boat, and bicycle rides through serene countryside, along scenic rivers and the bucolic shores of lakes and seas. Also of their rambles, sounding at times like marches, in the cities to visit extraordinary museums and cathedrals. She talked of immense wealth and crushing poverty, of conversations she had—sometimes in her halting French or Hubert's halting German, sometimes in others' halting English, often in a mixture of the two or three. She talked to laborers in Berlin and farmers in Provence, to journalists in London and business owners in Rome—and to their wives, girlfriends, mothers, and sisters everywhere.

"How could you ever stand to come home?"

She would answer, simply, "It *was* intoxicating, Maddie, you're right, but we had work to do. To be of use, to make a difference, that's what life is about, Maddie."

7

Friends Are Too Precious

Hubert and Iris returned home. Dolly had moved to Baltimore to attend medical school at Johns Hopkins. Violet was still living with her husband and three of her five children, the oldest two now having married and moved out. Pansy and her husband had bought a little house around the corner from Mama's boarding house. They had one baby and another on the way. Iris and Hubert took over the third floor of Mama's house for themselves, since everyone else was gone.

"It would have been silly, really, for us to get a place of our own," Gummie informed me. "I didn't want much to take care of, and anyway, Mama and Papa were getting on, so Hubert and I could help them out by living with them."

It was 1906; Mama was sixty-three and Papa was sixty-nine. Hubert opened his law practice in Minneapolis while Iris went back to the paper, where she immediately ran a series on her impressions of the "old world."

"It was good we were living with Mama and Papa," Gummie mused. "Otherwise I would have been even more lonesome than I was. Hubert traveled a great deal, going wherever he was needed. It was a fine arrangement, actually. Hubert was busy and happy with his life and I was, too, with mine. We shared our separate experiences with each other whenever he got home or worked in town for a week or two. I was too old to hang out with the boarders anymore, and Dolly was gone. It was nice to have Mama around."

I wondered if they had sex when Guppie was in town, but I wisely kept such speculations to myself. "Were you as busy as ever?" I didn't think she could be much help to her parents, as full as her life always seemed to be.

"No, not really. I cut back a little. Mama needed me." She rocked for a few minutes. "Much as I missed Hubert when he was gone, I missed Dolly even more."

"Dolly was your favorite, wasn't she?" I tried to imagine what it would be like to have a sister. As good as Annie, I wondered? I doubted that. Many of my classmates had sisters, and very few of them seemed to be as close as Annie and I were. That wasn't so with Gummie, at least not regarding Dolly.

"Yes, she was my favorite. Violet and I were awfully fond of each other, but she left home when I was just ten, and then she had all those kids, so we just didn't get much time with each other. Pansy was so much younger, and . . . different from me." For Gummie, that was a kinder-than-usual description of the schism between Pansy and her.

"Dolly was born just before Mama and Papa moved into Blue Earth, so—in lots of ways—I raised her. I was left to take care of her while Mama was busy running the hotel, and Papa indulged in his political work. Then there were those years, after I finished college and came home. Dolly was hungry to learn, and I had much to impart. It just drew us closer. We were . . ." she hesitated, searching for the right word, her grey eyes looking sad. "We were soul mates, I guess. We both worshipped at the altar of knowledge, we both wanted to examine every minute detail of life, we both loved books. We shared everything." After a pause, she added, "Or so it seemed."

"Except for her loving your husband," I supplied.

"Yes," she sighed, taking off her glasses and digging her thumb and forefinger into the corners of her eyes for a moment before replacing them. "Except that."

"When you came back from your honeymoon, were you surprised that she'd gone off to medical school?" I was familiar with most of these stories but always got a little more information each time Gummie repeated them. I also knew she couldn't always remember what she'd told me and what she hadn't. I didn't mind hearing them over and over. They were worth hearing more than once.

"Yes and no," Gummie replied. "I wasn't surprised she went to med school. She'd begun applying before we left. I was just startled that she'd departed without a letter, anything. I felt abandoned, I guess." She shook her head, as if in annoyance at herself. "I know how silly that is. After all, *I* got married and abandoned her! For a husband *and* a honeymoon. Still, she *knew* I was going. I didn't know she was going. And she'd been accepted at the University of Minnesota's medical school, so I couldn't understand why she'd decided to go so far away." This time, when she paused, she let her eyes drift out the window. I waited patiently, knowing she was not finished.

Without bringing her eyes back to me, she said, "You see, I was feeling sorry for myself. I'd never made many close friends because

I'd always had Dolly. I'd badger Mama—and Pansy, if she were around—endlessly complaining that Dolly had gone off when she could've stayed right here close to us. I'd written her when I returned home, but she hadn't written back. That bothered me, too. Everything bothered me.

"I was edgy and cranky, and finally one day, Pansy blurted out, 'Oh, Iris, will you just quit blathering on and on about Dolly leaving! Did you hesitate to leave her, to run off with the man she loved?'

"I wheeled on her and said, 'What? What are you babbling about, Pansy?' She shrugged and said, 'You might as well know. Everyone else does. Dolly and Hubert were keeping company before you ever came home from San Francisco. You just took him over and broke her heart. Think how it must have been for her those three long years of watching the two of you! Now you want to complain because she's building a life of her own somewhere else? Honestly, Iris.' Well. You could have knocked me over with a feather, I was that shocked."

"You had no idea?"

"None. I always berated myself after that for not being more perceptive."

"Would you have acted differently if you'd known?"

"Absolutely!" she said starchly. "Maddie, this is an important lesson: never let a man—or anyone, as far as that goes—come between you and a good friend. Friends are too precious to let *anything* jeopardize that relationship."

I did listen carefully, because tears welled up in her eyes when she said this, and she had to remove her glasses again, this time to dab at her eyes with her hankie. That was so uncharacteristic of her, I knew what she was saying was really significant. Actually, I couldn't imagine any silly boy ever coming between Annie and me, so this "lesson" seemed pretty obvious to me. Grown-up love, however . . . I suspected it might be different. "Even though you and Hubert loved each other, you would have given him up if you'd known Dolly loved him?"

"Maddie, if I'd *known* she loved him, I wouldn't even have taken up with him in the first place. I asked Mama if Pansy had told me the truth, and she answered, 'Yes, it did seem like something might be developing between Dolly and Hubert. When you came home, it all changed. I once asked Dolly if she didn't want to tell you that she herself was interested in Hubert, but she said no, that it was clear Hubert was more attracted to you than to her. She insisted none of us tell you.' I was devastated. I had wronged my dearly beloved sister, my best friend in the whole world, and I was afraid that she'd never be friends with me again."

"What did you do? It's not as if you could get divorced or anything."

Gummie frowned. "You're wrong. We *could've* gotten divorced, Maddie. It just wouldn't have solved anything. No, I did the only thing I could do. I wrote Dolly a letter begging her forgiveness, assuring her of my ignorance, and of the road I would've traveled had I known."

"And did she reply?"

"Yes. She was gracious and attempted to ameliorate my misery by assuring me that it was all over, and I needn't worry myself. It wasn't all over, though. We remained friends until her death, but—it was never the same."

An odd mask of grief and something else, something I guessed I was too young to identify, fell across Gummie's face. She never looked this way when she talked about Hubert. Since she'd brought up the subject of Dolly's death, I wondered if I could slip in a question or two, but—remembering Gummie's anger the last time I'd tried to elicit information about this death—I decided to let it be.

Years later, after Gummie had died, I found a box filled with letters—from Gummie to Dolly and vice versa. The following two made me remember Gummie's early version of this rift between the two of them.

> *Dear Dolly,*
> *I hope school is wonderful for you and that you are taking good care of yourself—eating well, getting fresh air and exercise, resting enough.*

I couldn't help smiling. Gummie was always full of advice, always knew what was best for everyone.

> *I have been so lonely without you. I miss you terribly, Dolly, and wish you could be closer to all of us here. Don't worry yourself; everything's fine. Papa gets tired easily, but we all pitch in and help. Mama is strong and happy as ever. Pansy's baby is due soon. If it's anything like the first one, it will run her ragged. She seems to have no inclination for discipline at all.*

I smiled again as she revealed more of her usual style. Meddling, Gramma would've called it, but Mom and I felt more benign toward her. It was just Gummie's way. It did make me wonder though—that judgmental tone regarding discipline—if she'd perhaps been a little harder on Gramma than she was on me or Mom.

> *Violet and all her merry throng are just fine.*
> *Dolly, I've written for a very specific reason.*
> *It has been brought to my attention that, before I returned from my trip out West, you had feelings*

for Hubert. You must believe me when I tell you, Dolly, I HAD NO IDEA. You must know, had I known, I would never have allowed myself or Hubert to entertain any notions of an alliance between us. You must know that you mean as much or more to me than any human being, and I never would've knowingly done anything to hurt you.

Please, Dolly, forgive me for being insensitive and lacking in observation. If there were anything I could do at this point to turn back the clock and undo all the pain I must have caused you, believe me, I would. Gladly. I love you and implore you to forgive me. I throw myself upon your kind mercy.

With love and sorrow, your beloved sister,
Iris

Dolly's reply, dated only two weeks following Iris's letter, was no less heartfelt.

Dearest Iris,

You must not distress yourself anymore. It's true I had feelings for Hubert, but it's also true that it was clear his feelings for you were much stronger than they were for me. Would you expect me to stand in the way of a man's happiness, particularly a man whose happiness was almost as dear to me as my own? Of course not. You know me well enough to know that I would never have expected—or wanted—Hubert to force himself to a false devotion to me when he was so clearly enchanted with you.

I never meant for you to know because I knew

*your high standards of morality would torture you
so. How did you come to know? Surely Hubert
didn't tell you. It must've been Pansy. It would be
just like her to blurt it out—wanting a little
drama, a little excitement. She is such a goose—
and really the most unanalytical person alive.*

*At any rate, I think you can understand when I
tell you—if I had to lose Hubert, I was glad it was
to you. Anyone else would've made me feel a fool,
but you—why naturally he would fall in love with
my clever, remarkable, and beautiful big sister.
Losing him to you is not shameful; it makes sense.*

*Please, Iris, know that I still love you and bear
you no ill will. Indeed, I wish you and Hubert all
the happiness in the world. It would only be a trav-
esty if you two weren't happy. So be happy.*

All my love,
Dolly

I thought of Gummie saying that it "was never the same"
between them. After reading Dolly's letter, I wondered about that.
It certainly was convincing to me: her tone, her words, her logic
all seemed perfectly reasonable and based on love for both Hubert
and Gummie. Why, I wondered, were things never the same? Or
was that just Gummie's guilt talking?

8

Both Work and Love

"Did you ask Guppie about him and Dolly?" I wanted to know.

"Dolly and him," Gummie automatically corrected me. "Oh yes, of course I did. A man and woman can't have secrets between them and expect to have a good marriage." Gummie's lips pressed against one another as she rocked rather furiously.

"What did he say?" I finally asked, giving up on her answering on her own.

"He had the grace to blush and stammer a little. He said something like, 'It's true, Iris, that I cared for Dolly. Given time, that feeling might have grown to something resembling love.' Then he spread his hands in a helpless gesture. 'After you came home, there was no other woman for me.'"

I thought about someone telling me that I was "the only woman" for him and thought about how nice that must be to hear. "Did you forgive him then? After he said that about you being the only woman?"

"I did not," Gummie said firmly. "I told him that he shouldn't have trifled with Dolly's feelings, and he should not have allowed his affection to be so easily swayed. I was angry, you see—at everyone for not having told me, for allowing me to hurt Dolly. Most of all, I was angry at myself. I should've paid more attention. I should've noticed what was going on."

"You wouldn't really want Guppie to *pretend* to love Dolly so as not to hurt her, would you, Gummie?" I thought of all the talk of ethics I'd endured from her. "That would be dishonest, and in the end, it would have hurt her more, don't you think?"

Gummie rocked silently for several minutes, her face stony, before she let her eyes rest on me and soften. "You're right, Maddie. I wouldn't have wanted a pretense for Hubert or Dolly. Or even myself, if it comes to that. I guess what I wanted was for Hubert to have just loved Dolly enough that he never paid me no mind."

"Then *you* would be hurt! Alone and unloved."

"Oh pshaw, Maddie, don't be silly. There would have been plenty of other men besides Hubert. Anyway, I had my work and my other activities. It wouldn't have bothered me much if I'd never had a husband. Dolly needed that more than I did."

"She had her work, too, didn't she?" I objected. "She was a doctor."

"Yes, and a fine one at that. You should understand this, though, Maddie—there are people who are more attached to people, and there are people who are more attached to doing. Dolly was a people-person and I am a doing-person. That doesn't mean you can't be both. I just mean one or the other seems to be your major passion. Do you understand?"

I nodded slowly, wondering about myself. I loved Annie and

Mom, Gummie and Gramma. I couldn't imagine life without them. Still, I loved reading, too, and learning. When all my class-mates bemoaned the return to school each fall, I was secretly delighted. I adored the long, lazy days of summer—lying in the hammock with a glass of warming lemonade on the ground next to me while I was entirely lost to one book after another or riding my bike, Jack trotting alongside, her large, floppy ears bouncing up and down like they were being tugged by invisible strings—but by fall, I was eager to be back in a classroom, to be challenged by the demands of a stern and exacting teacher. Was that like work? Mom always said that my job was school, so I guessed it was. Did I love work more than people? I didn't think I'd want to give up either.

Then I examined Mom and Gramma through this filter. Mom was a librarian. She obviously loved her job, was surrounded by books all day, and mostly had to interact with people who also loved books. She didn't, as I'd earlier noted, date anyone—or at least didn't seem to. She seemed to love Gloria, her best friend, like I did Annie. They did almost everything together. Gloria had been my teacher in the first grade. I adored her—Miss Foster I'd had to call her all that year—almost as much as Gummie and Gramma and Mom. She'd taught me to read, and I never doubted it was the greatest gift anyone ever gave me. For three or four years after first grade, I'd been sure I wanted to be a teacher so that I, too, could give the gift of reading to other children. As I grew older, though, I began to think about being a writer. To give the gift of books would be terrific, too.

Was Mom a lover or a doer? For her, it seemed to just be Gloria, Gummie, Gramma, and me. Annie, too, I guess. Of all of us, though, Mom was the least outgoing, the most introverted. If I had to push it hard, I think maybe Mom did love her job best of all.

With Gramma, it was no contest. She definitely was more attached to people than accomplishment. She would have been deliriously happy to have been married for her entire life, like Gummie was, and devoting herself to making that man happy, as Gummie had not. I asked Gummie about that once, and she answered, "You rarely make yourself or someone else happy by devoting your life to them. Oh, people often think that's what they want, but the best way to make someone happy is to *be* happy yourself."

I mulled this over, then asked, "What about Pansy? You said she and Uncle Albert were happy; it certainly seems that she devoted herself to him."

Gummie shook her head. "You're right, it looked that way. Pansy certainly would've said that's what she was doing, too, but it wasn't really. Pansy devoted herself to the *idea* of marriage and family. She did, in her own way, know what she wanted in life: to make a home. To clean, to arrange flowers, to plan and execute perfect meals, to decorate, to provide clean clothing and linens, to attend to her children's needs—these are the things Pansy wanted to do. Consequently, it made her happy to do them. That very happiness spilled over to her family. She took care of them by taking care of herself."

"And you? Did you take care of your family by working at a job you loved?"

"That's right," she agreed. "Absolutely right."

It seemed to me, that if I got to choose, I wanted to do it the way Gummie had—having both work and love.

9

The Whole Truth

Eventually, after a year or two, I got around to asking Gramma about Gummie and sex. We had a totally different kind of relationship than Gummie and I. Whereas Gummie and I could loll about for hours and talk, Gramma was far too active for "so much chatter," as she put it. Although I had scant inclination for the domestic arts, Gramma did have a pastime that enthralled me and in which she was pleased to include me. She liked to fix and make things.

"How did you come to be so handy, Gramma?" She could fix anything electrical or mechanical, it seemed to me, including the one car that the three adults in our household shared. She was a wonder at carpentry. Our house was filled with bookcases she'd built—and a good thing, too, since we were always needing more shelves for our growing collection. One did not expect a woman who efficiently and lovingly wielded a broom or whisk to do just the same with a screwdriver or hammer.

"Mom was always at work when I was growing up, so I spent a great deal of time with my daddy, probably more than most children did. He was very handy, always teaching me how to do everything he could do."

"Just like you do with me," I stated, and she would nod. Gramma, unlike either Gummie or me, was a woman of relatively few words. She would answer my questions usually, sometimes objecting to some of them, rarely offering much elaboration. Nonethless, I loved working with her. It was restful, speaking little and doing intricate or even boring things with one's hands: attaching tiny wires to other equally tiny wires; inserting miniature metal gadgets into miniscule apertures; gluing legs or arms back on chairs; sanding floors, shelves, bench tops, again and again. "Did you ever want to do this for a job, Gramma, instead of being a nurse?" I was trying to figure out what I wanted to be when I grew up, trying to figure out how anyone determined the direction they should go.

She worked for a long time without answering. She was whittling flutes into the splats of our dining room chairs, which she was remaking because they "are not particularly pretty." Finally, she said, "No. I never seriously thought about doing things men do."

I frowned, without letting up on my job sanding the finished splats. "Why not? You DO do things men do, all the time. Why didn't you think about doing them for a living?"

Again there was a long silence. I'd learned to wait her out on those silences. "Mostly, I guess, because Mom would've *liked* it so much if I'd insisted on doing men's work."

I was startled by such a frank answer. Gramma wasn't usually very analytical. "What?" I responded, not sure I'd heard right.

She waved her whittling knife in the air. "Oh, you know how Mom is. She *worships* the unconventional or controversial. She would've loved it if I had said I wanted to be a carpenter or electrician."

I laughed, thinking how accurate this picture of Gummie was, then asked, "*Did* you want to be those things?"

She shook her head, whittling silently again for several mintues. "Oh, I don't know. Maybe. I loved electrical stuff especially. Daddy taught me everything he knew. Then I learned more, from doing and from books."

She'd completely rewired lamps, added additional amps to our house to accommodate all the extra lighting she'd installed and the new appliances she bought for the kitchen and her workshop, fixed anything that went wrong, and put in a garage door opener when almost no one had heard of them. I don't remember us ever hiring an electrician to do anything around our house. I even had electricity in the tree house she built for me. I knew it was unusual, but I was also so used to her talents I took them for granted. It wasn't until I was an adult that I began to fully appreciate the individual paths my mothers had chosen.

"I loved working with wood, too, but I don't know if I seriously thought about doing any of it for a living. I mean, really, what I wanted was to have babies and cook and clean. Just stay home and take care of a family."

"Like Aunt Pansy?"

"Yeah. Just like her. Mom always had such disdain for Aunt Pansy, but I liked her. She was a little ditzy but sweet and simple and uncomplicated, too. Besides, there were always homemade cookies at her house. Always."

Just like there are for me now, I thought. "So, wanting to be like Pansy was sort of like wanting to *not* be like Gummie?"

I felt her looking at me, but I kept my eyes riveted to my work. "I suppose that's true. I wanted to be the mom my mom never was—the one who stayed home and made cookies." She let out a little bark of a laugh. "That didn't exactly work out, did it?"

I didn't respond, knowing I wasn't meant to. After a few minutes, I continued my questioning. "Why did you go into nursing?"

"Oh, Mom insisted I get an education before she'd let me get married. *Insisted.* I tried to stand up to her but . . . She has a pretty forceful personality, you know," she said dryly, so dryly I burst out laughing. She grinned. "I know. You and Jane are enchanted with her—understandably so, she is enchanting—but you didn't have to be her daughter. That's a whole different ball game."

I thought about that for a minute and figured she was probably right. Gummie undoubtedly was overbearing as a mother, something she rarely was as a grandmother or great-grandmother. "She wanted you to be a nurse?"

"Heavens no! She wanted me to go to college. If I must be in medicine, then she wanted me to be a doctor."

"Like Dolly."

"Yes. Like Dolly. Never taking into account what *I* wanted, what *I* had aptitude for. I chose nursing because it was, back then, an acceptable career for women, and—besides—I knew it would bug Mom."

Again I was surprised at her candor. "Were you right? Did she hate it?"

"Yes, sort of. She tried to accept it, acting as if it were my *choice* instead of a rebellion against her. Then Jordie died and . . . most of her energy was turned inward. She left me alone for awhile. We were all so devastated, as you can imagine. I actually did think about becoming a doctor. Like maybe I could've saved Jordie or something."

"You didn't, though."

"No, I was madly in love with George by then, graduated in December of 1932, and ran off to get married right away. A terrible gloom had fallen over our house after Jordie died. I was anxious to be out of there. Maybe a little too anxious."

That was the closest I had ever heard Gramma express even possible regret about her marriage to George Thoreson. I was torn between wanting to hear about the errant husband and wanting to hear about the dead son. Jordie was Gramma's little brother, Hubert Harris Jordan, Junior. I knew he was adopted in 1920 when Gramma was already nine years old and Gummie was approaching fifty.

"Did you resent a baby coming into the house after you'd been the only one for so long?" I tried to imagine what I'd feel like if Mom had another baby, but that made me think of her having sex and resulted in my shying away from the subject altogether. I concentrated on my sanding. I had to spend as much time smoothing each splat as Gramma had spent doing the fluting.

Gramma continued working in silence for several seconds before answering me. "I don't think so. I don't remember ever feeling bad about Jordie at all. Except when he died, of course." She was silent for a while longer, then added, "I guess it was because I was so much older, I had my own life by then and was pretty secure about my place in the family."

"Gummie and Guppie were gone a lot. Didn't you get stuck taking care of Jordie all the time?"

Gramma smiled at this. "Sometimes, but I didn't mind. You have to remember, Maddie—I was wild about babies. I always expected to have a bunch. Also, Mom had day help, so it wasn't like I was in charge or anything."

"Why'd Gummie get another baby, do you suppose? It wasn't as if she wanted to stay home and take care of babies or anything. Weren't you sufficient?"

Gramma laughed. "Oh, Maddie, you have such a funny way of putting things. Sufficient? Yes, I suppose I was sufficient. I don't think they ever intended to have more children. Then one night

71

we were all in town having dinner with Auntie Vi's family, and Vi was talking about this pitiful baby boy at the Maternity Hospital where she volunteered. That place where I was born."

She said nothing more, and I waited as patiently as I could, letting the rhythm of the sanding absorb me, knowing she'd continue when she was ready. "Auntie Vi told us he'd been born with some kind of problem and how he probably would never be adopted because of it. I saw, across Auntie Vi's enormous dining room table, a light in Gummie's eyes as she asked a half dozen questions. I knew—right away—I was about to become a big sister."

"What was wrong with Jordie?"

"He had a hole in his heart. The medical community thought it might be fixable, but it was going to take more than one surgery and was going to cost a lot."

"So Gummie wanted him because he needed her?"

"Something like that. She never could resist a cause, you know." I nodded. After a few minutes, she added, "Also, I think Mom knew Daddy really wanted a boy."

I frowned at this thought. "Did he say that? Did you overhear something that would make you believe such a thing?" This didn't seem right to me because, from everything I'd heard, Guppie doted on Hester, who worked side by side with him around the house and accompanied him on many of his out-of-town trips as she got older.

"No, nothing was ever said, so far as I know. It was . . ." she hesitated, resting her hands for a moment as she gazed into the past. "I think it was because they made him a junior. Hubert Harris Jordan, Jr. I think this made me realize Daddy wanted a boy because, you know, *I* could never be a junior."

This was a lot of talking for Gramma, so I didn't ask any more questions for a while. I went upstairs and got us some cocoa, letting Jack out to do her business. Large, puffy snowflakes—resembling tufts of quilting—were lazily drifting toward earth in the brittle cold of early winter. I remember the steam from the heating milk covering the window above the stove and me tracing my name in it.

The basement, where Gramma had created her bright workshop, was cozy and inviting, with the furnace I called The Octopus thumping away next to us and all the extra lighting Gramma had strung up to illuminate the room for her intricate work. The Octopus was a gravity furnace, very common in old houses, and Gramma and I had fixed it more than once.

She thanked me while sipping her chocolate. When she went back to her fluting, I asked, "How come you and Jordie were adopted?"

Without lifting her head, Gramma said, "What do you mean?"

"How come you were adopted?" I repeated. "How come Guppie and Gummie just didn't have babies the usual way?"

"Mom had female trouble before she and Daddy were ever even married and had a hysterectomy. You know what that means?" She peered at me.

"Sure. It means the doctors took out her baby-making stuff." She looked sharply at me, and I knew she wanted accuracy, so I elucidated, "Her uterus and ovaries." She nodded and said no more.

Okay, I thought, *how do I go on from here?* Finally, I blundered on, "So, a hysterectomy would prevent her from having her own babies, but it didn't mean she and Guppie . . ." I hesitated, not knowing what to say exactly and realizing if Gummie were here, I'd be getting her X-ray look plus a lecture on manners.

Gramma glanced up at me, a look of surprise on her face. "Why are you asking me this?"

I assumed—with no little relief—she knew what it was I was asking. "Because . . . because I heard Gummie'd never had, you know, ah . . . sex with Guppie, and I was just wondering . . ." *What was it I was wondering?* I suddenly thought.

Gramma stared at me with obvious surprise. "Wherever did you hear that?" she demanded to know.

"Oh, I don't know," I was purposefully vague. Gramma was extremely sour on my father, and I was afraid if I told her I'd heard him talking about it, she'd just clam up and talk no more. "It's not true, then?" I tried to dissuade her from focusing on where I'd heard about Gummie's sex life. Or lack thereof.

She shook her head slowly. "I don't know, Maddie. It might be true. It's not the sort of thing one would ask Mom." We smiled knowingly at each other. "Some people say they used to sew women's vaginas shut after a hysterectomy." Pretty much what Mom had told me. "I guess because the thinking was . . ." She hesitated here, peeking at me as if to remind herself, I thought, of whether or not I was old enough to hear this. Apparently I passed muster because she continued. "The thinking was—" she shook her head, obviously in some disgust, which made me think *she* thought sex was something you did for pleasure, not just for babies— "if you weren't going to have babies, you didn't need to have those openings for anything else."

She worked silently again, then surprised me by adding, without looking up, "Daddy was such an honorable man, he was impotent by the time he was thirty-five."

Impotent? I wasn't sure what that meant, but I was pretty sure she was telling me something important. "What do you mean, Gramma?" I asked carefully.

"Oh," she waved her whittling knife again, dismissing the subject, "Nothing. You're too young, really." Inwardly, I sputtered at her attitude, thinking I was perfectly old enough, but I knew that was the end of that.

Impotent. The word was curiously fascinating to me. I looked it up in the dictionary. "Incapable of sexual intercourse, often because unable to achieve or maintain an erection."

"That means," Annie told me importantly (she knew a great many things because of her older sister), "he couldn't get a hard-on." We giggled, in spite of ourselves. "Hard-on" was such a salacious term.

I thought about all of this and decided I was not certain what Gramma had been telling me. I understood about Guppie not being able to "get it up," but what was it she was saying about him being "so honorable?"

I finally gave up and asked Mom. She laughed, responding, "Oh, she told you, too, huh?"

I always felt a little disappointed when I discovered I wasn't the first repository of the family stories. I usually forgot that Mom, too, had once been a child, probably full of curiosity and questions, as well. "What does it mean, Mom? I know what impotence means, but what about the rest of it?" It was the first time that I'd heard a sentence in which I knew every word (not impotence, but I found out its meaning) and still didn't understand the sentence.

"Gramma is saying—when he couldn't have sex with his wife— Guppie didn't go elsewhere to get his needs met. The result was he lost his ability to have it at all."

"Oh," I said, pushing her words around in my head until the light dawned. "'Honorable' means he didn't go to a prostitute, you mean?" Mom nodded. "Do you think it's true?"

She shrugged. "I don't know. Gramma would believe it because she thought her father was perfect. It was true, I think, he adored Gummie, so maybe he would just accept the conditions of their marriage. All of this is assuming Gummie really was sewed up." She shook her head a little. "I once did some research on this subject, Maddie, just trying to find out if it could be true. Because with Gummie . . ."

She hesitated there, until I finished her sentence by saying, "It doesn't seem possible she wasn't sexually active."

Mom raised her eyebrows but agreed. "Yes. Well. I never could find anything very precise, but it's possible, I guess. There were no standardized procedures in that time; few medical schools even had gynecological courses; each doctor did it his own way."

"How is it Gramma would even know about Guppie's impotence, Mom? I wouldn't think her parents would ever tell her such things. Gummie's so adamant about privacy."

"Oh, people talk," Mom responded. "You don't have a bunch of cousins like Gramma did, so you don't know how a big family jabbers. Grown-ups talk about things in front of kids as if they don't have ears or something, and kids walk around like little sponges—absorbing all those conversations, then they share the details with each other, often trying to figure out what it all means. I'm sure that's how Mom found out."

Now, I thought with a thrill at the continuity of generations, *I know about it, too.* I still wondered if I'd *ever* know the whole truth.

10

As Legitimate As Anyone Else

"When did you move out of Minneapolis?" That was the usual way I got Gummie started, by asking a random question or two. We were sitting on the porch—the two of us and Jack, my dog—bundled up because, although the apple trees across the street were in lovely but tentative bloom, the edge of winter was still nibbling at our fingertips. Jack and I huddled together for extra warmth. We were ready, however, to start lingering on the porch—welcoming warm, green, noisy days after one of our long, black and white, silent winters—so there we were in sweaters and gloves and hats, pretending porch weather had arrived, a bit prematurely.

"Hester was just a baby. Papa had died the year before and Mama had lost her desire to run the boarding house alone, even with Hubert's and my help, which wasn't much actually, because we were both so busy. She sold the place and moved into Violet's enormous and mostly empty house, all her children but one being gone by then."

"That's when you moved to Riverton?"

"Not right away. We were not certain what to do next, so we stayed with Vi for a little while. It bought us a little time, but our stay was destined to be brief. Vi wouldn't have minded if we'd just moved in with her, but it was not like being in Mama and Papa's house. We were guests. Vi's husband . . . well. He was not so bad, really, but his politics were radically different from ours, and neither Guppie nor I were comfortable living in a mansion built on the backs of exploited mill workers. It was an untenable situation. I, especially, had a difficult time keeping myself from being drawn into constant arguments."

"I'll bet," I said, grinning. I had a bit of a problem with just such behavior in myself—more physical as a child, more verbal as I grew older.

She narrowed her eyes at me. "Don't be fresh now, child," but there was no rancor in her voice, and she continued, "I was starting to feel dissatisfied and restless at the paper. It was clear to me I was never going to get a chance at real responsibility. I did everything and a lot of it, but I was still, basically, a reporter. I wanted more challenge."

"That's when you thought about buying your own paper?"

"Maybe I would've, but Hubert thought of it first. He came home one day from one of his trips and told me about this weekly for sale in Riverton. *Riverton*? I thought. *A small town? A weekly?* I was pretty doubtful. Hubert and I went and talked to the owner, anyway, and walked all over the town. It was considerably smaller than it is now, Maddie." Riverton had a population of about 10,000 in the '60s, but in 1910—when Gummie and Guppie moved there— it was a sleepy little river town with about 1,200 people.

"We both fell in love with this dear little town sitting on the banks of the Mississippi. It reminded us of the villages we'd both grown up in. We got excited about the prospect of owning our own house, and I gradually got giddy at the thought of being in charge, doing a newspaper just the way I wanted to do it."

"So you went right back and got Hester and moved?"

"Just about. The train service was good; it was no problem for Guppie to get into the City or elsewhere. Trains were wonders in those days, Maddie, crisscrossing the state and going to nearly every small town so it wasn't difficult for someone like Hubert. Later we got a car, but in the beginning the trains were more than sufficient. Plus, it didn't matter where Guppie lived, he was on the road so much. Do you remember our little house on Maple Street?"

I nodded. Even though I'd only been eight when Guppie had died and Gummie moved in with us, I remembered the house well. There was a swing hanging on the big elm out back, so high my feet could barely reach the ground when I perched on it the last summer before Guppie died. "That's the house we had built in 1910. I wanted it small and compact because I knew I would never have much time or inclination to keep it up."

There were two little rooms under the eaves upstairs, Hester's and Jordie's rooms, and another bedroom on the first floor for Gummie and Guppie. I got to stay overnight when I was very little, sleeping in the room that had been Gramma's. It always seemed like a miniature house to me with its small front room, tiny dining room, and miniscule kitchen. The house I'd lived in all my life had a parlor, an enormous dining room, and a kitchen big enough to accomodate a table in its center, as well as a room at the back for the live-in help, which Gramma could never afford and which eventually became Gummie's room—plus four more bedrooms upstairs. There was an attic above the rest of it.

Once I asked Mom, "How come our house is so much bigger than Gummie's was?"

"When Gramma and her husband," Mom rarely referred to "that odious man" as her father, "bought this house, Mom thought she'd stay at home and fill it with babies."

"Was she very sad when George left?" I'd never been taught to call him *grandpa* and couldn't imagine doing so. He was the man who'd wronged my Gramma.

Mom nodded. "Very. It was probably for the best—I think even Mom knew this—but still, it hurt a lot. He never was going to settle down. He gambled, drank, womanized. That hurt, too. After he left, Mom actually had more dignity than she did when he was still at home."

"How was she able to keep the house?"

"Because she took in boarders . . ."

"Like Gummie's parents," I interrupted.

"That's right. She did that for some years, until it was paid for, which she was able to accomplish because she made good and steady money being a nurse, also. I was a teenager before we stopped having strangers living in the house with us."

"You never saw him again?" I switched back to the missing husband.

She shook her head. "Nope. He never even sent a postcard or anything. Except for that one note." This was said with considerable bitterness in her voice. I didn't understand entirely. Having never had a father who was part of my life, I couldn't quite imagine what it would be like to lose one.

"So," I said carefully, "it hurt you, too?"

She smiled her crooked smile, shrugged anything but nonchalantly, and said, "Yes. It hurt a lot. It wasn't as if he was ever much of a father to me. He was rarely even home. Even when he was home, he hardly noticed me. Still. He was my father. I could always *hope* he'd notice me."

The "one note" was a card postmarked in Bismarck, North Dakota, reading, "I won't be back. Sorry." That was it.

"If he walked in the door this very minute," I asked Mom, "would you throw your arms around his neck," I'd seen such a scene in a movie and liked the way it looked, "and forgive him?" He'd been gone about twenty-five years at that point.

It was a Sunday morning. We were in the kitchen, preparing the only meal each week that Mom cooked. Gramma had gone to church with Mom's friend, Gloria, who would join us for dinner afterward, and Gummie was listening to her regular Sunday news program on the radio. Mom was cutting onions, potatoes, and carrots for the pot roast while I was mixing the biscuit dough. I didn't like to cook very much, but Gramma had convinced me if I liked to eat, I should know how to cook.

"Certainly not," Mom answered crisply. "I'd probably get a gun and shoot him."

My eyes got very big. "Really?"

"No, not really, Maddie," she laughed at my astonishment, leaning over to press a kiss on my forehead. "I'd feel like it, though."

"Was he the reason you never married?" *And never had much sex,* I wondered but didn't quite have the temerity to ask. Nor was I sure I'd want her to answer.

She shrugged. "It might have had something to do with it. He certainly didn't leave me with a terribly good impression of men. On the other hand, I also had Guppie—who was more of a father to me than George had ever been. I don't know, Maddie. Guppie certainly made it clear men *could* be good and decent, and I did have that sterling example of Gummie and Guppie's successful marriage."

"You still didn't believe too many men were good though, did you?" I'd never actually heard her say anything like this, but I felt pretty certain that's what she thought.

She laughed. "I don't know about 'good.' I guess I don't trust many men. Really, men are different from women, Maddie, but in one way, they're just the same—there're good ones and bad ones. To tell the truth, I just don't think about them too much at all. Few men I've ever known were as smart or fun or caring as the women I've known: Mom, you, Gummie, my friends."

"Like Gloria."

She nodded. "Definitely Gloria."

"What about *my* father?" I asked. "Didn't you ever think about marrying him?"

She laughed even louder this time. "Oh no, Maddie. Never. I just wanted a baby. That's all. I've told you this before."

"I know, but I want to hear it again."

She sighed. "I knew Roman was headed for wrack and ruin—the drink, you know, but he was handsome and intelligent. His whole family was smart and good-looking. I figured a baby coming from our gene pool would be stunning. I was right, wasn't I? Look at you!" She reached over and tucked a piece of my nothing-colored hair—Mom called it blond, Gramma light brown—behind my ear.

I felt a warm spot on each of my cheeks. I *was* smart enough, I'd give her that, but I wasn't so certain about the good-looking part. I was short and sort of scrawny, all legs and arms. While Annie was filling out and acquiring curves—both desired and dreaded—I just seemed to stay the same. My face was painfully ordinary, I thought, dominated—it seemed to me, anyway—by my glasses. What was it Dorothy Parker said? "Men seldom make passes at girls who wear glasses." That was probably written twenty or thirty years before I was even born. I wasn't so sure I wanted anyone to be making "passes" at me, but I got the underlying message: girls with glasses were unattractive.

"How come, if you didn't think he was the one, Mom, you never married anyone else?" *Of course*, I thought to myself, *it would be hard to marry someone if you never even* dated *anyone.*

"I never had any intention of getting married, Maddie." There was amusement in her voice. "It simply wasn't in the cards for me."

"Really?" I asked, looking at her out of the corner of my eye. She was just my mom to me, but I had to think—if I looked at her as an outsider might—she was pretty nice to look at. She wasn't exactly slender, but her roundness wasn't unpleasing. Her large brown eyes—inherited from that odious man—were soft and expressive; her honey-colored hair was cut short in a no-nonsense style that nicely framed her face. "How come?"

Because Gummie had been married forever, I think I just sort of thought marriage was the norm. Even though neither Gramma nor Mom were married, Gummie always seemed to set the standards for my life. Now that I thought about it, Gummie would've been just as happy unmarried as not. She always preached "women should make conscious choices, not just drift through their lives."

Mom shook her head. "I don't know if I can explain, Maddie. I just knew at a very young age I was never going to live that kind of life, the married-wife-mother life. I wanted something different for myself. Honestly, I just wasn't very interested in men." *Like maybe you didn't like sex?* "I never met a man I thought I would want to spend the rest of my life with. I did want a child, however, so I took care of that and moved on into the life of my choosing."

"Wasn't it an awful scandal? You having a baby without a husband?" Actually, I *knew* it was a scandal. There had been plenty of times I'd heard—been meant to hear, actually— whisperings of the words "illegitimate" and "immoral." Many mothers wouldn't let their kids have anything to do with me.

The first time I'd heard such talk, when I started school, I'd asked Gummie what "illegitimate" meant, stumbling on the pronunciation but obviously conveying it well enough. She was livid. "It means, Madelaine, some people have small, dreary minds, and nothing better to do than judge others."

This was not at all helpful to me, so I asked Gramma. She looked very sad, took me on her lap and rocked me, before answering. "It's just a word, Maddie, and it's important you learn young not to let other people have power with words of their making. What it *actually* means is your mother wasn't married when you were born." This had little meaning to me because, so far, my mother not being married had just been ordinary to me. I hadn't, yet, realized this was somehow different. Or wrong.

Gramma may not have approved of her daughter's choices, but she knew what was important: the love we all had for one another. She was fiercely protective and loving, always. She squeezed me, almost too hard, and said, "You just tell me if anyone ever gives you a hard time, and believe you me, I'll take care of them." I never doubted she would.

When I finally asked Mom about the word, she said, also angrily, "You're just as legitimate as anyone else in this world, Maddie, and don't you forget it."

"What does that mean?" I wailed. "Ligimite or igimite?"

"Legitimate or illegitimate," Mom automatically corrected my pronunciation. "It's stupid, Maddie. It has to do with the law and common practices. It has to do with whether someone is a 'legitimate'—meaning *legal*—heir, based on marriage or lack of it. The word almost implies the child of unmarried parents is not real, not genuine. Are you real?"

"Yes." Being real, however, didn't aid in clearing my confusion.

"Like I said, it's a stupid, medieval concept. Anyone who talks like that is not worth knowing. *Do you understand?*" she underlined. I nodded dutifully, even though I understood almost nothing. "*They are not worth knowing.* I know it hurts to be treated like there's something wrong with you, but you must learn right now—this is their problem, not yours."

So, I did know all about the scandal of Mom's choices, but she replied anyway, as if it was the first time I'd asked. "Sure, it was a scandal. I just decided what I wanted was more important than what other people thought. You know what Gummie always says?"

I rifled through my catalog of Gummie's aphorisms before replying, "'The odder you are, the more freedom you have?'"

Mom smiled again. "That's the one. It's true, Maddie. I have more freedom than almost any woman I know, and I'm happy. Isn't happiness more important than having a lot of people think you're acceptable?"

I guessed so, although I did realize—in a way I couldn't quite put into words then—I had never really known what it would be like to be "legitimate." Or acceptable. Or even ordinary.

11

A Capacity for Joy

Unlike Dolly's death, Jordie's death was not shrouded in mystery. He'd had two experimental surgeries before he was five to fix his heart. They were successful—or so they thought. What the doctors didn't tell the family, probably because they didn't know in those days, Gramma said, was that his heart would never be as strong as it would've been if he'd been born with a good one in the first place. Iris and Hubert never treated Jordie as if he had any limitations, as if he should be careful.

He was a lively boy—climbing trees, building rafts to sail a la Huck Finn and Tom Sawyer down the Mississippi (although the Mississippi was a good bit smaller this far north than it was down in Huck's and Tom's region), playing sandlot baseball. He was not, Gummie always said, as good at school as she and Guppie would've liked.

"He was a little too squirmy, a little too impulsive to settle down and attend to his studies properly. Not that I'm making excuses for the boy. I never did hold with that boys-will-be-boys nonsense. Pansy excused a multitude of sins for her sons, using that excuse. I thought it was criminal. No, I'm not making any excuses for Jordie. I'm just stating the facts. We tried, but we just couldn't get him to settle down. His mind was like a humming-bird, just flitting from one subject to another without lighting anywhere."

"He wasn't dumb, was he?"

"Oh no, he was bright enough. Who knows? If he'd lived . . ." Her face would be inexpressibly sad at this utterance, then she'd perk up again and say, "Let me tell you, Maddie, he had a capacity for joy like nobody's business! Why Jordie just brightened up everyone's life! He never took a piano lesson but could sit down and pick out tunes, just from listening to them! He told tall tales that made you howl—they were so outrageous and absurd! His smile was like fireworks, it just exploded all over his face and lit up the sky!" Her own face would be soft and happy in the memory of her son.

I might say something like, "Maybe he was just here to make everybody happy for a little bit of time, Gummie, don't you think?" Gramma had once told me that was what she believed, and it made sense to me.

Gummie'd stare across the road at some boys on bikes, then nod slowly but firmly. "Might just be, Maddie, might just be, indeed. He certainly did make everyone happy. I would get so frustrated, and so would Hubert, trying to work with him about his lessons. Just when I thought I would lose my temper, that boy would throw his arms around me and plant a big kiss on my cheek and sing a song he'd made up about irises. Why, you just couldn't stay mad at him."

I used to paw through Gummie's old picture albums, wanting to see pictures of the ones who died before I was born: Mama and Papa and Dolly and Violet and Jordie. I especially liked a special family snapshot. It must have been taken shortly before Jordie's death because it was summer, and he looked to be about ten. He died during his tenth summer. Gramma was sitting on a blanket with a young man and lots of food spread around them. Gummie had confirmed my supposition that this was "that odious man," but his head was bent away from the camera, so I could not see his face clearly.

Gramma wore a pretty, flowered summer frock, carefully pulled below her knees although she was comfortably reclining, and Gummie was sitting on a chair at the edge of the blanket, in pants and a middy top. Both had their mouths open and were laughing. Hubert must've been taking the picture because he was not in sight. Jordie—with short pants and a cowboy hat—was riding a bicycle on the grass right next to the blanket, and the front wheel was in the air, so he resembled a man on a bucking stallion. His head was thrown back, the cowboy hat sliding off to reveal his tangle of brown curls, his mouth wide open in what appeared to be a shout of triumph. How could somebody with so much life suddenly be dead?

"We had no warning," Gummie would tell me when I asked her.

I was a little obsessed with the idea of Jordie's death. Guppie was an old man when he died. To my mind, that made sense. But a little boy? It scared me. Could I die? With no warning? Could Annie?

"One minute he was fine, laughing even, the next he was gone." I always imagined him on his bike, popping wheelies, shouting gleefully, and then the bike tumbling over as Jordie fell dead— even though I knew that wasn't how it happened.

"He was coming down the stairs, rushing down them actually,

like he always did, sounding like a herd of elephants, and I said something inconsequential like, 'Slow down, boy, there's no fire in this house.'" Gummie would pause here; I knew, from experience, her voice had to swallow its quaver before she could continue. "Then he collapsed."

She rocked and sniffed; I waited. After a few minutes, Gummie continued. I'd heard the story many times. Now that I'm an adult and have lost some of my own loved ones, I understand better Gummie's compulsion to tell this story over and over again. People seem to comprehend women's need to tell their birthing stories endlessly; why don't they understand that death stories need to be repeated, too?

"I ran to Jordie, yelling for Hubert who was out back with Dolly, who just happened to be visiting. They both came running, Dolly yelling for her bag upstairs. I ran up and got it, thundering back down. It was a miracle I didn't fall and break my neck. Hubert was on the phone, demanding an ambulance. Dolly was pushing on Jordie's chest, insisting, 'Breathe, Jordie, breathe.'"

She rocked some more, and I waited some more. "She never quit. Climbed right in the ambulance with him and kept pushing and begging him to breathe. He was probably dead right away, they told us later. His little heart just gave out, but Dolly kept thinking she could revive him. Hubert and I? We kept hoping she was right, but he was gone, our dear, sweet boy—so full of life and promise—he was gone. Death is hard, Maddie, especially when it takes a youngster."

By now, tears would be streaming down Gummie's face. Mine, too. She would dig around in her sleeve, fetching her hankie, yank off her glasses almost angrily, wipe her eyes, and blow her nose with a resounding honk. I'd go to the bathroom to get some tissue, never being able to stand the idea of a hankie.

I asked Gramma once if she felt that her parents loved Jordie more than her, "you know, because he died so young, and almost perfect." She shook her head, impatiently, "No, Maddie, I sure never did. Love is not like that. There's always room for everyone."

"You think so?" I asked, wondering if I'd want to share Mom's and Gramma's and Gummie's love with siblings.

"Sure. Let me show you." She pulled the four brass candle-holders, which always stood in the center of our oak table in the dining room, to the edge of the table. She lit the first one, then took the second candle and lit it off of the first one and took the third one and repeated that action, until they were all lit. Then she said, "See these candles, Maddie?" I nodded. "Is the flame bigger on any of them?" I shook my head. "They're all just the same size, right?" I nodded again. "That's how love is, Maddie. Doesn't matter how many times you get someone new to love, the flame is just as strong, just as bright. These candles don't get weaker by sharing this flame with others, there's just more light and more flame. That's how love is, too. The more you love, the bigger the light and warmth."

I'd think about how much I loved her and Gummie and Mom, my best friend, Annie, and Mom's best friend, Gloria, and I'd guess she was right. I loved all of them differently, but I still loved all of them—big and wide and deep and hot. And they loved me back, the same way.

12

Jack

It had been years earlier that the patterns of our lives together had been set. During my preschool days, I spent most of my time alone or with one of my mothers. I didn't mind, didn't know enough to mind. I went to work with Gummie or trailed around the kitchen or workroom after Gramma, ending most days snuggled in my mom's arms as she read to me. I loved the hustle and bustle of the newspaper office, the smell of fresh ink on paper, the sense of urgency. I equally loved the moist, sweet odor of oatmeal cookies or the smooth elasticity of bread dough under the palms of my hands as well as the feel of heavy and unyielding tools, their very bulk promising function. The billowy softness of another's body and the smell of lilacs, my mother's favorite perfume, still trigger drowsiness in me. All of these elements came to mean love and security. The world outside this world did not beckon to me. I did not know I was missing anything.

Then I started school. It seemed to me, right away, that everyone else had a friend. Someone to eat lunch with, walk home with, exchange confidences with. I not only had no such person in my life, I was continually rebuffed whenever I tried to create such a connection.

"My mom says I can't play with you because you're illegitimate." Or "Your mother's not married, and you're atheists, too."

Once the concept of illegitimacy was clear, I went on to tackle atheism. "What's an atheist, Gramma?"

"Someone who doesn't believe in God," was Gramma's indifferent answer.

I thought about that, turning it over in my head. "Are we atheists?" I figured we must be because I didn't exactly know who God was, let alone whether or not I believed in him.

"Certainly not!" was her sharp response, then she softened, "I'm not. Your Gummie probably would say she is and . . ." saying this in a way that made me think she didn't believe Gummie, even if she said she was an atheist. Here she hesitated, stilling the beating of her sauce for a moment while she gazed out the window at the leaves drifting to the earth. I took advantage of her inattention and snatched a fingerful out of the bowl. "I guess I don't know for certain what your mother would call herself. You'd best ask her." She pursed her lips. "Better ask Gummie, too. She'll surely want to talk it over with you."

"What about me?"

She bestowed one of her serene smiles on me and said, "Lovey, you're too young to know, I guess. You'll decide later."

"Atheists," Gummie pronounced, "are the thinking people in the world. They're folk who refuse to accept nonsense on blind faith. An atheist knows life is what you make of it, not just a big stage with someone else pulling the strings. Maddie, listen carefully for this is important: an atheist has faith in concrete things, like people or systems, not in something that's made up because people need an authority-figure in their lives."

Mom's response was an interesting counterpoint to Gummie's. "I guess I think atheists are just as arrogant as Christians or other people who believe in some kind of god. Atheists say they know there is no god and Christians say they know there is a god. How can anyone know for sure? I call myself agnostic, Maddie, which means I just don't know. There might be a god and there might not be. Either way, it's okay with me. It's also okay I don't know. I think questions are more important than answers, anyway."

None of this was particularly helpful. I still didn't know who God was, and I still didn't know why other kids couldn't play with me. "Why would anyone tell me they can't play with me because we're atheists?"

"Who said such a thing?" Gramma wanted to know. "Is this the same child who called you illegitimate?"

"You just tell anyone who talks that way," Gummie insisted, "they're poor misguided souls who've never learned to think for themselves."

Mom took me into her lap and cuddled me. "Maddie, kids won't play with you because you don't have a daddy who lives with you and someone in your family might be an atheist?" I nodded, burrowing deep into her softness and drinking in her odor. "Oh, honey," her voice was stricken and she rocked me, patting my back absentmindedly. "Oh, honey," she repeated, "some things I just didn't think of. I never wanted you to pay the price for my decisions." I didn't exactly know what she meant, but I liked it that somehow it was her fault.

By the beginning of first grade, I quit trying to make friends. I spent my recesses reading, leaning against brick walls warmed by the sun in the fall and spring. During cold weather, I either stayed inside or—if I was forced to go outside all bundled up against the elements (as we all were, our elders being convinced "fresh air" was good for us, although I suspected those elders just wanted a break)—I walked around the edges of our shoveled playground, making no attempt to join the other children in their games of angel-making or snowman-building or sliding down the slight rise behind our school. That way, I gave no one the opportunity to reject me.

Mom and Gramma didn't really notice, at first, so content in their own lives were they. When they became more aware, especially after I had asked questions about illegitimacy and atheism, they had whispered conferences with one another, invited strange kids over who just ended up staring at me, talked to teachers, and finally gave up—trying to explain to me it wasn't about me, it wasn't my fault. I didn't like or appreciate their efforts. They never seemed to understand: I had to make my own friends. Or else just be left alone.

It certainly wasn't that I was miserable. I loved books and was happy to live on pages most of the time. I had Boo-Boo, my imaginary playmate from preschool days who took on a new kind of presence in my life. He was a cross between a boy—a very nice boy, nothing like the horrid examples of boyhood at school—and a cuddly teddy bear in polka-dotted trousers, dark purple on bright yellow. I made up stories for him, making him laugh, and he made up stories for me, making me cry. I learned to live inside of myself, not to rely on others, but still, truth be told, I longed for a friend. I wanted the "kindred spirit" of the *Anne of Green Gable's* books my mom read to me.

Mom and Gramma came up with a solution to usurp Boo-Boo and banish my friendless state. Entering the kitchen after school on my sixth birthday, I was greeted with the sight of a fluffy, reddish-brown, big pawed, black-nosed creature who was ignoring the newspapers laid out for her and peeing directly on the linoleum.

"A puppy!" I squealed.

"Oh no," Gramma moaned. "Not again. Puppy!" She scooped the dog up and tossed her out the back door. Gramma shook her finger sternly at the puppy, who was already ignoring her. "Outside! Don't pee in my house!"

I followed the animal, kneeling down and putting my fingers out. She licked them, then nibbled a little—her tiny, sharp teeth feeling like a dozen pinpricks, and finally she put her big paws on my chest and began slathering my face with her soft, wet tongue. I laughed, falling backward, holding the puppy up in the air. She was squirming and yelping, and immediately dribbled urine on my face. "Oh, yech!" I screamed, laughing, as we rolled around together. Then I jumped to my feet and raced around the back-yard, the dog following, yipping excitedly.

Gramma sat on the back steps, watching us and smiling. "What are you going to call her, Maddie?"

"I don't know. What kind of dog is she, Gramma?"

"Heinz 57, I guess."

"What does that mean?"

"A mutt. Brand unknown. A mix of different kinds of dogs. Her mother was a springer and some kind of terrier. We don't know what her father was, but she shouldn't be too large." Gramma was wrong, though. The puppy weighed seventy pounds before she was a year old. "Should have paid attention to those humongous paws," Gramma would mumble.

"Jack," I announced at dinner. "I'm gonna call her Jack."

"After Laura's dog?" Mom asked me. She was reading me *The Little House in the Big Woods* series by Laura Ingalls Wilder, and Laura had a dog named Jack in her books. I nodded.

"It's a girl," Gramma pointed out.

"So?"

Jack became my constant companion. She presumably slept on the rug next to my bed, but as soon as Mom checked me before she went to bed herself—I was only supposed to read one chapter of one book before I turned my light out, but I always read until I heard Mom coming up the stairs, then would quickly extinguish my light, pretending to be asleep—Jack would hop up on my bed and curl at my feet.

She would whimper when I left for school in the morning and be waiting on the porch, alert and tense, when I returned at the end of the day. Her fuzzy, baby fur gave way to long, sleek, brown-and-white hair as she grew and grew that first year, her sweet face helping to offset her formidable size. She was fierce and protective if she thought anything or anyone might harm me, but otherwise was loving and good-natured and playful.

I brushed her daily and took her for long walks at least twice a day. We would romp together and go swimming together, and I would slip her little bits of "people" food under the table, even though I wasn't supposed to. Our photo albums are filled with pictures of me on the porch glider, reading, Jack curled precariously next to me; me in the hammock, reading, Jack slumped next to me, head peeking over the hammock edge at the photo-taker; Jack and me sitting on a sled together; the two of us sitting on the back steps, my arm slung around her neck, her tongue lolling out of her mouth as she rested against me.

She was a fine friend, loving me with an unconditional devotion even my mothers couldn't match. When I felt sad or lonely, Jack always seemed to know and would come and lean against me or push her cold, damp nose into my ear. I would bury my face in her neck and tell her things I'd only shared with Boo-Boo before.

Then she'd force her big, old head under my hand, making me

laugh and say, "That's your cure for everything, isn't it, Jack? I should pet you, then I'll feel better, right?" It was clear she agreed with me. She was right, too. I did feel better—loving and being loved. My friend Annie once said, "Have you noticed? Jack loves us by letting us love her." But that was much later.

Mom was affectionately distant with her—the way she was with almost everyone but me. Gramma continuously sniped at her—"Get your nose out of that wastebasket, Jack!" or "Jack! Get out in the back hall until those muddy feet are dry!" or "Get out of my kitchen, Jack! I can't stand to have you underfoot!"—but it was abundantly clear to me she was abundantly fond of Jack, in spite of her irritation.

She once confided to me, "I always wanted a dog, Maddie. Something Mom could never understand."

Gummie was the only one who totally resisted Jack's charms, muttering things under her breath like, "Marx was wrong. *Pets* are the opiate of the people." When I brought Jack with me to the newspaper, she would snap, "Get that dog out of here! We don't allow dogs in our office!" I would ignore her, and—after her perfunctory objection—she would pretend not to notice Jack's presence. She undoubtedly figured out that, without Jack, I wouldn't come to the office.

When Gummie moved in with us she did insist that Jack could not come in her bedroom. Gummie had a right to make decisions about her own room, Gramma pointed out to me. Jack would lie on the floor in the bedroom door, looking sorrowful, but she learned to accept this rule.

In these ways, Jack became a member of the family—wiggling her way into all our hearts, whether we each admitted it or not. I had no trouble admitting it. She was my heart's joy, the "concrete thing" in which I had faith.

13

Best Friends

Jack was my best—and only—friend until the beginning of third grade. There was a new girl in our class that year, Annie Rees, a transfer from the Catholic school. The kids held back from her, trying to gauge her mettle before making overtures of friendship. I watched her from an even greater distance than the other kids, with no intention of making any kind of overture. She seemed aloof, content to be separate. She intrigued me, and part of me wanted to get to know her, but most of me just refused the risk.

One day, that first week of school, I was sitting on the wall between the playground and the sports field, book in hand. Annie was walking by me, and I was aware of her nearness. I was wondering if she was as aware of me as I was of her when Randy Eastlund and a pack of his pals came sauntering by, and he taunted me with, "Oh look, there's Maddie Jordan. Maddie has no daddy!"

His buddies all chorused, "Maddie has no daddy! Maddie has no daddy!"

My shoulder blades tightened, but I didn't look up from my book until I heard an unfamiliar voice retort, "Big deal, Randy Eastlund, you might as well not have a daddy yourself since *your* daddy is drunk as a skunk every night and twice on Sunday." It was Annie speaking, and I stared at her in astonishment. No one ever took up my side.

What happened next occurred so quickly that I could barely discern one action from the next. Randy Eastlund's arm reached out and smacked Annie's face. Blood arced from her nose and spattered across the front of his shirt and I leaped on his back and was pounding on his head before I could even think. When he threw me to the ground, my glasses went flying, and he straddled me and began pummeling my face. I was only peripherally aware of Annie hitting him over the head with her fists. The three of us were rolling around on the concrete playground—caterwauling and scratching and hitting and biting—attacking whatever body part we could reach and in whatever mode was at hand.

A large group of kids immediately circled us, and almost as immediately, the teachers had reached us and were pulling us apart, upbraiding Randy for "striking a girl" and admonishing Annie and me for not "acting like ladies." After finding my smashed glasses, I managed to spit on Randy before I was tugged away, and he shouted, "I'll get you, Maddie Jordan! You'll be sorry, you bastard you!"

There was a sharp intake of breath—children did not use language like that in front of grown-ups—and Randy was quickly bustled off, presumably to the principal's office. Annie and I were taken to the nurse's office, all the time our teacher clucking about "behavior unbecoming to young ladies." We hardly heard her; we were busy eyeing one another curiously, finally grinning at each other.

The nurse tended our wounds—scraped elbows and knees, Annie's bloody nose, my darkening eye, and various other cuts and bruises. Gramma arrived, quickly followed by my mother, who had a hurried conference with the principal and took me home just as Annie's mother arrived to pick her up.

Gramma left me alone the rest of the day. I knew, once she'd heard the story about Randy Eastlund, she was madder at him than me and couldn't bring herself to punish me. As for myself, I could not stop thinking of Annie. Could not stop thinking of her sharp-tongued response to mean old Randy Eastlund, her beating on his head when he got me down, her staying with me throughout the fracas. *Annie Rees.* I whispered her name to Jack, who was licking all my cuts, then wrote it down, let it sing in my head. I tried, in vain, not to think of her.

That night, she and her parents arrived at our door. We looked at one another wordlessly, breathlessly. The array of bandages scattered across our bodies attested to our bond. Her parents— her mom tall and rather fat (imposing, Gummie would've said), her father even taller with a grim countenance—looked stern and disapproving. My mom and Gramma and Gummie looked equally solemn. I shuddered to think what this meeting meant.

"Girls," Gramma said softly, "why don't you get some lemonade and go out back?" Annie looked at her parents; her mother nodded briefly.

We sat on the back steps, Jack leaning against me but glancing hopefully toward Annie. I dared not talk to her. I felt that the possibility of our having an alliance hung in the fall evening like a flimsy spiderweb blowing in the breeze, and if I made any connection at all, it was likely to be snatched away by a hefty gust of wind. I did not know, then, how strong and tenacious spider-webs were. Annie also did not talk or make eye contact with me. I tickled Jack's ears as I resolutely stared at unresponsive treetops.

Even though it was a warm fall evening, someone closed the door behind us. We peeped a look at each other. I could hear the low trumpet of a man's voice. Mr. Rees, naturally. He sounded angry. I heard my own mother's voice rising and Gramma's quieter murmur. I heard a thud, like someone maybe slapped a hand on the table. I would bet on Gummie for that gesture. I couldn't bear it. I couldn't stand the thought of grown-ups getting to decide our fate, and we had to just sit there and wait it out.

Jack scampered off after a squirrel and, when she returned, pressed her nose against Annie's hand. I thought that was a good sign and smiled tentatively, breaking the unspoken pact of silence between us. "Her name is Jack."

Annie scratched Jack's ears. "After Laura Ingalls' dog?"

"Yes!" I was thrilled. "You knew." By then, Mom had read all the Laura books to me, and I was now reading them myself.

"I love the *Little House* books," Annie intoned seriously, smiling back at me.

"Me too!" *Oh gosh,* I thought, *this is like a dream.* "Wanna see my tree house?"

She nodded, and we left our lemonade on the steps with the stormy rumblings emanating from within the house. I reassured Jack, and we scurried up the rope ladder. I pulled it up after us, as if I could protect us from the rest of the world by doing so. The tree house was two offset levels, one slightly higher than the other. The higher platform had walls with two shuttered but glassless windows and a shingled roof, while the lower platform was merely a deck with railings.

Annie was properly impressed. "Wow! This is super! How'd you get it?"

"My Gramma made it for me. She can make just about anything," I boasted.

"It's keen," she insisted. "Even lights?"

"Yup. Gramma's a whiz with electrical stuff." On the outside, the lights were like a string of Christmas bulbs running around the edges of the roof. There were single bulbs on two walls, on the inside. I turned them on and off a couple of times.

We plopped on our stomachs on the wooden platform, and I thought I *must* be dreaming. This was just what it would be like to have a best friend, I always knew, and I dared not even think such a thing. Our parents, I had no doubt, were already making certain that our future would never be together.

Annie looked around some more and said, "This must be a neat place to get away from everything."

"Yeah," I agreed. "It's one of my favorite places in the whole, wide world. Except for Jack can't come up." I leaned over the side and waved at Jack, who was sitting patiently below us, waiting sadly.

Annie said suddenly, "Gosh, it must be awful. People always being mean like that."

I knew she was talking about Randy Eastlund and those other boys. I felt a sting of tears behind my eyes, tears I was determined not to shed, and shrugged. "I'm used to it."

She looked at me inquisitively, then said, "I'd *never* get used to it. It's terrible."

I looked away, afraid of crying, then said, "How'd you know that about Randy's dad?" A sudden thought occurred to me. "Or did you make it up?"

"Oh no! I didn't make it up." She giggled a little. "That's a good idea, though, isn't it?" We grinned at each other. "Everyone knows what a drunk his dad is. At least everyone at our church. I guess it was kinda mean of me to say something, but he was mean first.

You were swell to just pounce on him like that when he hit me. Wow, what a fighter you are!"

"You're not so bad yourself. How's your nose?"

She touched her nose tenderly. "It's okay. Sore. How about your eye?"

I shrugged again. "It's okay. I think we got him pretty good, too."

Annie giggled again. "Yeah. He was pretty well dinged up."

I asked her, then, about Catholic school—what it was like and why she had transferred. She asked me about Gramma and Mom and Gummie. Her father, she informed me, admired Gummie although he often disagreed with her. "My father always says, 'That Iris Jordan has spunk, she does. Gotta give her credit for that.'" We both laughed at her gruff imitation of her father's voice.

In spite of myself, I felt a flicker of hope. We were far enough away from the house so that we couldn't hear the decisions being made there, and it was almost possible to believe that we could just go on lying on our bellies in this tree house, talking to each other, for the rest of our lives.

She was just describing holy communion, a total mystery to a girl like me who'd only rarely been to a Protestant service, when the back door opened, and Mom said, "You girls want to come in here now?" Even though it was a question, I knew it was an order. My stomach flip-flopped, and I stopped looking at Annie. I didn't want to see her brown eyes with the yellow flecks in them, her riot of reddish-brown curls, her slightly discolored nose, if I couldn't count on seeing them regularly.

As we walked to the door, Annie did an extraordinary thing. She slipped her hand in mine and tightly clasped it, pulling it away so quickly I almost thought I'd imagined it. Still, I knew, even if our parents decided we could never see each other again, the warmth of her hand, the pressure of that quick squeeze would get me through the entire third grade. Annie Rees liked me.

When we walked into the dining room, the first thing I noticed was my grandmother's decanter of homemade dandelion wine standing on the table, and all the adults—except Gummie who never "indulged" under any circumstances—had little glasses of it. My heart leapt with joy because only the most special people were ever served Gramma's wine. Without thinking or hesitating, I grabbed Annie's hand back and leaned toward her, whispering, "It's going to be okay." She had no idea what I was talking about, but she smiled at me anyway.

And it *was* okay. We got seriously lectured on appropriate behavior. We had to promise not to settle differences by fighting in the future (a promise we weren't so good at keeping). We were ordered to apologize to the principal, our teacher, and even Randy Eastlund. We didn't care. We would have done anything, anything at all just to be assured that we could be friends. Because we knew—the way people do sometimes—we *knew* that we were meant to be best friends.

14

Kind of a Tomboy

M om and Gramma and Gummie embraced Annie almost as thoroughly as I did, making her feel so welcome at our house that, sometimes, she didn't want to go home at all. Annie wasn't enough for Gramma, however; she thought I should have more than one friend. So, the summer after third grade, she enrolled me in the Brownies.

"Brownies? That's the Girl Scouts, isn't it?" Gummie frowned at dinner the night Gramma announced it. "They're awfully conservative, aren't they? Don't they kind of push God and Country and all that? Almost military, with their uniforms and medals."

"Badges, Mother, not medals." Gramma shrugged indifferently. I looked down at my plate, suppressing a smile, because I knew what was coming. "I guess they *could* be kind of conservative, but it probably depends on the leader."

Gummie looked up from her food. "So? Who's the leader of this group?"

I almost snickered as Gramma said, "I am."

"Oh," Gummie chewed slowly, looking thoughtfully at her daughter. "How come you're doing this, Hester?"

Gramma dropped her game playing and stated emphatically, "It's a good organization, Mother. It teaches girls responsibility and resourcefulness, independence and competency. It provides them with female role models. It gives them active, physical opportunities—allowing them to know girls can have outdoor adventures, too—not just boys. More important, it gives them a taste of friendship in a girl-only setting." After a little pause during which Gummie stared in surprise at this outburst from Gramma, she added, without looking up from her food, "I *always* wanted to be a Girl Scout."

"I don't suppose I was very encouraging," Gummie remarked offhandedly.

"You certainly were not," Gramma responded tersely. "In fact, you forbid it."

Gummie glared fiercely at Gramma, who glared just as fiercely back. Mom and I glanced at each other. "This obviously upset you a great deal, Hester. What was the attraction?"

"Where else was I going to get to go camping and hiking and canoeing? You and Dad never had any time or interest in those activities."

"And you did?"

"Yes," Gramma said sharply. "I was kind of a tomboy, if you remember. You probably never noticed, though, did you? You were so busy with your own life."

I'd never heard such a note of bitterness sneak into Gramma's voice. I looked from her to Gummie to Mom, who was looking as suprised as I felt. Gummie was gaping at Gramma and had carefully put her fork down. After a moment of silence during which Gramma kept eating and Mom and I held our breath, Gummie picked her fork up again, saying very gently, "I'm sorry, Hester."

Gramma nodded briefly and, through the sudden moistness in her eyes, she said cheerfully, "It's okay. I get to be a Girl Scout now."

Did she ever. It was as if she'd been *born* to lead a Girl Scout troop. During the summer months, we went on endless hikes. We learned to identify wildflowers and trees and other plants as well as birds and animals and their scat. We would squat, uncomfortably and quietly, for hours in the reeds surrounding ponds, so we could observe the activities of ducks and other waterfowl.

These nature forays reminded me of Gummie's stories of going home after college to lead Dolly and Pansy on scientific expeditions into the fields and woods, and I mentioned this one night at the dinner table. Gummie looked a little startled, then pleased, saying to Gramma, "That sounds fine. Yes indeed, just fine."

We also learned to swim, dive, paddle a canoe, identify bird calls. We had overnight camp-outs where we dug latrines, gathered wood, and stripped green sticks for roasting. We wrapped potatoes and carrots in tinfoil and placed them right into the coals, then stuck hot dogs on the ends of our sticks, jockeyed for position around the fire, and thrust them into the flames where they made popping and sizzling sounds as the juices dripped into the fire. We always ended our meals with s'mores, marshmallows replacing our hot dogs on the sticks—followed by debates over the merits of toasting the marshmallows golden-brown or burning them to a crisp—finally sandwiching them between graham crackers and chocolate bars.

Following the meal, we'd dump all the remaining wood into the fire, building it to bonfire strength. We'd sing songs—

"Make new friends" and "I've got something in my pocket" and "She'll be coming around the mountain"—and tell chilling ghost stories about limping thuds progressing up a staircase or hooks left dangling on a car door. Telling the stories, we would all move closer to the fire and one another, peering continuously over our shoulders.

In the winter months, we learned to cook and sew and knit and build things. We made birdhouses and frames for photos of ourselves for our families for Christmas that first year. If we had siblings, we knit stockings and mittens for them. I gave my birdhouse to Mom, who liked birds the best of all of us, while everyone—Gummie and Gramma and Mom and Gloria and Annie—got mittens and stockings and framed pictures of me. I thought it was the best Christmas I ever had.

Over the years, we built many other things, too. Bookcases, sleds, small tables, benches, buckets, salad bowls, lamps. One summer, we built a storage shed for one of the girls' fathers because Gramma wanted us to learn we could build houses, if we wanted.

We also had speakers during those indoor months—women who came to tell us about their lives. Mom talked about being a librarian, Gloria about being a teacher, and Gummie, of course, about being a newspaperwoman. Others came, too—women who were nurses, lawyers, bankers, secretaries, homemakers, waitresses, truck drivers, farmers, doctors, and carpenters—all giving us information about possible career choices.

We also went on field trips to see women at work—to the library, the bank, insurance offices, the hospital. The only places we didn't go were those having no women employees. We wrote letters to our local police department and our local fire station, sending copies to our mayor and city council, decrying the fact that neither had women officers or firefighters. Gramma was far ahead of the times in her views, sometimes surprising everyone in the family. Gummie printed some of our letters on her "op ed" page.

We read books about women living full, active lives—women who were explorers and photographers and writers and social workers and doctors and just about anything. Frosty afternoons often found us in Gramma's parlor knitting or sewing or just listening while we took turns reading aloud. Mary Kingston and Margaret Bourke-White and Mary Shelley and Jane Addams and Elizabeth Blackwell and many other interesting, unique women quietly stepped into the room with us, unobtrusively entering our lives.

We didn't stay inside all winter, though; Gramma introduced us to outdoor activities, too. At first, we just went sliding and skating. Then we learned to ski and snowshoe. Finally, we started winter camping.

I don't know what other troops were like, but I can't imagine any of them being as wonderful as ours was. There were five of us to start with—Annie and me and Patty Hanson, Donna White, and Shari Adams. Eventually, there were ten of us, but Gramma insisted that was enough, even though many other girls wanted to join when the word began to circulate about how much fun we had.

Every one of us in our troop loved Girl Scouts. We were proud to wear our brown Brownie uniforms to school on meeting days and then our green Girl Scout uniforms with our sashes displaying our prodigious number of badges—awards for botany, friendship, cooking, sewing, service, camping, knots, government, boating, kindness. Slackers were not attracted to our troop. We bustled to our meetings every Tuesday with joyous anticipation.

Eventually, Annie and I and some of the other girls got to go to Greenwood Camp in the summer. We missed Gramma; it didn't quite seem like Girl Scouts without her, but we loved it, too. Those wonderful overnights we'd done around home were suddenly expanded into a week, then two weeks—repeating most of the same activity plus pulling pranks on one another or our counselors, whispering late into the night in our tents over all the forbidden subjects, and sleeping that deep sleep only bodies saturated with physical activity and fresh air get.

All the fun activities we had, all the things we learned, all of this paled—for me—in comparison to the major component of scouting: camaraderie. In my troop, and later at camp, it did not matter whether or not I had a father, a church, a left-wing great-grandmother. What mattered was we all had to work together as a team to accomplish the things we were doing. What mattered was one voice singing was rarely impressive, but a dozen or more voices raised in song were thrilling. What mattered was we all had stories to share, futures to explore.

I finally had the friends I'd never had in my younger years. Annie was always going to be my best friend, but scouting introduced me to many other girls whom I also got to call friends. Our troop became Annie's and my own circle of closest friends, the girls with whom, as we got older, we had slumber parties—talking endlessly of boys, sharing countless pizzas, joining demonstrations, and finally examining college choices.

Maybe I would've had a nice circle of friends anyway. I don't know. What I *do* know is that this troop Gramma created for me (and for her, I later realized) became my home and my family, too.

15

A Good Friend Is One of Life's Finest Treasures

From the beginning of our relationship, aside from those early cuts and bruises from our fight with Randy Eastlund, Annie's and my biggest bond had always been books. I can still remember, all these years later, how Annie—after our parents had felt we were sufficiently chastised that first night—had wandered around our house, gaping at all the books.

"I've never seen so many books outside of a library," she breathed reverentially, and I felt warmer and warmer toward her.

"Well," I tried to say casually, "there are four of us, you know, and we all love books. So . . ."

"I bet your grandma built these bookcases, didn't she?"

"Yep."

"Have you read all these books?" she asked, running her hand lightly across the spines of the books on one shelf.

"No, of course not. Some of them I don't want to read. For instance, Gramma reads a lot of how-to books. They aren't so interesting to me. And Gummie mostly likes nonfiction. Some of it I like, but I like novels best of all. I'm going to write novels someday," I bragged, having just decided at that very moment.

Annie was not impressed. She did not even take her eyes off the books as she said, "I bet you will." I didn't know if that was a compliment or not but decided it must be. "We could read these books together, you and I," Annie continued, her eyes still riveted to the books themselves. A shiver of pure pleasure and anticipation raced through my body. "We could even read them to each other," she finally tore her eyes away long enough to look at me, "don't you think?"

I didn't trust my voice, so I just nodded seriously. I was absolutely certain I must be dreaming. *How was this possible?*—I was trying to puzzle out. *This morning I had no friends, and now I not only have a best friend but one who loves books, maybe as much as I do.*

Suddenly, the shelves were teeming with more than books: wild horses galloped across broad plains, spiky mountain ridges creating a backdrop; women in white strolled down perfumed lanes, carrying ruffled parasols and wearing wide-brimmed hats; babies, weak from hunger, made pitiful mewling sounds; the din and roar of humanity pressed all around me in a Hong Kong alley; a moustachioed man brandished a rifle while another grasped a Bible as they both made their way up swollen rivers winding through African rain forests. The myriad possibilities were intoxicating, making me feel dizzy with pleasure and hope.

We did just as she'd fantasized. We lay on each other's beds, on the hammock in her backyard, the floor of my tree house, snugged into opposite corners of the window seat halfway up the stairs at her house, or on the front-porch glider at my house, Jack always nearby—talking and reading, reading and talking—sometimes to ourselves and sometimes aloud to each other. There were times we'd be in bed with a flashlight, some parent or other admonishing us earlier to "turn that light off," in spite of our pleas to finish the book first. Even on camping trips, books were tucked into our backpacks.

A couple of years later, one or both of us—I can't remember now—read a book in which two girls became blood sisters. It completely enchanted us, naturally, and we knew we had to do it. I brought the needle and matches and a glass of water, while she brought the silk scarf, purloined from her mother's "best things" drawer. We met up in the tree house, a place where no adults ever intruded on us.

I carefully held the needle in the flame of a lit match to sterilize it, then stuck it in the glass of water so it wouldn't be too hot. Next, I pricked Annie's middle finger. "Keep squeezing it," I advised as I repeated the same action with another match and my own finger. Then we placed our bleeding fingers together, and Annie awkwardly tied the scarf around our kissing fingers as she chanted a ditty she'd made up for this ritual.

> *"Best friends forever*
> *Blood sisters, too.*
> *Never to betray*
> *Always to be true.*
Your turn now, Maddie."

I repeated the chant. I was smiling but also felt like crying. Annie looked like she might cry, too, so I didn't place too much importance on the intensity of my feelings. After a moment, we removed the scarf and tugged at our fingers, which were lightly stuck together. They began to bleed anew when we separated them, and we both reflexively put them in our mouths to stanch the blood.

Around her finger, Annie said, "Sister, we are related by blood now."

I nodded, feeling both solemn and elated, echoing, "That's so, Sister, we are."

Then, feeling a little silly and overwhelmed by our emotions, we both let out whoops, barrelled down the rope ladder, and hopped on our bikes. We tore through town, Jack galloping behind us, barely missing moving cars and annoying no end of pedestrians, finally arriving at a wide spot on a creek we'd discovered the summer before—where we jumped right in, fully clothed, and swam to our delight. Jack joined us—barking gleefully and trying to climb up on us, pushing us underwater. We would surface, sputtering and coughing and laughing.

Afterward, we lay on the grass in the sun, trying to dry off, but Jack kept going back in the water—staring intently into the murky liquid, then snapping eagerly at small fish flitting by. When she'd rejoin us on the bank, she'd vigorously shake, getting us wet all over again. It was warm enough so our clothes dried on our bodies as we slowly pedalled home.

At dinner, I told Mom and Gramma and Gummie about Annie and me becoming blood sisters. They listened indulgently. When I was done, I asked, "Gummie, how come you don't have any friends?" I quickly amended my question, as I realized it sounded awful, plus I knew she had dozens of friends, but I meant someone *real* close to her. "I mean like Mom has Gloria and Gramma has her stitch and b. . ." I swerved adeptly, knowing I wasn't supposed to say a word like bitch, " . . . her sewing group and I have Annie. Someone real special."

Gummie continued chewing, and Gramma grinned, saying, "Haven't you told her about the Gummies, Mom?"

"The Gummies?" I asked. Could it be there were stories I hadn't heard? "What are the Gummies? Is this how you got to be called

Gummie?" I'd never thought about it before. It was just her name, or rather, *our* name for her. My mother, I guess, used it first, and I came along and just learned it from her.

"Who," Gummie responded. "The Gummies were a 'who,' not a 'what.'"

"Okay, *who* were they?"

After finishing her mouthful, Gummie began, meditatively, "In some ways, I've never had enough time for girlfriends. I mean I had my friend Bertha out in San Francisco, you remember, the one who went to Carleton with me. There was Dolly, only she was gone for a lot of years. Your Guppie and I had lots of friends in our political work, both men and women. That was about all I had time for."

Gramma was shooing us. "You two go out on the porch. Jane and I will do the dishes and bring you some iced tea and gingerbread." I thought this must be an important story; I rarely got out of doing the dishes. Gummie and I settled ourselves, the familiar squeak of the old swing blending with the other evening noises to create a kind of summer concerto—squeak-squeak and the swishing of sprinklers and the peeping of the tree frogs and the chirping of the crickets. It was drowsy-making on a warm summer night.

After a couple of minutes of no words, I got impatient and repeated, "So Gummie, who are the Gummies?"

"Mmm," she hummed. "When we moved here, I lost touch with a lot of my friends in the City. Your guppie still had an office there and saw them oftener because he went in frequently. I was really busy with the paper and didn't have much time to get down to the Cities or keep contact with other folks I'd known.

"Even though I was busy, I was lonely, too. Hubert was gone a lot, as always, and often took Hester with him—this was before Jordie was born. So, finally, I started a book club. I figured it would force me to take time to read more and also help me to meet some women I'd like."

"Here's your iced tea, Mom," Gramma interrupted, "and ginger-bread for both of you." I got a glass of milk. Gramma smiled at me, placing her lips against the top of my head, and said, "I'm glad you and Annie are sisters now, Maddie. You're both so special." I grinned back at her.

"Have you got to the part about the Gummies yet?" Mom asked as she joined us on the porch.

"Just started," Gummie answered. "If you all would quit inter-rupting, I could finish this story and get to bed." Mom and Gramma sat down, and Gummie recommenced her story. "Women came and went in our book club that first year, but eventually it settled down to five of us regularly—AliceMae Evans, Jeanne Schlosser, Lizzie Solberg, and Maud McCleary. And me, of course."

I was startled to see tears in Gummie's eyes. She didn't cry often or easily. I looked at Mom and Gramma; they looked kind of sad, too.

"We became the best of friends. Jeanne Schlosser and I were the only ones who had jobs, paying jobs, I mean. All of us *worked*. Jeanne was a teacher at the high school. Never did get married. She had a special friend for a while, woman she met in the Cities at a teacher's convention, but that woman—what was her name? Edith. That was it. Edith Budroe. Anyway, she couldn't stand liv-ing in a small town like this, so she moved back to the Cities, and Jeanne spent most of her life alone. She had her students—who adored her—and her friends."

"I remember Miss Schlosser, Gummie! Or . . . I think I do. When I was real little, she lived in that nursing home on the river?"

Gummie nodded, smiling. "That's right. I took you there with me sometimes, Maddie, when I went to visit her." I remembered her because she barely had any hair and what she did have was pure white, sort of just waving around her head like threads unraveling from a ball of yarn. The best part, though, was her teeth residing in a glass next to her bed. I found them fascinating and stared at them while she and Gummie chattered away about incomprehensible events and people I didn't know. Also, she talked funny, sort of garbled and gooey. I could rarely make out what she was saying, but Gummie always seemed to know.

"It's surprising you remember her. She died before Guppie did. You couldn't have been more than four or five when I took you there." Gummie looked sad again. "She was my best friend in the world, Maddie. She was *my* Annie."

I thought about Annie and me being old and best friends still. I felt almost happy until I thought about her dying before me. "I'm going to die first," I blurted out, and they all laughed, but not unkindly.

"Uh-huh," Gummie agreed, "that's what we mostly want. Doesn't always happen the way we want, though."

"What about the others?"

"Oh, they were good friends, too. They were all married and did what most women did in those days—stayed home to look after their husbands and children. Still, they didn't let their minds go fallow. We read interesting books, had lively discussions about them, but also shared with one another everything about our lives—our anger, our pain, our joy—everything.

"AliceMae's husband—well—he wasn't such a swell fella. Surly and drank too much. He did *let* her come to our meetings, but he didn't like it. Never let her forget how *fine* he was for letting her come. I'm surprised, when I look back now, that he did let her come. He'd drive her there and pick her up. Always wanted to be in charge. Left the kids, two little girls, at home asleep in their beds when he came to get AliceMae. Always said they'd 'be okay for a few moments.' None of us liked him. Dumber than a box of rocks and mean as an old bobcat who'd had a foot cut off in a trap. We thought she should leave him, but not many women did that back then. We knew he hurt her. She never said anything, but we noticed those bruises on her arms. No, he wasn't a likeable man."

She swung and hummed, and I waited, fully engaged now. "Lizzie and Maud were married, too. Lizzie had a girl and two boys, and her husband was just as sweet as AliceMae's husband was sour. A kind man, a man who made a woman feel soft and cared for and appreciated, too. Maud only had the one boy. Her husband was an officer in the local Farmer-Labor Party; he and Hubert were great buddies and worked on projects together, too.

"These were my friends. Women I laughed with and argued with and agreed with and *knew*, without a shred of doubt, *knew* I could count on. We met once a month to talk about the books we'd chosen to read, but we gradually began spending lots more time together: taking our children on picnics in the summer, walks in the woods in the fall, skating sprees in the winter, and tea parties in our backyards when the plum and apple trees were in full, radiant bloom."

"Anyone want more iced tea or sweets?" Gramma asked quietly as Gummie subsided into humming and rocking again, a soft smile resting on her lips. I held out my plate for more gingerbread while everyone else shook their heads.

Mom said, "I'll get it," and took our plates.

"Thanks, Jane," Gramma smiled and stretched.

Gummie continued, "Sometimes, the five of us would get all dressed up and take the train into the City on a Saturday. We'd go shopping and have lunch at Dayton's Tea Room or walk around Loring Park or go to the Minneapolis Art Institute, then have dinner at Murray's. We might take in a play or a concert, spending the night afterward at Violet's house. It was like a grand slumber party for us. What a lark!"

After a moment of the swing squeaking without her voice accompanying it, she said, "It was the four of us, actually. Leonard, AliceMae's husband, would *never* let her go with us into the City. Oh no! Who would feed him if she were gone? When we got back home, we would tell her in minute detail everything we saw and did and said, so it helped a little to take the sting out of her not getting to join us.

"We swapped kids and recipes and home remedies. We were all at AliceMae's in August, to help her cook for the harvest crew. Lizzie had a huge garden so part of the same month, one or the other or all of us would be out at her place, helping her pick, clean, cut up, scald, and can her tomatoes, beans, and corn, make pickles from the cucumbers and watermelon, and jellies from the plums and crab apples. In the winter, we'd sometimes help her with her quilting, all of us ending up, sooner or later, with one of her quilts on our beds. We'd have mailing parties at Maud's house, helping her and her husband disseminate information to farmers and workers all over the Midwest. Also, she was a fine painter and relied on us, one by one, to be her models at various times."

I interrupted. "Is that Lizzie's quilt on your bed, Gummie? And did Maud do that picture on the wall?"

"That's right, sweetie. Two of my prized possessions, yes indeed." She looked happy, even though her eyes glimmered. "All of us, at one time or another, were guest speakers in Jeanne's classes. If we needed an extra hand or two for a spell at the paper, you'd better believe one of the Gummies was there to pitch in. Oh yes, we could count on one another."

When she paused this time, I asked, "I don't get it. How did you get to be called the Gummies?"

It went very still on our porch, that kind of stillness you feel on a blistering summer night just before a thunderstorm explodes. I almost held my breath, in anticipation of what was to come next.

"We just stuck together, you know, and—as time went by—we got to standing up for each other over one thing or another."

"Like what?" I inquired.

"Maud decided, once her son was in school, to go back to school herself, and her husband put his foot down, insisting her place was at home. Him so *progressive* and all. Humph. We just bombarded Stan with information and ideas from progressive publications all over the country, insisting women's labor was just as essential to a healthy economy as men's. We never let an opportunity pass to harangue him about his small-mindedness and his unfairness, talking to him when we ran into him in the street or in a store or if he came into the paper to place an announcement about some meeting or other. In the end, he capitulated, as he should have in the first place.

"Then there was an incident at Merklee's," our general store, a kind of small department store. "They told Lizzie her credit had run too high, and she couldn't shop there any longer. We all knew, however, it wasn't any higher than anyone else's in a small, rural area where profits are often a future matter. We found out they were really keeping her out because Janine Merklee had discovered that Lizzie was part Indian. We all wrote letters and refused to do business there and informed and prodded others to follow our lead. I even made certain an article was written for the paper and followed it up with a series on discrimination. Needless to say, Lizzie's eviction was rescinded.

"So it went like that, for anything happening to any of us. Some of the men of this town, our own husbands included, started to say things like 'Oh those women, they're just like gum on your shoe—sticky as glue and fierce nuisances.' Eventually, they just started calling us the Gummies." She paused, sipping some tepid iced tea, pushing the swing to swaying again.

"What happened to the other Gummies? Are they all dead? Are you the last one?" The questions tumbled out of my mouth.

"Don't get ahead of me now, Maddie. A good story goes along at its own speed. The big incident, making it absolutely clear to the five of us how much we could count on one other, how much we would always stick together, happened when AliceMae killed her husband."

My eyes, getting a little droopy before this, snapped wide open at this astonishing statement. "She killed him?" I shrilled.

Gummie silenced me with a look, then proceeded. "One night, on our regular book meeting, Lizzie and Maud and I were at Maud's house, waiting for Jeanne and AliceMae to come. We were drinking coffee and eating Maud's prizewinning snickerdoodles and just talking.

"When Jeanne finally arrived, she had AliceMae in tow, and AliceMae looked—well, she looked a bit vacant. Jeanne herself looked rattled. 'Whatever is wrong?' I asked right away and, 'How come Leonard didn't bring you?' AliceMae just sort of collapsed into a chair and pressed her hand against her mouth, not seeming capable of saying anything. Jeanne told us the story. She was just leaving to come to the book club when the phone rang. It was AliceMae, who said, 'Jeanne, you have to come out here right now. Right now. I think I killed him.'

"So Jeanne got in her car and drove out to AliceMae's farm. She walked in the kitchen, and there was Leonard, AliceMae's husband, lying on the floor with blood all over the place and AliceMae just speechless, twisting her apron in her hands. 'What happened? What happened?' Jeanne kept asking as she took the blood-splattered apron off of AliceMae, using it to wipe the blood off the large iron frying pan lying on the floor next to Leonard, then hanging the pan back up above the stove where it usually went.

"Next, she put AliceMae's apron in the kitchen sink and lit fire to it. 'I didn't know what I was doing for sure,' Jeanne told us, 'I was just acting out of some instinct I didn't even know I had.' AliceMae kept repeating, 'Thank God the girls are over to their grandparents. Oh thank God they weren't here.'

"Jeanne made a quick visual survey of the kitchen, then hustled AliceMae out of there. All the way to Maud's house, she kept telling AliceMae, 'Now AliceMae, you have been at Maud's with the rest of us all evening. Leonard dropped you off at the customary time,' it was, by then, an hour or so later than we usually got started, 'and then never did come back to get you. You hear me, AliceMae?'

"We spent the next couple of hours going over this story, again and again, determined AliceMae would never have to pay any more than she was already going to have to for doing what not one of us doubted—protecting herself. We were giving her an airtight alibi. Who, after all, could contradict it? The only person was the one lying dead on her kitchen floor."

Gummie stood up suddenly and said, "Lordy, I've got to go to the bathroom."

"Gummie," I wailed, "what happened?"

"Don't fret, Maddie, I'll be right back." I got up and ran out in the yard with Jack for a minute, zigzagging back and forth as she followed me, barking excitedly. When Gummie returned, I came back and sat in front of Mom, leaning against her legs. She tickled my hair, and I relaxed into the delicious feeling of bubbles tap dancing across my scalp. Jack came and plopped her head in my lap, so I tickled her head, too.

Gummie picked up where she'd left off. "When the usual time for picking up AliceMae had come and gone, she called the sheriff and told him Leonard hadn't shown and didn't answer the phone out to their place, and she was a little worried. The sheriff assured her he'd take a run out to check and let her know 'what was what.'

"We practiced our story a few more times, then waited. And waited and waited for quite some time. Imagine our amazement when the sheriff finally came by and told AliceMae that Leonard was in the hospital over at the county seat and 'would she like him to drive her over there?' AliceMae said, somewhat stupidly, 'Hospital?' *Did they take corpses to hospitals*, we were all wondering? The sheriff said he'd gotten out to the farm and found the back door unlocked and walked into a kitchen with blood all over the floor, but there was no sign of Leonard anywhere. 'No Leonard?' AliceMae asked, daring a glance at the rest of us.

"'Nope,' the sheriff answered, 'No Leonard.' So he checked the outbuildings. There was no sign of Leonard there either, and Leonard's truck was gone.

"'The truck is gone?' AliceMae was beginning to sound almost retarded. We understood, though, because we all felt a little slow. *What in heaven's name*, we were all thinking, *is going on?*

"'So,' the sheriff continued, 'first thing I did was call Doc Andrews and sure enough, Leonard had been there. Had driven himself there. The doc took him on over to the hospital.'

"AliceMae looked absolutely stunned, was white as if she'd seen a ghost or maybe *was* one herself, and said, 'He drove himself there?' while Jeanne piped up quickly, 'What happened, Sheriff?' The sheriff told us he'd gone on over to the hospital, before coming here to get AliceMae all upset, and talked to Leonard himself. We all braced ourselves.

"'He's a little disoriented, ma'am,' the sheriff informed AliceMae. 'Head wound. He doesn't seem to know how it happened, just came to in a puddle of his own blood, and drove himself right to the hospital. Doc says there's a slight concussion, so he'll have to stay overnight, at least. Doc's kind of wondering if he had a spell or something and hit his head, falling down, but he was lucky.

Bled a lot, apparently, not uncommon with head wounds, but the wound scabbed on its own. Otherwise, he might've bled to death.'

"At that word, 'death,' AliceMae seemed to come alive a little, and exclaimed, 'Oh my!' and started to cry. We assured the sheriff we would take AliceMae over to see Leonard and get her home, too. We weren't sure, now, what our plan was since we weren't sure what Leonard was going to do or say. Jeanne and Maud took AliceMae over to the hospital, where she just kept moaning, 'I'm so sorry, Leonard, I'm so sorry.' She was obviously terrified, Jeanne and Maud told us later. Lizzie and I went out to the farm and scoured that kitchen, probably the cleanest it'd ever been."

When Gummie paused and hummed a little, I couldn't wait. "What happened then, Gummie? Did Leonard ever tell? Did he hurt her bad for hurting him?"

Gummie shook her head. "Nope. He never said a word. We didn't know whether he didn't remember or whether he was just too embarrassed to have been damn-near killed by his own woman. He never laid a hand on her again, although he didn't have much time left actually. It was just a little over a year later when a cow kicked him in the head, in that weak spot caused by the earlier accident, the doctor said, and he had an aneurism in his brain and died." She added unemotionally, "He was not missed." Then she chuckled a little and added, "Of course, we never did let Jeanne forget she hadn't even checked to see if Leonard was dead or not, just assumed he was. 'Well, he looked dead,' she assured us."

The four of us sat in companionable silence. The sprinklers in the neighborhood had been quieted, and some houses were already dark. I felt a stirring in me when I thought of the next day, getting to tell this story to Annie. Gramma got up, muttering about her old bones, and went inside. Mom stood and stretched, saying, "C'mon, Maddie. We have to walk."

Startled, I said, "This late?"

She smiled, "We'll make it short."

Before we left, I asked, "So what happened to all the other Gummies?"

"Oh," Gummie exhaled a long, slow breath, "they all died, eventually. Everyone does, Maddie, sooner or later." I didn't want to hear that, didn't want to think about Gummie or Gramma or Mom dying. Ever. Or even Annie or me.

"Let me tell you, AliceMae surprised everyone. She sure did. This whole town expected her to sell off her dairy herd, sell the farm even, but she did what she'd always wanted to do since she was a wee girl on her daddy's farm. She farmed it all by herself. She hummed and lullabied and cooed to those cows as she was milking them—Leonard had always been rough and nasty with them, getting poor milk production and finally kicked in the head—but she got the best milk production in the county and the sweetest cream and butter you could ever imagine.

"She leased the land in exchange for fodder for the cows; she taught her girls to be strong and independent; and she never did marry again, even though many a farmer came courting her. 'What good's life's lessons if you don't learn from them?' she'd say and then giggle until we all joined her. She ran that farm herself and keeled over dead, milking her beloved cows one morning— oh, about twenty years ago. She was seventy-two or seventy-three.

"Lizzie just went on doing what she'd always done—raising her kids, being a good wife to her good man, gardening, and quilting. She was the first of us to go. Got cancer and died within months. She was only in her fifties. They cut both breasts off, but nothing helped. She just died anyway." Gummie's voice was like a dull knife, cutting raggedly through the air. After a moment of silence, she continued. "Maud surprised us all. As soon as her boy graduated from high school, she divorced Stan and ran off with another man, an artist and union organizer from Chicago. She kept in touch with us and died only about ten years ago."

Only? I thought. Ten years is a long time.

"Jeanne kept teaching until they forced her to retire. She was nearly seventy by then. She threw herself into volunteer work with kids, continuing until her stroke. That's how she ended up in the nursing home where she died about five years ago now.

"So, I'm the only one left, Maddie. This is the worst thing about living as long as I have. Most of the people you love die before you. I'm lucky because I have the three of you, but—oh those girls—" even in the darkness of the front porch, I could see her eyes brighten, hear the lilt in her voice "—those girls and me, how we laughed and cried and loved one another. Yes, Maddie, you cherish Annie. Always remember, a good friend is one of life's finest treasures."

16

Ninety

Sometimes, I worried about Gummie. Mostly, she seemed indestructible, untouchable, but she was—after all—pretty old. In 1963, we had a surprise party for her ninetieth birthday. In advance, she insisted, "No fuss now."

"Okay," Gramma agreed.

"Gummie!" Mom had objected. "It's a milestone! Don't you think we should mark it in some way or other?"

"No," Gummie shook her head. "No fuss. It's just another year. That's all."

Then we ignored her and planned the grandest gala imaginable. It was pretty easy to do. Even at ninety, Gummie still went to work every day. At that point, she'd run the *Prairie Voice* for fifty-three years. Everyone always asked her when she was going to retire, and she'd just shoot back, "When I'm dead and buried. Not before." Then she'd add, with a twinkle in her eye, "Which is going to be never since I don't intend to be buried." Guppie had been cremated, and we knew she intended the same for herself.

"A little backyard barbecue," she'd chuckle, and Gramma would warn, "Mother," while Mom and I laughed.

We lost count of the number of invitations that went out. It kept shifting as we continually added folks to the list. Everyone who'd ever worked with her—at both papers and on her various projects over the years. The family—Pansy and her children and Violet's surviving children (two of them were already dead) and subsequent generations, cousins I didn't even know existed, and Guppie's family members, too. All the folks over in her old neighborhood on Maple Street as well as our neighbors on Oak Street. Guppie's friends and coworkers. The children and grandchildren of the original Gummies. Gramma's friends and Mom's friends and my friends. The list grew longer and longer.

As she left for work the morning of her birthday, she reminded us, shaking her cane, "Remember, no fuss."

When Gummie began using a cane, she declared, "It's not so much that I need it but that I can strike someone with it if they give me any grief."

"Mother," Gramma had admonished, not appreciating that kind of violent image, even in jest, but Gummie had merely waved her cane at Gramma and replied, "See? It's already coming in handy."

We all solemnly nodded our heads, breaking out in giggles the minute she was out of the house. It was a warm day in early September. The minute she left, Gramma began pulling things out of the freezer. She'd been cooking for weeks and now began thawing and warming, as well as creating the last-minute fresh items. Gloria and Mom had both taken the day off. Even I got to stay home from school. Gloria helped Gramma in the kitchen while Mom and I festooned the backyard with crepe paper,

Chinese lanterns, and balloons. Tables and chairs were loaned to us by local churches and other organizations. All day, they were delivered to our house, and people kept joining us to help set up.

By the time Gummie was expected home from work, the backyard was filled with people I knew, and even more I didn't know —celebrities and community members; people she'd helped; some admired and liked her; others merely respected her. Jack frolicked around this throng, assuming everyone had come to feed and pet her.

Pansy's children had brought her in a wheelchair, since she was no longer mobile. She sat in the center of the hubbub, totally baffled, and kept shouting things like, "Who are all these people?" One or the other of her children would bend over her, explaining, but a few minutes later, she'd forget again and yell, "What am I doing here?"

Three o'clock came and went. No Gummie. Four o'clock came and went. Still no Gummie. Mom called the paper. No one was left at the offices; they were all in our backyard, having closed down right after Gummie left at three.

Gramma was moaning and wringing her hands. "She knew. She knew all along, and now she's hiding somewhere. Just to thwart us. She told us 'no fuss,' and now she's going to punish us for ignoring her."

Mom tried to calm Gramma down. "Now Mom, don't worry. Even if Gummie did know, she'll come. She'd never humiliate us by not coming."

"Mmphh," Gramma snorted. "You don't know her like I do."

Annie and Jack and I took up sentinel posts on the front porch. I tended to agree with Gramma. I thought it quite possible Gummie was hiding out somewhere. I could almost hear her saying, "Serve you right. Go and plan a party after I told you not to."

We talked in hushed voices, as if there were some need to be quiet. There would be no surprise anyway, once Gummie was within a block of the house. People were making a lot of noise, eating Gramma's exquisite food and drinking glass after glass of lemonade and iced tea and punch with islands of sherbert melting into it. No dandelion wine or other strong spirits today; it was Gummie's day, and Gramma respected her temperance stance. I hoped there would be some food left by the time Gummie did arrive.

When it was nearly five o'clock, even Mom was getting a little desperate. She would come out on the porch about every three minutes. "No sign of her yet? Where could she be? I can't even think where to call or look for her. Almost everyone in town is here." Then she'd be back in a couple of minutes. "No sign of her yet?"

The first thing we heard was music. Annie and I looked at each other and then stood and looked up and down the street. Nothing. There was nothing to be seen, but we definitely could hear music—faint at first, but growing stronger. "It's a Sousa march," Annie said. She played trombone in band and knew about such things. We left the porch, went down the front steps, and hung over the picket fence, gazing up and down the street again. Still nothing in sight.

By then, Mom and Gramma had come out on the porch. "What is it?" Gramma called. "Do you girls see anything?"

We shook our heads. "Nope. Nothing."

Other people started to drift around to the front of the house as the music grew yet louder and their curiosity grew with it. Suddenly, Annie shouted, "Look!" her arm stretched out and pointing toward the end of the block. We all looked. Coming around the corner was a marching band, all decked out in bright red suits and swaying to the music. By then, they had switched from Sousa to Dixieland, Gummie's favorite. I felt the stirrings of something . . . excitement? Apprehension? Everyone started coming from behind the house, filling up our smaller front yard and spilling over to the neighbors' yards.

"What is it? What's happening?"

I looked back to the front steps where my mom and gramma were still standing. Mom had her arm around Gramma's waist, and both were smiling, like they knew what was happening. Tears were rolling down Gramma's cheeks, and I felt my throat tighten. The band was loud now and almost upon us. As it grew nearer, it was clear there was a float right behind it. Everyone was craning their necks and buzzing.

It wasn't until the float practically pulled up in front of the house that I saw Gummie sitting on it with a huge grin splitting her face. The float was covered with violets and irises and dahlias and pansies—real dahlias and pansies and violets, but the irises were plastic or paper because you couldn't get live ones in the fall. There was a huge banner across the back of the float, proclaiming:

IRIS JORDAN WANTS TO THANK
ALL HER FAMILY AND FRIENDS!
HAPPY BIRTHDAY TO YOU, TOO!

Then the band stopped playing, and Gummie got up and started talking. It was lucky her voice, like her personality, tended to boom. She announced, "Thank you all for coming today. Thank you all for trying to surprise me, for honoring me for merely enduring these past ninety years. Before you applaud me, let me applaud you. I could never do the things I've done, accomplish the amount I have without all of you. Your love, your friendship, your support, your work, your dedication, your devotion—all the things you've showered me with these past ninety years—have made my life possible. I am honored by you, I am grateful, I appreciate you, but most of all—I SALUTE YOU! Thank you!"

At that point, the drums and cymbals did a crescendo and the crowd roared. Gummie continued, "I heard you didn't have a band. So I brought one—" more drum rolls "—and also an ice cream truck," she indicated a vehicle hiding behind the float. "The street will be closed to traffic," we could see there were police cars on either end of the street, setting up barriers, "so don't hesitate to get out here and dance, eat all the ice cream you want as well as that fabulous food I'm sure my daughter has prepared for you. Oh yes," and she paused until a hush fell over the crowd, "a special thanks to the rest of those Jordan girls: Hester and Jane and Madelaine." At the sound of my name, Jack barked. Gummie frowned a little, then laughed. "Even you, Jack." She extended her arms up in the air and waved them. "Thanks for coming! Everyone!" With that, the band swung into "For He's a Jolly Good Fellow," and we all sang, "For she's a jolly good woman."

The party was a smashing success. Old and young danced in the street. Children climbed all over the vacated float. Everyone plucked flowers off of it all night as souvenirs until it was almost naked at the end of the evening. Sometimes the band played old standards, and we would sing along. The food kept coming, and the ice cream truck seemed to be bottomless. I think nearly everyone in Riverton, and a good many people from the Cities, too, were there.

We were cleaning up for days afterward, but it was worth it. Gramma scolded Gummie, "You just couldn't let us do it, could you, old lady? You were so sure we couldn't do it on our own. You had to top our efforts."

"You *didn't* have a band, did you?" Gummie responded, then laughed and protested. "Don't be cross, Hester. I wasn't topping your efforts. I was thanking you—and surprising you back. I figured if you couldn't resist making a fuss, then I'd make one, too. I just wanted people to know—in a big way—how much they mean to me."

Mom hugged Gummie. "It was fabulous, Gummie. Just fabulous! It was overflowing with love. You've always taught us so much, and here you are at ninety with still more surprises. You know, you can't *ever* die. I won't let you."

Even though I was feeling warm and rosy all over, I felt—at that exact moment—a chilly little breeze blowing on my heart. *Gummie was ninety*, I thought. *Most people don't live even that long. How much longer could she have?* I couldn't bear the thought of her dying, of her no longer being in my life. I felt sad when Guppie died, but mostly for Gummie. I never knew him as well, and he'd been ill the last years of his life, so I didn't really miss him. But Gummie! How could she die? How could I keep her alive? How could I find out everything I needed to know before she died?

She hung in with us for a long time after that birthday, but I never felt entirely secure once she'd crossed the boundary into her nineties. Sometimes I'd forget and really believe, without really thinking about it, she was going to live forever. Then, she'd do something like fall asleep in the middle of a story, and I would watch her—her snowy white head bobbing a little, mouth open in a droning snore with drool snaking out of one of the corners, veins on her hands so prominent they made me shudder—and I'd know she might die any moment. Each breath she took might be her last. Then I'd want to hang on to her. Desperately, tenaciously.

17

Sins of the Fathers

"Gummie? What does it mean when someone says 'the sins of the fathers are visited on the children?'"

We were checking the layout of the paper, something Gummie always reviewed before allowing it to go to press. She reached over and rearranged two articles, one of which she thought should be more prominently displayed.

Without looking at me, she asked, "Did someone say this to you, Maddie?"

I was used to veiled and sometimes not-so-veiled remarks being addressed toward me regarding my lineage. However, I had never heard this particular phrase before. I shrugged, pointing out a white space on the third page. "Sort of."

Gummie lifted an eyebrow but still did not look at me. "What does that mean? 'Sort of?'"

I sighed. "She didn't say it to me directly. She said it to someone with her. But it was clear to me that I was *meant* to hear it. Why? Did my father commit some heinous sin that I will now have to pay for?" I had just looked "heinous" up, having read it in a book. I was pleased to be able to find a way to use it so soon.

Gummie snorted, and we spent several minutes retrieving cut-up articles, which had fluttered to the floor from the onslaught of her exhaled breath. When we had the page back in order, Gummie moved on to the next one as I did my job, gluing the loose articles to the approved page, and said, "Undoubtedly the man who contributed to your gene pool," she rarely referred to him as my father, "has committed countless sins, but Maddie, that's probably not whom she was talking about when she said that. By the way, who said it?"

I shrugged again. "I don't know. I mean, I know she's Aurora Peterson's mom," Aurora was a girl in my class who was a little standoffish, but I didn't know her well enough to know if she was snobby or just shy; given my own circumstances in life, I was loathe to pass facile judgements, "but I don't know her. And I don't know the woman who was with her."

Gummie nodded at the city editor to "put the paper to bed," and preceded me into her office where she picked up the phone. "Judy Peterson needs something to occupy her time. Unintelligent utterances have more to do—" she interrupted herself to say, "Joe? Ready to roll," then replaced the receiver and finished, "—with idleness than with actual stupidity. Ready to go?" She blew her nose, pulled on a sweater, and plopped a hat on her head. She never went out of doors without a hat, mostly just simple straw boats that no one wore anymore. Except in the winter, when she wore horrifyingly odd caps with furry earflaps that I was certain no one would *ever* have worn. Gummie never cared a whit about style or others' opinions.

She raised a hand and nodded as we ambled through the offices and her coworkers called out, "Good night, Miz Jordan."

"See you tomorrow, Iris."

"Take good care of your grannie, Maddie."

Because Gummie had always been old throughout my lifetime—almost eighty at my birth—I never knew her when she walked fast. As a little girl, I'd loved walking with her because she moved so slowly that I could examine every wonder that our footfalls came across: leaves, caterpillars, stones, twigs, ants. At eleven, I sometimes felt a little impatient with our slow progress, and so did Jack, who often scurried ahead of us—periodially checking our advancement. I would remind myself, *She's ninety*, and repeated, also inside my head, one of her favorite admonitions to me, "What's your hurry, Maddie? Life's too short already. Slow down and savor it."

Life's too short? It was hard for me to understand her saying that. Wouldn't you think at ninety she'd be thinking that life had been long? I had no concept, yet, of how time appeared to speed up as you grew older, no way of understanding that life wasn't really forever.

Between greetings from other folks on the sidewalks, Gummie returned to our conversation. "'Sins of the fathers,' Maddie, is a biblical quote. What most Christians mean when they use that verse is that they expect children to be as 'bad as their parents.'"

After a few moments of silent shuffling, I asked, "So that phrase means—what? I might grow up to be an unwed mother like my mom?"

"Maybe," Gummie agreed. "Or something only in the speaker's mind. Like you might be promiscuous, which your mother wasn't, but some people think she was because their imagination is so *shriveled* they can't conceive of someone choosing to be a mother without bothering with matrimony."

The idea of my being promiscuous was pretty intriguing. *How,* I wondered, *could I be both sexually active and not interested in sex,* as that man who was my father had so clearly stated? Plus, there was something indefinably *thrilling* about the idea of promiscuity. *Slut,* I silently labeled myself and almost giggled out loud.

"Or it might not be about your mother at all. It might be about me or your grandmother. Like maybe you're going to be an atheist or commie or an outspoken, opinionated hell-raiser like me or . . . what? What could they possibly fault your grandmother with? She lives an exemplary life! Still, her husband *did* abandon her, and some folks think that must mean there's something wrong with her. So you see? You have lots of options regarding your sinful future." She stated this quite cheerfully.

We strolled on, and I pondered all her words. After a few moments, I said, "So what that biblical phrase is about is how children end up repeating the same sins their parents committed?" When she nodded, I finished, "You think that's silly, right?" Gummie thought most religious stuff was claptrap.

She walked on without comment, smiling a little, then finally said, "Not really, Maddie. The Bible is a book of philosophy. Even though some misguided folks want to believe it was written by God Himself—whoever the hell that is—we know it was written by people. Some people are, after all, pretty smart. What I think that verse and chapter out of the Bible is *really* about is the result of environment.

"For instance, if you're raised in a household where everyone shouts, then you'll probably be a shouter when you're grown. It's what you learned to be natural. Or if your father hits your mother, there's a good chance you'll marry a hitter—if you're a girl—or you'll be a hitter—if you're a boy. Again, it's what seems natural to you because it was common in your home.

"How we might apply that to you, Maddie, is to say there's a good chance—having grown up with the illustrious womenfolk in your family—you'll be an independent thinker, making conscious choices for yourself rather than following trends or the stultifying expectations of an unimaginative society. So you might choose not to get married or you might choose to be a carpenter or you might choose to be an atheist—all of which might *look* like you were repeating the 'sins' of your foremothers instead of merely exercising your free will. Your choices may well be influenced by the choices the women in your family have made because that is what is natural in your home. Do you follow me?"

I nodded but didn't say anything, because I could tell she was just warming up. "Part of the problem is the word 'sin.' It's so arbitrary. I certainly think none of the choices my daughter, granddaughter, or myself have made are sinful, so that's where such thinking becomes unendurably silly. Then there's the other issue: inheritance. Some people, genetically, are just destined to have problems and some aren't."

We were climbing the front steps to our porch now. "Do you mean to say you think some people are just born . . . *bad*, Gummie?"

She stopped and wrinkled her nose. "Not necessarily bad, Maddie. More like troubled. Their genes are such that they might have a predilection toward depression or negativity or unhealthy addictions—like drinking or drugs—or just an inability to make good choices."

"You think all that's inherited?"

"Sure," she nodded, stepping into the porch. "Take that man who's your father. He's a good example. Dissolution runs in his family. His father and his grandfather both had drinking problems. So does he. Fact is, they're probably all alcoholics."

"Gummie, if you're right, doesn't that mean I'll probably be an alcoholic, too?"

"Could be, could be indeed," she agreed affably, which was a little chilling to me. "However, you know that's a possibility now, so maybe you could avert it by making careful choices. The truth is, in spite of their stupid drinking, those men are all real brainy—unfortunately they just let their minds rot, mostly in the bottom of a bottle. How much of that was genetic and how much was learned behavior? Hard to tell exactly, but for you, Maddie, you've inherited intelligence from both sides of your family. Now you have awareness to boot so you might be able to outwit those tendencies."

"If it's genetic, how could I do that?"

"Probably just the *tendency* to drink is genetic, Maddie. You could just drift into a life of dissolution, which the men in that family seemed to do, or you could do as I always have encouraged you to do—make careful choices about how you live your life, choices that don't include imbibing, for example. One way to avoid such a problem is to simply avoid the catalyst."

"Mmm." Jack nuzzled my hand until I absentmindedly began petting her.

Gummie lowered herself to the porch swing. "I've got to take a nap, honey, but listen: I think the Bible has a great deal of wisdom in it. Unfortunately, way too many people who read it don't have much wisdom and consequently twist good advice or information to use in their own little, petty ways. That statement about the 'sins of the fathers,' I believe, makes a lot of sense if looked at from the proper perspective. It's not about 'sin' at all. It's about the impact of a family on any individual. If Judy Peterson were smart enough, she'd realize just how much of a compliment she paid you. Your environment and most of your genes are such, there is no way in this world you aren't going to grow up to be one amazing person! Yes indeed, amazing!"

I couldn't help beaming at this pronouncement from the closest thing to God I was pretty sure I was ever going to encounter.

18

Enough

On the surface, Gramma seemed to be the most conventional member of the family, the one who seemed easiest to predict. Maybe because of that, she was often the most surprising. I remember once being in the supermarket with her on a Saturday morning and bumping into Mrs. Conrad. The Conrads were probably the richest people in Riverton. He owned the mill, which harnessed the hydroelectic power generated by the river to fuel the enormous millstones to grind wheat, resulting in flour sent, subsequently, to the large cities where bread was made. Mrs. Conrad always acted as if they were royalty or something—and the rest of us were mere peons.

"Hester! How are you?" she pronounced in a voice thick with fake honey. "And—what's your name again, child?"

I narrowed my eyes at her but knew Gramma would expect me to be courteous. "Maddie."

"Oh yes. Maddie. Such a dear little name, isn't it?" Neither Gramma nor I responded. When she realized we weren't going to say anything, she went on mellifluously, "Well now, Maddie, are you going to the dance tonight? I believe you're in my Sonja's class, aren't you?" I nodded but said nothing. I wasn't going to the dance, had not been invited. I had not felt bad about my lack of suitors until that very moment, because few girls my age were going. We were only in the seventh grade, and the dance was mostly for high schoolers. "Of course," she continued airily, "we had to go down to the Cities to get Sonja a dress. There's just *nothing* to be had in Riverton. Were you able to find something here, dear?" She peered at me, obviously assuming I would be forced to make do with Riverton's inadequate resources.

"I'm not going," I answered, almost sullenly.

Gramma interjected, a certain iciness with which I was not familiar creeping into her usually warm voice, "Madelaine is not attending the dance because she will be dining this evening at the Governor's mansion." This astonishing statement hit me like a bolt of lightning, and I had to steel myself to keep from gawking open-mouthed at Gramma. "With her great-grandmother, naturally." Everyone knew Gummie was friends with our then governor so it wasn't without possibility. Still, I couldn't believe this lie had slipped so easily out of Gramma's mouth.

"Oh!" Mrs. Conrad gasped. "Well . . ." She was clearly uncertain how to proceed. "Well, that *would* take precedence, wouldn't it?"

Gramma, whose conscience I suspected was fiercely pinching her by then, responded, "Yes, it certainly would. We must run now. So much to do, don't you know? Nice to see you, Hazel."

We finished shopping in silence, both of us wordlessly agreeing we couldn't say anything in the store for fear of being overheard. When we made it to our car, Gramma slapped her hand to her forehead as she bent over the steering wheel, exclaiming, "I don't believe I did that! I just don't believe it!"

"Oh, Gramma, Mrs. Conrad is such a bossy, show-offy cow—she made you do it!"

Gramma was shaking her head. "No, no, Maddie. No one *makes* you do anything. It doesn't matter how awful someone else is, that's no excuse for lying. Ever."

"I suppose," I agreed reluctantly, but then couldn't help smiling, remembering the look on Hazel Conrad's face when Gramma told her I'd be dining with the governor. I giggled a little. "You sure did knock her dead, though, didn't you, Gramma?"

"Oh, oh, oh," Gramma was wailing. "I can't believe I did that. That woman . . . that woman . . ." Then she chuckled a little, too, and said, "It really did impress her, didn't it?" Then she started to laugh, I joined her, and our laughter moved into gales of mania until tears were rolling down both our cheeks.

When our hilarity subsided enough so Gramma could catch her breath, she said, "Oh my, that *was* fun, wasn't it? Knocking the wind out of that old bag's sails?" We started to laugh again.

When we got home, Gramma told Gummie to "call your friend Karl Rolvaag and see if you and Maddie can join him for dinner tonight."

"What?" Gummie returned. "What are you talking about?"

"Oh, Mother," Gramma said irritably, "for once in your life, just do what I ask you. Call Karl. Otherwise," she looked at me with a twinkle in her eye, "I'll be the worst liar in Riverton. You want to make me an honest woman, don't you?"

Gummie looked from Gramma to me and back at Gramma again, finally snapping, "What in heaven's name is going on here?"—at which point, Gramma and I started laughing uproariously again.

That's how Gummie and I—and Gramma and Mom, too—happened to have a little potluck with Karl and Florence Rolvaag at the governor's mansion one spring evening. It was one of those rare moments of good fortune—they had no other plans.

On the way down to St. Paul, I said, "If those Conrads weren't so rich and always trying to show off, Gramma would never have put her foot in her mouth." The two of us started giggling, and Mom and Gummie just rolled their eyes, getting a little tired of our irrepressible giddiness.

"You had to be there . . ." Gramma tried to explain, then just started to laugh again.

When Gramma and I seemed to be somewhat under control, Gummie asked, "Maddie? What do you think 'rich' means?"

Oh-oh, one of Gummie's tests.

What does lazy mean? What does it mean if you say 'I'm bored'? Who's an immigrant?

I was used to it, but it always made me a little apprehensive because I knew I wasn't going to get it right. Actually, I wasn't supposed to get it right, but that had taken me years to figure out, and by then, the pattern of nervousness had already been established.

How could Gummie teach me anything if I knew all the answers? Sometimes, I did get it right. Then she would just glow, treating me as if I were, indeed, the most brilliant person alive. That always felt so good, I wanted it oftener. Mostly, however, I knew she wanted me *not* to know so I'd learn it from her.

When she asked me this question, I examined it for a few moments, like maybe I could answer correctly if I thought about it long enough. I mean, it was obvious, wasn't it? "Rich" meant you had lots of money, didn't it? What else could it mean? I knew, from long experience, it could mean lots of other things. Finally, I said slowly, like I was still thinking it through, "I guess 'rich' means having more money than you need."

"That's not a bad answer, Maddie," Gummie responded generously, never making me feel like I was the total idiot she must've sometimes thought I was, "but perhaps a little limited in its scope."

Undoubtedly.

"What *I* think," the whole point of this exercise, giving her an opportunity to expound on what *she* thought, "is most of us are rich in some ways but don't realize it because of our limited scope. You see, I don't think rich is about having too much. I think it's about having enough."

"Enough?" I knew my script.

"That's right. Enough. Not just money, either. Enough attention. Time. Food. Sleep. Shelter. Work to enjoy. Free time for relaxation. Friends. Enough of whatever we care about. Like things to fix, for Hester. Children and a home to fuss over, for Pansy. A career and causes, for me. Books, for your mother. And maybe the most important one—enough love."

"Don't forget enough laughter," Gramma said, and she and I started chuckling again. Gummie frowned so Gramma suppressed her merriment, winking at me.

"Mmmm," I responded, turning over what Gummie had said in my head.

"What do you think, Maddie?" Gummie prodded.

Rich is really about having tons of excess money, I thought, but said, because I knew I was supposed to, "We're probably pretty rich."

She smiled her approval and nodded, just once. "That's right, dear. We're very rich. The trick is, to be aware of it. Then we can appreciate it properly. Do you know how to do that?"

Oh, God, another test! I shook my head. Actually, I was still thinking about what it would be like if we did have a lot of money.

"Lots of folks don't have enough. In this country, not to speak of the rest of the world, probably *most* folks don't have enough. In something. Like enough to eat. Or enough living space. Maybe they have enough love. Or enough attention. The point is: almost everyone has enough of *something*. It's important to focus on that fact, not lose sight of it, when some of the ways you don't have enough get you down.

"Undoubtedly some people don't have enough of *anything*. All the more reason why those of us who have enough of most things should be grateful for what we do have. Always think about how we can share what we have. Not just money, Maddie, but skills, ideas, time, whatever excess we have. It's important to never forget how fortunate you are if you have enough in most things. The best way to appreciate your wealth is to give some of it back. It's an essential part of your own gratitude."

I nodded, my mind elsewhere. I was imagining having too much money. Not just enough. *Too much.* We had enough, I guessed, to be okay-comfortable. *Too much* would mean we could live in a mansion on the river like the Conrads did. I could have a new bike like Marijo Jensen's, not the repainted secondhand one I had. It would mean we could carpet all our floors, like Janie Alman's parents just did, and I would never have to help clean all those awful old wood floors again. We could have a color TV, like Keith MacPherson's family did; then we could watch "The Ed Sullivan Show" in vibrant, living color. I could have a lot of clothes, and Mom could have a new car instead of our old beat-up Hudson, which Gramma kept going. We could even go to Europe or somewhere exciting together. We could bring Annie and Gloria with! Oh yes, I kept thinking, it would be nice to have too much money, it would be nice to be *really* rich.

Gummie's words on "enough" kept tickling around at the back of my head, too. We weren't rich, by my definition, although I couldn't help thinking we sure were rich compared to Jannie Barnes, who had two outfits to her name and both were frayed and faded from constant washings. Or Alberta Campion, whose hair was lank and clumped together and how I complained because she never washed it and she kinda smelled, until my mother pointed out to me that some people just couldn't afford soap or shampoo. Things we took for granted were luxuries to some families. I also remembered when our civics teacher told us to bring a newspaper article to class once a week to share and discuss, and Gerald Berg got an "F" because he didn't do it. The teacher just assumed he was being lazy, but we found out later, when he dropped out of school and joined the Army, that his family couldn't afford to spend money on newspapers—what with eleven mouths to feed and a father laid off work and a mother working only part-time at Curly's Cafe.

Yeah, we looked pretty rich compared to lots of folks, when I thought about it. Especially with our big old barn of a house. I didn't have a lot of clothes, but I had plenty more than two outfits, and I got some new ones at least once a year. It was true, we didn't have a color TV, but some folks didn't have *any* TV—black and white *or* color. Our furniture was pretty shabby, none of it much matched with any of the rest of it, and the floors were covered with scrappy-to-threadbare rugs, but we had books! Hundreds of them! Probably thousands of them! I had a multi-level tree house out back in the big maple tree.

When I thought about the other things Gummie had listed—attention, time, food, sleep, work we enjoy, friends, love—I started to think maybe she was right. Because we seemed to have plenty of enough of everything really important to us. I mean, I wouldn't *mind* more clothes or a new bike or a color TV, but I wasn't hurting or anything, not having them. What became clear, the more I thought about this, was how much more I had than didn't have.

Eventually, the thing I realized I had the most of—not just enough but an abundance—was role models. It's not as if I really grasped that entirely at twelve; it's just I gleaned it in some unwordable way. With Gummie, who was in her nineties and still going to a job she adored every day, with Gramma who could fix and mix anything and taught me to do both, too, with Mom who also had a job she loved, and with all of them being strong and independent and fiercely intelligent and showering me with affection and appreciation and encouragement—how could I go wrong? How could I ever be richer?

After all, wasn't I on my way to have dinner with the governor of Minnesota? I looked at Gramma and, again, with no word passing between us, we started to laugh.

19

Born to Be a Newspaperwoman

The story Gummie loved to tell about my first visit at two and a half to the paper was that she turned her attention away for a moment, and I climbed on a desk and yelled, "Stop the presses!" ensuing in a moment of stunned silence and then general mirth. I don't remember the incident, even though I have some memories from that age. I've always suspected that Gummie fabricated the tale. After all, there was no explanation for how I'd ever learned that phrase.

When I was older and questioned her, she would shrug and say, "I have no idea. You must've seen it in a movie or something." I would point out I was not taken to movies that young, and we had no TV yet. "I don't know, Maddie. Maybe the radio?" This was one of the reasons why I was suspicious: she was *never* disingenuous. Then, she would throw her arms in the air, smiling broadly, and say, "I guess you were just born to be a newspaperwoman."

This final statement cooked her goose, as far as I was concerned, and made me certain she'd made the whole story up. She wanted to know, before she died, that there was a family member to whom she could pass the wand. Even though she never said this, I knew it to be true. I thought, because her daughter and grand-daughter had found other lives, I'd been elected. I believed she made up the whole story about me because she wanted to ensure my fate by pretending it was a foregone conclusion.

At the time, I didn't mind. It seemed unimaginable to me that she would ever die, plus I knew, if she did die, I was free to do whatever I wanted. What would it cost me to indulge her in this fantasy I thought she needed so badly? I wasn't sure, during my childhood, what I wanted to be when I grew up, anyway. After a while, I was pretty certain I wanted to be a novelist, not a journal-ist. Nonetheless, it was true, the paper did hold a certain allure for me, too.

I loved to be there—smoke swirling about the room like a thick, London fog, phones ringing, the smell of ink permeating everything, the sense of urgency, importance, essentiality. To this day, a whiff of cigarette smoke—maybe clinging to someone's hair or sweater—doesn't conjure scuzzy bars for me. It evokes a news-paper office.

I never really understood why Gummie wanted this so badly, since there was no guarantee—even if I did want to take over—it would happen. In 1911, the year after she bought the *Riverton Weekly,* she transformed it into a worker-owned operation called *The Prairie Voice.* There were only four workers, counting Gummie, but she shared ownership equally with them all. Every new staff member automatically became an owner—just a small percentage their first year at the paper. After that trial year, they owned a proportionate share, according to the number of hours they worked and the total number of staff.

"How come you did that, Gummie? Didn't you buy the paper because you wanted to be in charge and do it your own way?"

"Sure, but I spent my adult life railing against unjust bosses and supporting workers' rights. I had to put my money where my mouth was, Maddie. Otherwise, I'd be totally devoid of integrity." A fate worse than death for her.

"By making the paper worker-owned, didn't you risk giving up control?"

She nodded. "Yes, but Maddie? If I didn't trust my workers, then I didn't trust the systems I'd been advocating all my life. If you believe in a system, you have to trust it. If you believe in people, you have to trust them. If I got deposed, then I had to *trust* that it was meant to be."

I was skeptical. I could not imagine Gummie simply accepting being dethroned. The paper was not a collective. Even though it was worker-owned, it was always set up with a hierarchy of responsibility. The workers did, however, get to vote on the major decisions, just like a board would—including selecting who was going to be the managing editor, the position with the most power. They continued to vote, year after year, to keep Gummie in this position.

As I grew older and more knowledgeable, this was increasingly confusing. "How come they do that?" I asked my mother once on one of our evening strolls. "I'm sure Gummie does a good job, but it seems odd to me that not once in all those years, anyone came along and tried to topple her off her throne. I mean, she is sort of . . ." I hesitated here, not feeling very comfortable in criticizing my idol.

"Autocratic?" Mom supplied for me, and I nodded assent. "I think it's a number of things, Maddie. For one thing, the workers are a little scared of your gummie."

I nodded again, having witnessed this myself. "That's what I mean, Mom. Wouldn't they want to get rid of someone who scares them?"

She shook her head. "It's not that simple. Mixed in with their fear, they have fierce loyalty and respect for her. She may rule with an iron hand, Maddie, but the other hand is a velvet glove."

"What does that mean?"

"She knows her coworkers. She remembers the details of their personal lives—their spouses' and kids' names or who they're dating. She inquires after them, keeps track of who's sick or who's graduating from high school or who's won an award and acknowledges it or offers help. She has high expectations of her coworkers—no less than she has for herself—but she is also quick to give them time off when they need it or to lend a sympathetic ear when one of them just needs to talk about some personal problem or even dig in her own pocket to close the gap between need and payday. She appreciates them. That may seem obvious, but not every employer does that so well. She *never* takes their contributions for granted, and she always lets them know that.

"They don't always like her, Maddie, but they respect her. Besides which, because they're owners, they have access to the books—and other aspects of the operation. Not having any secrets goes a long way toward producing good relations between everyone. They all know Gummie doesn't make an exorbitant amount of money, any more than any of the rest of them. In fact, that's one of their responsibilities as owners—they get to set the wages every year. Gummie is continually awarded a higher income than everyone else, but just barely. She accepts this with grace and appreciation, and they respect her for it.

"Here's another thing, Maddie. This paper has won more awards than any other paper in the state, including the big city dailies. It garners a huge readership, reaching well beyond its own county boundaries, because it's controversial, well-written, thorough, and honest. This kind of journalism makes people proud to be a part of it. It also keeps securing your gummie's position as the in-charge."

"Doesn't the paper *ever* get dissatisfied workers? People who think they could do better than Gummie? Or people who just want to be in charge themselves? Or even people who think, you know, this paper is a little too pinko for them?"

Mom shrugged. "Sometimes. Mostly not the ones who think it's too left-wing. People like that just wouldn't come to work at a newspaper like *The Prairie Voice*. Other disgruntled folks? Sure, it's happened. It's part of the beauty of the worker-owned operation, Maddie. Or maybe Gummie has just been lucky, I don't know. A handful *have* tried to take over, but the other workers never backed any of them sufficiently for them to succeed."

I thought this over, then asked her, "Do you think Gummie would really just accept it, if the workers ever voted her out?"

Mom laughed and answered, "Not without a fight. There was one time I know of—you should ask her about it. It was after the War. I know she says she'd just 'have to accept it' if she got voted out. The fact is, I don't think she's ever *really* believed that that would happen."

I nodded my agreement. I didn't even think she believed that, if I did want to carry on her tradition, the workers would thwart me, either.

"When you were growing up, Mom, did you work at the paper like I do? Did she want you to take it over?"

"I didn't work there quite as much as you do because we didn't live with Gummie. She always wanted me to work more, though, and learn the business. She wanted an heir." I nodded. She still wanted an heir.

20

The Smell of Fresh Ink

In some ways, it feels like I grew up at Gummie's paper—at first just hanging around, later handling increasingly more difficult jobs. I probably would've been there every day if Gramma hadn't insisted there were other things for me to do. I went in after school one or two days, most Saturday mornings, and usually three times a week during the summer months. When Annie and I became friends, it was easier for me to spend less time there.

I started out cleaning the bathroom, sweeping the floors, and doing some careful tidying—believe me, these were not people who wanted *anyone* touching their work areas—and being a "runner," doing whatever errand running anyone required of me. In addition, by the time I was in school, I was stuffing envelopes and licking stamps. I soon learned how to post payments in the ledgers, solicit new customers door-to-door, process new orders by phone, and update files. As I grew older, I was allowed to proofread ads and even sell some of them. I learned to set print and load paper into the press. Working with Gummie, I became an expert scrutinizer of layouts. Running a paper route was expected of me by the time I turned ten. Long before I was allowed to write copy—for ads or articles—I was a proofreader and a fact checker and even a researcher. Every job at the newspaper, at some point or another, was assigned to me. I was both apprentice and general dogsbody.

I clearly remember bending over proofs spread out on Gummie's desk, seriously discussing headlines, layout, ads—just as if I were a peer, rather than a child. The smell of fresh ink would mingle with the heady sense of being treated like a grown-up, lodging itself—so it seemed to me—permanently in my nasal cavities.

I asked Gummie about the takeover Mom had mentioned. "Oh yeah. That would be Donald Keller." She repeated the name slowly, shaking her head a little, blowing her breath out in this way she had, making me know she wanted to expell the memory. "Donald Keller." After another pause, she continued, "He came back from the War angry. About everything. Who could blame him? War is terrible."

"He tried to get your job?"

"Yes, that's what he wanted, all right. Thought he *should* have it, actually."

When she didn't proceed, I inserted, "I guess he didn't get it, though, did he?"

"No, he didn't. He came back, as I said, angry. During the War, Beatrice Allen was our city editor. We were all women running the paper throughout those years, except for Henry. Do you remember Henry?" I shook my head. "I guess he died when you were just a baby. He was our printer, had been since I took the paper over back in '10. Anyway, he was too old to go off to war, but the rest of us? All women."

She hummed as she rearranged items on her desk; I was patient, knowing she'd gotten started now. "I thought these women might stay on after the War, that they'd gotten a taste of the working world and would want to continue. Some of them did. Mostly— not just at the paper but everywhere—women quit their jobs and went home to take care of their returning men or else took jobs where there were GI's looking for brides.

"We were being bombarded by messages telling us to 'go home and put our aprons on.' Just as there'd been campaigns to 'do our patriotic duty' at the beginning of the war by taking up the positions made vacant by men who'd done '*their* duty' by signing up and going off to make the world safe for their women and children, there were campaigns afterward for the opposite. Women were then exhorted to 'do our duty' by giving up our jobs to men who *had* made the world safe for them, supposedly, and now needed jobs to restore order and meaning to their lives. What a lot of hooey! Unfortunately, most women swallowed this hooey."

"That must've rankled you."

She grimaced. "Some. It *was* annoying. I ran more than one article about how women needed work, too; they also needed 'to be of use.' I wrote about how keeping a house and raising children was honorable work, but it wasn't what all women wanted. Or needed. Most people thought my opinions were heretical. I even did some articles on the need for child care facilities. Whoo-ee! I really got it, then, for being a commie! In the late forties and early fifties, only the commies and Jews—one and the same to many people—advocated state-funded child care."

"Why was that, Gummie?" It wasn't as if there were lots of day care facilities in the mid-sixties, but it certainly made sense to me.

"Very controversial. You're too young to remember the witch hunts of those days. McCarthyism. Believe me, people believed communists were lurking under every bush, just waiting to snatch folks up and brainwash them. Actually, many still cradle that belief. Child care was viewed as a tool of the state, a way to separate children from their parents and indoctrinate them, too. The scare tactics were enormous."

"What was it like for you, Gummie, during those years?"

"The so-called witch hunts were never very vigorous here in the Midwest, at least not as much as they were on the coasts."

"Why not?"

"It didn't matter that much of what occurred in this country in terms of radical organizing got started here in the Midwest. The real power lay mostly on the East Coast, and those folks?—they never saw us as any more than a bunch of hayseeds. It was one of the few times when we actually benefitted from that kind of arrogance. They didn't take us seriously enough to muster forces against us. Public opinion still ran high against left-wingers. At the paper, we danced a careful dance."

She said nothing for several minutes. "You see, Maddie, the thing you have to be—if you want to survive and especially if you have a business that you want to survive—is flexible."

If "flexible" meant compromising, I couldn't imagine Gummie doing it, and I said as much. "You mean you watered down the news?"

She snorted. "No, I don't mean that. I gave them enough of what they wanted so that I could keep slipping in the stuff they didn't want, but *I* thought they needed. We could stay in business, not get tarred and feathered and run out of town."

"Was that ever a possibility?"

"A possibility? Sure. It happened to lots of people. Mostly, though, it was more likely we would've just had to close our doors. It's about faith, Maddie. I *had* to believe if I did what was right and used my common sense, the paper would weather the onslaught of the McCarthyites."

"How did you actually do that?" Again, I couldn't imagine her compromising or diluting the news.

"Men were coming back from the war disgruntled about working conditions and the general exploitation of workers—as they should've been—consequently, enormous labor activity spread across the country. Blacks, who'd tasted 'equal opportunity' in the War—equal opportunity to die, that is—were not particularly inclined to accept massive discrimination in job, housing, voting, or other situations.

"You know, Maddie, history likes to characterize the fifties as this bland decade when nothing more exciting than Marilyn Monroe happened. It's true, women were mostly shooed back into the kitchen and nursery, but lots of men came home mad and determined to change the world. We had widespread labor unrest, leading to the creation of more and more unions, strikes, and workers' demands. We had the burgeoning Civil Rights movement. Just because white folks got involved in the '60s doesn't mean there was no movement until then. It started in the forties, mostly with those returning black soldiers.

"On the other side, we had an increase of Ku Klux Klan activity, comparable only to the rise during the decade following the Civil War. We had McCarthy's "witch" hunts, which were just a way for the right-wing folks to scare everyone into low expectations and scant respect for those who did demand rights. Organizations like the John Birch Society became prominent. All over the South, racist organizations not as blatant or violent as the KKK—but just as pernicious—attracted moderates."

"You covered all of this activity in the paper, didn't you?"

"Of course, but it was also a time for pablum. People wanted less controversy. The War had taken its toll on all of us—too many fine young men never coming back, too many coming back with awful physical or mental problems, too much trauma for a nation to easily absorb. People wanted things to be easy for a while. Or at least to pretend a simple, uncomplicated life was possible. So, in order to sell newspapers, in order to sell ads, actually in order to survive at all, and also in order to sneak in the *really important* news, I had to give them some hope, some ease, some fluff."

"Fluff?" That word made me smile, thinking how no one would *ever* connect it with Gummie. Pansy maybe, but definitely not Gummie. "How did you do that?"

She smiled this time. "The *Voice* had never had a 'women's' page since I took it over. I had this radical notion that women were *people*—imagine!—and all news was for *all* people. I just thought the whole paper was for everyone, women and men. In 1949, for the first time, we created a women's section. We ran recipes and fashion tidbits and child-rearing tips next to articles about child care and education. We'd also sneak in something about home repair because more women fix stuff than men would ever want to admit, and I thought they should be able to find out how to do it right. We got a lot of ads for those pages; consumerism was just warming up and every business wanted to reach those star consumers—housewives.

"As for the so-called hard news, I'd run banner headlines about some school or community celebration or event, then I'd run—still on the front page but a little less prominently than the so-called 'good' news—articles about strikes or new Civil Rights legislation or Klan activity or demonstrations in the South.

"We'd never had a large international section, most weeklies don't, but it had expanded during the War when, naturally, people wanted to understand the wider context of a world in which their sons, husbands, brothers, or fathers were killing or being killed. I continued that expansion following the War because I thought context was always important for people to understand what was happening, but I also could find lots of happy things to write about, too. Princess Elizabeth's wedding, for instance, and her subsequent crowning as the Queen of England. Movie star dreck—people love that stuff, Maddie. Who's marrying whom and who's divorcing whom and who's dating whom and what were they wearing?"

Her face had the look of someone who'd just gotten a rotten piece of food on her tongue and was trying to figure out how to get it out without just spitting. It made me laugh. "Did it work, Gummie? Did it sell newspapers?"

"Oh yes, it worked. Sometimes I hated it, but—gradually—I started to see that this information was still news, even if *I* wasn't so interested in it. People had a right to all of it. It created a kind of balance I wasn't even looking for when I started using these tactics. It actually taught an old dog like me a few new tricks. After the War, our circulation decreased some, but by the mid-fifties, it was stronger than ever."

"What about this Donald fellow?"

"Yes. Donald. He was all a part of this transition." Gummie, as usual, acted as though her long digression was just part of the major story. When I grew older, I realized she was probably right. "Donald Keller came to us in 1949. He'd had newspaper experience before the War, went to college on the GI bill afterward, and got a degree in journalism. Came to us full of energy and ideas—and anger.

"He took Beatrice's job as city editor. She'd stayed on for a while after the war, while her returning husband recovered from his wounds and shell shock. When she quit, wanting to start a family, Donald came to us—and I thought we were lucky. I was aware of the anger, but I thought we could just channel all of it into useful newspaper work—and he'd heal. He was, after all, AVC, so I thought he'd be fine."

"AVC? What's AVC?"

"American Veterans Committee. This was a veterans' group differing from other similar organizations, like the VFW—Veterans of Foreign Wars—or the American Legion, which mostly glorified war. AVC was for men who didn't believe in war, who believed in a world community. Some of the AVC's were communists; all were liberal, left-wing types. I always thought we could count on those men to be on the side of women's rights, like Guppie. Some of them were. Unfortunately, I was often disappointed.

"Donald had his own agenda. He began fomenting trouble right away. While workers all over our nation were rising up against exploitative bosses, Donald merely wanted the power I had and felt he could get it by removing me. He hated it that any woman might be any man's boss—particularly *his* boss."

"Did a lot of men who worked for you have those attitudes, Gummie?"

She wrinkled her nose. "A lot? No, not *a lot*. It did happen, though. Donald wasn't the first to squirm at the thought of being under a woman's thumb. See, Maddie," and she leaned forward in her conspiratorial way, "all men are toilet trained by some woman, leaving an indelible mark on them, making them feel they have to spend the rest of their lives proving they can piss without help from a woman." We both laughed. "Having a woman boss reminds them of those years they were so dependent on their mothers, and it makes many of them nervous. As a woman who's in charge, I just always have to remember to combine the best of men's and women's styles. In essence, I have to nudge them toward their best efforts—sometimes even going so far as to shove them—while showering them with tender and continuous praise."

21

The End Justifies the Means

"And Donald?" I prodded Gummie again.

"He came with a chip on his shoulder, and—as I said—an agenda. I thought the chip was mostly about the War, but I was wrong. Or maybe I wasn't wrong, but he'd transformed it to be about women and blacks and just about everyone whom he thought was a threat to his manhood. I suspect the real threat to his manhood had been his feeling of terror and helplessness during the War, his natural desire to just cut and run. War is horrible, and it makes men feel like scared little boys. Some of them just can't handle that.

"He started poking and prodding, gradually, saying things like, 'How could a woman run a newspaper? A woman can't report about the *real* things in life—war and government—because she can never experience those things.' I ignored his swagger, but maybe I should've starting fighting back right away.

"What he did, mostly behind my back, was convince the other workers that I was past my prime (I was, after all, in my seventies), and that the paper needed new blood, aggressive people (he meant *men*) who knew the inside of news in ways that an old woman never could. Also, he harped about my pinko leanings, my godlessness, my alliances with well-known, card-carrying commies—he used all the scare tactics and rhetoric of the time to discredit me, minimize my power, and undermine my authority."

"If he was—what was it called?—AVC?" Gummie nodded, "—wasn't he on the side of the communists?"

"I thought so when we hired him, but somehow he got caught up in McCarthyism. Or maybe he was just faking his liberality to get hired. I never knew, one way or the other, for sure.

"All I knew was that Donald wanted to create a rebellion. I thought I could just ride it out. I was operating on that faith principle, having faith in the people and the system, but Maddie? Sometimes you have to give faith a little boost. You have to remember that human beings are frail and can easily be led to slaughter, especially in times of recovery from some trauma or other. Even the best systems need an overhaul occasionally.

"I wasn't remembering these things and blithely let Donald have his say—although I pulled him up short once or twice when I thought he had gone too far. The annual owners' meeting, at which company positions were determined, was approaching when Henry came to me.

"Henry was my oldest colleague, the only one left from the original workforce when I bought the paper. He was probably about seventy by then, almost as ancient as I was. He told me exactly what had been going on behind my back and to what extent Donald had garnered support.

"'Iris,' he said to me, 'if I thought it was just time for a change, and this young fella was aiming to accomplish that, I wouldn't say anything. I don't think that's it, though. I think he wants power, and he wants to get it by taking your job. What's worse, he's not going to share that power; he's going to wield it like a club over our heads. Even though we can get rid of him if all that happens, it will take a long time for most people to admit they made a bad mistake, and he's likely to do a lot of damage by then. You gotta fight, Iris. You can't let him do this to us.'"

She paused here, sipping some coffee, tapping her fingers against her desk edge, and staring vacantly at the article she'd been perusing before I'd begun questioning her. I waited as long as I could, then asked, "What happened, Gummie? How did you beat him?"

She looked up, her eyes sad, and sighed. "I started by talking to the rest of the staff, one by one, thinking I could dissuade them individually. They listened intently; many nodded as if they agreed with me, but I felt, with a chilling certainty, that it was just the *appearance* of agreement. Mostly, they didn't want to openly disagree with me, out of respect, if nothing else. Some actually argued with me, told me how it was a 'new day' and we needed to 'open the windows and let a fresh breeze' blow through our company. I could tell they'd bought Donald's line.

"So how to get them to see Donald as the potential tyrant that I was becoming convinced he was going to be? You have to understand, Maddie, I was a little unsure myself. It did occur to me, believe it or not, that maybe he was right, and maybe it was time for me to move on, to let the next generation take over."

I snorted in true Gummie-style, and she chuckled.

"I was trying to be fair," she insisted, "and consider the possibility of my being wrong." Another snort issued from me, and this time she shook her head. "Anyway, it gradually became apparent I needed to unmask him, reveal his true intentions."

"How'd you do that?"

"At first, I couldn't think how to do it. When I stumbled on an idea, I enlisted Henry. He was a sweet, lovable guy; everyone knew they could count on him. That's partially why I'd paid attention to him in the first place. Henry simply had no malicious tendencies. If he had something bad to say about someone, it meant that person had grave problems. I knew, because Henry was so universally liked, that if he got attacked, the others would be protective of him and suspicious of anyone who would assault him.

"Henry and I decided that he was going to make a deliberate mistake. As you know, Maddie, a certain amount of mistakes happen when setting the print, even when a machine does it." She shot me a look that made me squirm, thinking of some of the mistakes I'd made. "After all, machines are run by people, and people aren't perfect."

I interrupted, saying gravely, "Some of us less so than others."

She pursed her lips to control her grin and nodded seriously. "That's true. Mistakes always upset us at the paper, but you live with them, and if they're serious enough, you print retractions or corrections. Henry and I cooked up a scheme in which he would make a serious, strategic mistake in one of Donald's stories.

"Now keep in mind, Maddie, I didn't feel very good about doing this. Henry, on the other hand, loved the idea, insisting 'the end justifies the means.' I, personally, think that's a dangerous concept, but I couldn't see any other way out of it. Also, if we were wrong about Donald, if he didn't react the way we suspected he would, then it would've proved to *us*—to Henry and me—that we were misjudging the fellow."

"Would you have just let him take over then? If you thought you were wrong about him?"

She rocked back in her chair, looking thoughtful. "I'd like to just say 'yes' to your question, but I honestly don't know, Maddie. I mean, I would have had to, wouldn't I? Would I do it gracefully?

I just don't know. Luckily, I didn't have to find out. The first time we manufactured the mistake—Henry changed a couple of letters in one or two words, which completely altered the meaning of the entire story—Donald was livid."

"Which letters, Gummie? Which words?"

She waved her hand, dismissively. "I don't know. That was a long time ago. I can't remember every detail," but she looked at the ceiling and squinted her eyes in concentration. Then she chortled, saying, "I remember. It was a story about a politician, one Donald particularly liked. This man was quoted as 'wanting to serve his community'—or something like that—and Henry switched the 'er' in serve to 'a,' resulting in him saying he wanted to 'save his community.' In another quote, this same politician talked about the experience of campaigning as being 'humbling,' and it came out 'bumbling.'" She grinned in appreciation of the memory.

"Wow! That makes the politician look like a fool. What did Donald do?"

"He stormed back to the press and chewed Henry out nastily. You know how small this place is. Everyone heard him. Believe me, you could see a parade of doubtful emotions marching across every face in this office that day.

"People do yell at one another in this business. Quite a lot, in fact. Most journalists are passionate people—and passionate people tend to be explosive, in both positive and negative ways. There's a difference, however, between being angry and being *mean*. The first time, Donald was straddling that difference. Just enough to get people worried. So, we just pushed him over the edge by repeating our experiment the next week.

"Donald played his part beautifully. Wouldn't you think he'd be a *little* suspicious when destructive mistakes occurred in his stories—and only *his* stories—two weeks in a row?" Gummie shook her head. "He never seemed to have a clue. Later maybe, when it was too late, but not when it was happening."

She put her hand up to ward off the question about to pop out of my mouth. "I don't know, Maddie, I can't remember everything," but she scrunched her brow again and continued, "Something like *bland* instead of *band*." She shrugged.

"How did Donald handle it this time?"

"He was more than mean. He attacked Henry personally and viciously, deriding him for his age, his infirmities, his stupidity. This was pretty funny, considering Henry had figured out a way—two weeks in a row—to make a simple change, resulting in a major shift in the meaning of a story. Donald yelled at Henry, insisting he 'should retire, had no business attempting to do this job.' Then, luckily, he really went too far. He shouted—and everyone either heard him or was told by someone else at the paper—'Believe me, the first thing I'm going to do when *I'm* the managing editor is dump you. And every other doddering old fool who shouldn't be here.' Well." She swiveled her chair a little and hummed, her attention drifting out the window.

Finally, I said, "That was the end of it?"

"Yes, it was over. Donald's pronouncement engulfed our newsroom like a tsunami. Certainly, some of them were a little apprehensive of Donald and his tactics already, after he'd attacked Henry so fiercely the week before. This—this convinced them of his true colors. We had plenty of older people working on the paper in those days, and they all felt the shock of what Donald was predicting as their fate."

"Did you fire Donald?"

She shook her head, her lips pursed. "Nope. Didn't have to. He kept trying to whip up sentiment against me. After the things he'd said to Henry and *how* he'd said them, everything he said about me or my editorial decisions seemed just what they were:

venomous, vile assaults. His real nature had been revealed, and no one could go back to seeing him the way he'd initially painted himself. He was desperate to reinstate his ascendancy with them, and desperation is rarely a good motivator. It forced him to escalate his charges against me, and the more he raised the ante, the more everyone saw exactly who he was and what he was trying to do. In the end, he just quit."

"Did everything get back to normal, then?"

"Not exactly. We had a series of meetings in which we talked about some of the real problems Donald had uncovered. I also began, gradually, to hire more and more young people, to provide some balance in perspectives. It wasn't all bad, what his ambition had started."

"Do you think it'll ever happen again?" I wondered.

"Not now, Maddie. I'm too old now. You know what I mean."

I shook my head slowly, saying, "I'm not sure . . . You mean because they respect you too much?"

Her lips twitched in amusement. "No, it's not that. They do respect me, and I don't want to minimize that, but mostly—they just know they can wait me out now. If they want to get rid of me, they know I'll die before they actually have to take any action."

I hated this thought, even though I knew it was undoubtedly true.

22

Part of the Problem

The spring before I turned thirteen, 1965, was when I truly lost my innocence. It had certainly taken a blow when I was eleven and JFK had been assassinated, and it had been further damaged reading about the violent resistance—including murder—to integration in the South, but I had lived an unbelievably sheltered life—growing up in a small, mostly white town in a northern state. To be sure, there were hateful people who lived in our town; some spite had been directed toward me, even. However, loathsome acts were rarely overt—or direct—in small-town Minnesota, where most people were polite, even about their animosities.

"That's just because northerners scarcely ever have to come face-to-face with it," Gummie insisted when I was outraged by pictures on TV of white southerners trying to overturn a bus with a handful of black children in it.

"They were kids!" I shrieked. "Just little kids! Think how terrified they must have been! And the white people? They were women! Ladies! How could they do that?"

"You're right, Maddie, it's horrible," Gummie soothed, "but it could happen here, too."

I shook my head adamantly. "I know people are prejudiced here, too, Gummie. I get into arguments at school, and I know those kids are just parroting their parents' ignorance." Gummie beamed—being proud, I know, of my taking a stand—and I decided not to tell her that sometimes those arguments were actually fights and sometimes the fights were the result of my being informed that I didn't know what I was talking about because I was just a bastard. "Still, I can't believe anyone here would try to knock over a bus full of kids. Kids!"

Gummie would just shake her head in response, saying, "They might, Maddie. You just don't know, because no one here has been tested."

"You make it sound like it's okay those white ladies wanted to tip that bus over!" I accused.

"Maddie. You know that isn't true. I just don't want you to think the South is the only place where this could happen. I don't want you to assume we're somehow better in the North. People are people. There are good people everywhere, even in the South, and there are bad people everywhere, even in the North."

I knew she was right, but still . . . There were no black families living in Riverton. We had a couple of native families and one adopted Asian girl from the Korean War. Multiculturalism didn't exist.

"They have to deal with it in Minneapolis," I insisted, "and nothing really violent or awful is happening there."

She shrugged. "Okay, Maddie, maybe it's *worse* in the South, maybe it's *more* ingrained—this adamant attitude of separation, but don't be misled by 'worse.' Prejudice and racial hatred exist in the North, too. It's just not as obvious because the numbers are different. There are places in the South, even in rural areas, where the blacks outnumber the whites. The whites get scared—scared about their jobs, scared of the voting power of such a large group, scared their kids are going to start falling in love with their new black classmates, and that they're going to end up with little black grandchildren."

"So? What would be wrong with that?"

Gummie shook her head. "Nothing, Maddie, nothing at all. Except most people would be appalled by it. Believe me, even in the North."

"Would you? Gramma or Mom?"

"No, it wouldn't matter to me at all. Nor to your grandmother or mother, I'm sure. It would to most people, though. A lot."

I squirmed, knowing there was truth to what she was saying. I'd been amazed when Annie's father, one night at his dinner table, had said he thought blacks should have all the rights whites had and he certainly couldn't understand why all those folks in the South were putting up such a fuss about school integration but how glad he was we didn't have to worry about such things here and how he hoped blacks wouldn't get it into their heads to start moving out to Riverton or something.

I'd been astonished at this swift progression from what seemed to be a reasonable assertion to blatant prejudice. I was so surprised, I blurted out, "Why?"

"Oh, Maddie," he hastened to assure me, "now don't go and get the wrong idea. I know where your family stands on all these issues. I agree, one hundred percent, with the stuff your great-grandmother is writing about the Civil Rights movement. I just

don't want our property values to be lowered. The sad truth is—
they would be if a bunch of those people moved in." *Those people*,
I thought? "Anyway," he chuckled at this point, looking around
the table at me and Annie and her mom and brother, "I sure don't
want any pickaninny grandchildren!" He chuckled again, and
Annie's brother, Gary, sniggered. When the rest of us didn't even
smile, he said jovially and a little peevishly, "It was a joke, people,
a joke."

Annie's mother smiled faintly, but Annie and I just bent our
heads to our food. Later, when Annie and I had turned the light
off in her bedroom and were hunkering down for that whispering
we did before drifting into sleep, I asked her about it. She
defended her father. "It's true, Maddie, about the property values.
It's common knowledge. I agree with you, though, his remark
about pickaninnies was really stupid." Her defense of him put me
on guard so I said nothing when she paused. She added, "He just
wasn't thinking, I guess."

I dropped the subject. This was Annie, my best and dearest
friend in the world. How could she defend her father? How could
she not see he was . . . I was unsure of what he was. Prejudiced?
Racist? Was it reasonable to be concerned about property values?
I lay awake for a long time after Annie had fallen asleep, considering the human heart. Or maybe it wasn't the human heart at all;
maybe it was how the human brain interferes with what the
human heart knows.

Back home, I reluctantly asked Gummie about Mr. Rees's comments. I didn't want anyone in my family to know Annie's family
was ever less than perfect, but I needed to talk to someone, to
tickle out all the conflicting information I kept getting. I steeled
myself, when I told Gummie, for a blast of ire from her. Instead,
she just shook her head sadly and said, "Oh, Maddie, I'm so sorry
to hear about Frank Rees saying things like that. So sorry."

"So, it's not true? The stuff about property values?"

She shook her head again. "No, it is true, Maddie. When blacks move into an all-white neighborhood, some whites immediately want to move out, not wanting blacks for neighbors. When other whites discover there's a black family in the neighborhood, they won't buy in that neighborhood. Everyone—the whites moving out, the whites refusing to move in—pretends it's about property values when, in fact, it's about racism. Of course, the property values *are* affected by this racism, thereby allowing racist folks to focus on this and ignore their racism. Are you following me?"

I nodded slowly. "So, Mr. Rees was telling the truth about property values, but he was probably not being honest about his—and other people's—underlying racism?"

"That's right, Maddie."

"That crack about pickaninnies . . ." I exhaled a large sigh of sadness and dismay.

"Yes, it surely revealed the truth more clearly. Lots of people, like Frank Rees, couch their racism in humor or supposed ignorance—the I-didn't-know defense. Neither ignorance nor humor are excuses for prejudice. Racism is *always* a bad thing. Always."

So when Gummie talked about northerners handling their racism differently but still being as bad as southerners, I knew she was right. Racism was subtle or hidden in the North. Still, it couldn't possibly be as bad as what was happening in the South, could it?

Another time when I was at Annie's, her father made a disparaging remark about "all these northern do-gooders going to the South to stir up trouble." It was startling, hearing this man whom I believed to be a good man saying the kinds of things prejudiced southerners seemed to be saying. I didn't respond, carefully biting my lip.

Annie challenged him, though. "Dad, shouldn't people commit

themselves to stirring things up when changes are needed? Shouldn't we stand up for what we believe in and help others?"

"Sure, Annie, those are good and admirable ideals. It's just we don't always know what's help and what's meddling. The newspapers—no offense, Maddie—" I guess I was the newspaper representative, "and TV like to focus on the worst stuff. We never hear about all the blacks who are happy with things just the way they are. Or all the whites who are good people who'd never hurt any of their neighbors—black or white. Newspeople just like to report the bad stuff because it's more interesting, so how can we be sure what's right—or best—for other people? Northerners should just stay home and tend to their own."

I still didn't say anything and didn't intend to say anything to Annie when we were alone, either, not wanting to rock this fragile boat. Luckily, she said it all herself. She was angry at her father for expressing such prejudice and for the way he attempted to mask it with "niceness."

"Robin and her husband are even worse," she informed me (Robin being her big sister). She added, about her brother, "I don't mind Gary being such an idiot. He just lives for sports and 'babes,' but Robin! She just goes along with everything her husband thinks, and he makes Dad look like Gandhi. Mom agrees with me, but she thinks we should keep the peace. Maddie, how can he be so awful? I just hate it! It's not like he's dumb or anything, but every day it gets worse. He makes jokes or else seemingly reasonable observations—all just cover-ups for his own prejudice. I hate it!"

I said little, knowing—no matter what—Annie wasn't going to be able to bear much against her dad from anyone else. I commiserated with her, then went home and reported to Gummie (*like the good little commie-spy you are*, I sometimes teased myself).

"That isn't true, is it, Gummie, what he said about good and bad news, is it? It sounds like he's accusing the media of manipulation."

"Mmmm. Maddie, I think I'd be less than honest not to admit there is manipulation in newsmaking. When the 'other folks' do it—the right-wing-McCarthyites-would-be-Nazis-sometimes-Republicans—then we call it manipulation. When we—the avowedly good guys—do it, we call it 'the truth.' And vice versa, naturally." We smiled at each other.

"So he *is* right, then? The news is just focusing on the bad stuff in the South, and we don't really know what's going on?"

"There's probably *some* truth to what he's saying, Maddie. I really doubt there are any 'happy blacks' down there—or much anywhere in this country—happy in some ways, of course, but I mean there are almost for sure no blacks who are happy with the way things are. It's just there are many who don't want to mess with the status quo—it's too hard and too dangerous. They could lose their jobs, or even worse, their lives.

"I know we aren't seeing much in the news about the good whites in the South—those who don't go out and lynch black men and those who don't think integration is bad and even those who are joining the demonstrations and sit-ins and marches. When I went to Montgomery in 1956 to cover the bus boycott, I became part of a car pool there, mostly for the black day helpers. There were plenty of white women helping in the car pool—women who were defying their husbands, their parents, their culture to do what was right. I'm sure there are southern whites doing that now, too.

"If the news seems to focus on the whites who are doing awful things—and this is the manipulative part, Maddie—it's because change usually only comes from people being exposed to the worst of humanity. I doubt the news is making bad people in the South worse.

"The truth is—there probably is not much balance in depicting southerners right now. Part of that is because too many good southerners are not taking a *strong enough* stand against their bad neighbors, which would give us some positive images to portray. They may be privately bemoaning others' actions, but they aren't putting themselves in harm's way by getting out in those lines and protecting little black kids or sitting in the back of the bus or sitting next to black people at lunch counters. There's so much southerners could do to convince the rest of us they really do 'love their coloreds'—as they're always saying, but unfortunately, few of them *are* putting their words into action.

"Remember, Maddie, if you're not part of the solution, you're part of the problem."

Soon thereafter, in 1965, our entire household joined a march from Selma to Montgomery, Alabama. Gummie had decided it was necessary for her to take stronger action herself, to become a participant, as well as to observe firsthand the kinds of things she was reporting in her newspaper. She also felt it was time that I see, up close, just what it was I was so fervently supporting. There was no problem convincing Mom to join, but Gramma was not so sure.

"I hear you, Mom," she said to Gummie, "and I think everything you're saying is true. You seem to forget, though, you're ninety-two years old, and it's hotter than hell in Alabama. You can hardly endure the heat and humidity of a Minnesota summer, how do you think you're going to fare down there?"

Gummie shook her head fiercely. "Hester, you are no doubt absolutely right. However, if one is going to make moral decisions on the basis of one's comfort, then we've come to a pretty sorry state, haven't we? Anyway, it's March, Hester. It's not going to be all that hot."

"Comfort?" Gramma shouted. "You think I care about your *comfort*, you stubborn old goat? I'm worrying about your health! I'm worried you'll just drop dead on this march, old woman!"

Gramma and Gummie stared stonily at one another, then Gummie said, cool as the basement on a blistering, summer day, "Hester, can you think of a better way for me to drop dead? If I don't get to choose how I want to live and die at ninety-two, when do I?"

Mother suppressed a smile, and we exchanged knowing looks. Gramma, of course, capitulated. How could you argue with such sense?

Gramma intoned, "I guess *someone* will have to drag your body around while the rest of you are busy being revolutionaries, won't they? I don't have much choice, do I?"

Mom and I cheered while Gummie grinned. Our "adventure" began in this manner—feeling like a family outing, maybe a picnic down by the river. When I look back now, I am amazed at our unbearable naivete. I think Gummie was the only one of us who had an inkling what we were in for, and she didn't prepare us thoroughly. Probably because she believed we had to learn by experience. You'd have thought we would've known better, having been bombarded by images in the media for ten years. Or at least the grown-ups would've known. What I discovered on our trip (although I didn't realize it until years later) is that the human brain—or maybe heart?—doesn't retain hate. Maybe doesn't even really believe in it. We were doing what was "right." How could that be anything but good?

23

The Edmund Pettus Bridge

After more than a decade of Civil Rights organizing, Alabama was still holding out regarding blacks and the vote. In Selma, Alabama, a town of about 30,000 people, half of them black, only about 150 of these 15,000 blacks were registered to vote. When others attempted to register, one roadblock after another was erected to prevent this from happening—roadblocks including physical and emotional harassment and threats. Nightsticks and cattle prods were used frequently in the dispersal of orderly lines of black people at the courthouse, waiting to register.

Beginning in January of 1965, there was a barrage of campaigns, encouraged by Martin Luther King. In the first week in February alone, over 1,000 blacks were arrested, most of them children protesting their elders' arrests.

The march from Selma to the state capital at Montgomery—fifty miles away—was intended to bring many people together to dramatize the unbelievable injustices in Selma, the state of Alabama, and the South in general. When Jimmie Lee Jackson, a local voting rights activist, was murdered by the police shortly before the scheduled march, the need to focus the resistance in Alabama on constitutional grounds as well as in memory of Jackson's life and commitment was even more crucial.

When Gummie decided this was the demonstration we would be joining, none of us guessed we were going to be part of a major historic event. We also didn't know we were walking into a simmering cauldron of fury, poised to boil over. We *thought* we knew. We didn't, though. We couldn't even *imagine*, yet, the magnitude of hate and the tenacity with which some clung to a vanishing way of life.

Mom's friend Gloria had a colleague who had converted an old school bus into a camper for his family. He loaned it to us so we'd have a place to sleep, thereby eliminating the need to find a place to rent in a hostile community. We headed for Alabama on a blustery, wintry March day in high spirits. I was getting out of school for a week, so I thought it doubly exciting.

Gloria wanted to go, too, but could not easily get days off from her teaching, so she remained behind, bemoaning her fate. "Dr. King was not thinking of all the schoolteachers when he planned this event in March," she whined. Such single-minded self-centeredness was soon going to be proof of our general inexperience.

I was secretly glad Gloria didn't join us because the bus had only four beds, and I would have had to sleep on the floor if she had come. I tried to convince Mom to let Jack come, too. She would be good protection, I persuaded, but I didn't succeed. We left her behind at Annie's house.

We headed for Chicago, belting out all the protest songs we knew and learning new ones from Gummie. "We Shall

Overcome," "Keep Your Eyes on the Prize," "Hallelujah, I'm a Bum!" and "Which Side Are You On?" mingled with the odd burps and sputters and clanks of our decrepit bus and the steady swish-swish of tires on pavement, carrying us further and further into what seemed like a foreign country. I secretly relished the notion that we were *almost* a "hippie family"—breaking free of conventional ties and sailing out into the world in search of justice.

We stopped at a motel just beyond Chicago at the end of our first day. Gramma insisted we sleep inside, with real beds and toilets and showers. I thought that was pretty boring, but no one else argued. I scribbled a postcard to Annie before retiring.

> *We are on our way to striking a*
> *blow for freedom! Tomorrow, we turn*
> *into "enemy territory"—the*
> *South. Gee, I wish you were here!*
> *Love, Maddie*

I think that night was the last time, in my entire life, when I was so filled with and buoyed by the sweet headiness of innocent, hopeful idealism.

"Where you folks headed?" the woman in the motel office asked Mom when she was registering on our second night, in Nashville, Tennesee.

"Selma, Alabama," Mom answered cheerfully.

A mask seemed to drop over the woman's face, and she said, coldly, "You Civil Rights workers?"

Mom's smile faltered a little, but she answered pleasantly. "Just supporters."

The woman pulled back the keys she'd pushed across the counter, saying, "I forgot. We're all filled up."

Mom stared at her in amazement. "What? You can't do this. It's against the law." It wasn't actually, but it would be soon, and it should've been.

The woman turned her back on us and said, as she was stalking, stiff-backed, out of the room, "So sue me."

Mom and I hurried out to the bus to report to Gramma and Gummie. Gummie said, grimly, "It's started."

We found another motel; this time Gramma registered us and answered, when asked about our destination, "We're just taking a little break from winter. Heading south, you know." True enough.

The next day, we were a little less giddy. Our balloons had been burst, and it was just beginning. Whenever we stopped for food or gas, our license plates and northern accents gave us away. Sometimes, we were turned away or refused service altogether. Waitresses ignored us, gas station attendants left us sitting in our vehicle, "Closed" or "No Vacancy" signs appeared as we pulled into parking lots. It was clear that the infamous southern hospitality did not extend to anyone southerners perceived as Civil Rights' workers.

In spite of this, we were still unaware of the events, by then, careening toward us. We reached Selma in the late afternoon of the third day. It wasn't hard to find the gathering supporters, in the vicinity of Brown's Chapel.

The demonstration was set for the next day: March 7. All of us "outsiders"—blacks and whites from other parts of the country— gathered for a meeting that night to be informed by SCLC (Southern Christian Leadership Conference) people about nonviolent tactics. We were instructed, for instance, to offer no resistance if we were arrested—to simply go limp. We were warned not to strike back at anyone who struck us—no matter what—but to retreat quickly. We were sobered by the information, beginning to come to grips with the real possibility of violence being directed toward us.

Afterward, we sat together—blacks and whites, singing songs and talking of justice. Our flagging spirits rose. I remember feeling an enormous bubble of excitement swell within me. I knew we were part of a good thing, taking a stand against injustice. I felt we could do anything, change the world even, because of this tremendous sense of connectedness we all had that night.

There were about 600 of us marching through Selma the next morning, marching unknowingly into "Bloody Sunday." We were mostly blacks and a handful of whites from the South and other places. We whites symbolically marched at the "back of the bus," thereby escaping the worst of the attacks.

It was a cool day; even our emotional commitment couldn't lift the greyness of that morning. The blacks, far more experienced and savvy than we, were somber. The streets were oddly empty; we had been led to believe there would be nasty hecklers and opposers lining our path out of town. Few were in evidence, at least at first.

Gramma had convinced Gummie to ride in a wheelchair so she wouldn't end up trailing behind the main body of marchers or slowing them down with her measured pace. As we ambled through Selma, Gummie was not in the wheelchair. Gramma fussed at her, but Gummie said, "Don't natter on so, Hester. I'll get in the chair as soon as we cross the bridge."

We didn't know we were not going to cross the Edmund Pettus Bridge, didn't know the opposition forces were committed to not letting us cross that bridge, didn't know Gummie was going to win a Pulitzer Prize with her newspaper article, beginning with these words: *The name of the Edmund Pettus Bridge should be burned into the American psyche in the same way the name Enola Gay should be.*

When the deliberate movement of our progress faltered, then halted altogether, we didn't know what was happening, thought it was a mere slowdown trickling back to us, at first. Suddenly, we began to hear hollering and screaming and realized something was up. Much of what occurred we didn't find out about until later. We couldn't see the attacks on the bridge itself, where waves of Alabama state troopers in conjunction with murderous citizens, replete with nightsticks and tear gas and bullwhips, awaited the marchers.

The physical impact quickly reached back to us as the group of protestors began to sway, and bloodied and sobbing individuals started straggling through the crowd. Gramma thrust Gummie into the wheelchair, swiveled it around, and beat a hasty retreat, yelling for us to follow. Mom and I were momentarily transfixed by the shoving, stumbling crowd, then separated from each other.

Mom was yelling and waving at me as we were pulled further apart and, somehow, swept forward. Just as inexplicably, a surge placed us next to one another again. All around us were the lurching bodies of retreating demonstrators and the threatening bodies of others. We resisted the push and pull of the mob, our arms around each other, as we gawked in horror at a solid phalanx of helmeted and gas-masked state troopers, descending on our now-dispersed, ragtag procession of bodies. They were wielding billy clubs and cattle prods while others were using little rocket-launchers to shoot tear gas containers into the crowd. Dozens of mounted police urged their horses to charge on stumbling, retreating, wounded people—pounding on them from their saddles and knocking them off their feet, the horses walking right over the downed bodies.

People rushed by us on all sides, blood pouring out of wounds on their heads and other parts of their bodies while others were doubled over, vomiting on the pavement, all of them white-eyed in their terrified attempts to escape. Those in the front of the line were on the ground, and I was horrified by the sight of troopers standing over these folks, who were offering no opposition whatsoever, yet the troopers' arms were pumping up and down, up and down as they relentlessly brought their clubs to smack against these inert bodies.

I'd never known before—never had any reason to know—that blood and panic had an overwhelming stench of its own, searing my nostrils. It did not compare, however, to the effects of the tear gas on my body. My eyes were burning, and I was sputtering and gagging, feeling like I could retch my insides out. We'd been warned the night before to drop to the ground if they used tear gas, but the sight of those downed bodies being mercilessly beaten made such an action unthinkable.

I got a brief impression of people standing on the side of the road: arms crossed righteously over their chests, lips snarled in vicious hatred, eyes blazing with malice and smug complacency—or the extreme opposite, almost worse, glazed eyes staring out of blank, emotionless faces. They were office workers—men in dark suits with white shirts and women in tidy frocks and high heels, shop owners leaning in their doorways, teenagers in jeans, ordinary-looking housewives, workers in uniforms. I can see those troopers' pumping arms and the watchers' twisted faces in my head still—animated by a zeal to kill, maim, destroy, blot out.

All of this only took moments. Mom and I were being jostled and bumped, mostly by our own comrades as they rushed to escape the savage intent of this swelling wave of malevolence. Spectators were also dispersing, perhaps to avoid the tear gas or else to join the hate troops. Stunned and emotionally bruised, we began to move backward, finally.

24

Hold On, Hold On

White people were yelling "nigger-lover" and "cunt" and "whore" in our faces while jostling or shoving us. My mother held tightly to my arm and shouted, "Maddie! Just ignore them!" I felt she'd read my mind because I was thinking of handling this the way I did schoolyard tussles. I'd never heard some of the words being hurtled at us. I followed her with my head down, trying to block out the viciousness all around us.

At one point, a white woman pushed my mother so hard, she fell to her knees. Without thinking, I threw my body—legs and arms whirling like a human windmill—against this woman's body.

"Maddie!" I heard my mother call, but I was on a mission.

Suddenly, strong arms went around my midsection, stilling my flailing limbs as I was firmly carried onward. A deep voice said calmly, "You forget about nonviolence, child?" I looked up into a dark, placid face in stark contrast with the enormous goosebump on her forehead and collapsed into the comfort of her soft, yielding body, tears streaming down my own face.

"Mom?"

"She's coming. You just keep movin' now." She gave me a little hug before releasing me. Then Mom was at my side, arm around me, thanking the woman. She was limping a little, and tears continued to stream down my cheeks, even as the worst of the attackers were beginning to leave us alone.

By the time we found Gummie and Gramma, Gummie was on a pay phone—dictating her story to the *Minneapolis Star* at home. She'd already called her own paper, but she'd arranged to call in a news report to the evening daily in Minneapolis as well, to make certain fresh news was reaching the outside.

I looked around apprehensively, worrying about someone snatching the phone out of Gummie's hands and hurting her. We were on the black end of town now, near Brown's Chapel where so many of us had started out with high hopes such a short time earlier. Troopers were everywhere around us—on foot and horseback, but they were no longer approaching or attacking people. The street was filled with moaning and wailing, and I couldn't seem to stop crying.

"Are you okay?" Gramma had sprawled in Gummie's abandoned wheelchair but jumped up as we approached, gathering both of us into her arms. She started to cry. "I was so afraid."

Mom and I hugged back. "We're okay. How about you?"

"I think we missed the worst of it. You'd better tell Gummie what you saw."

When Mom went over to describe the horror we'd witnessed and Gummie relayed it to the news desk, I said to Gramma, "Someone pushed Mom down."

"Oh, sweetie," Gramma fell back in the chair again, "come here."

I climbed into her lap, not caring what anyone thought, even though I was almost thirteen. "Gramma," I managed between hiccoughing sobs, "they were so hateful. How can people be that way?"

She didn't answer, just shook her head and rocked me as though I were a little girl.

"Are you okay?" A black man with a doctor's bag asked us.

Gramma nodded. "We're okay. Unless you can mend broken hearts." He patted her arm and hurried on, as she added, "Thank you for asking."

Then we heard what sounded like a low rumbling at first, and I felt my spine stiffen. Quickly though, we realized that someone had started singing. People came out on the steps of Brown's Chapel to add their mournful but firm voices to those that had begun the chorus,

> *"I know one thing we did right*
> *was the day we started to fight.*
> *Keep your eyes on the prize,*
> *hold on, hold on."*

I stood up and started singing, too, in a teetering voice filled with grief and tears. Mom came and stood next to me, her arm around me, then Gramma stood up, too, also linking arms with us. All of us had tears rolling down our faces. I glanced over at Gummie, who was holding the phone out in the air so whoever was on the other end could hear what was happening. I realized these voices pouring out determination and faith rendered this song in a manner I'd never before heard. I felt a great welling up inside of me, pride and sorrow mixed in equal measures perhaps, I wasn't sure. I just knew, without a doubt, my life was changed forever.

Gummie's award-winning article also contained these words: *The unquenchable spirit of these seekers of justice was most apparent as they stumbled back to a tenuous semblance of safety—blood gushing from their heads, ears, noses, and mouths; arms and shoulders and ribs held stiffly from the raining blows; dried spittle upon their clothing— and still, en masse, their voices ballooned out in melancholy dignity.*

First aid stations were set up in the church and throughout the nearby campground. Mom got her scraped knees cleaned out and dabbed with iodine. We were lucky. All around us were people with their heads wrapped in white gauze and their arms in slings. Others were being transported to hospitals. People were sorrowful and dispirited. A keening seemed to emanate from the low murmurs surrounding us.

"Get your stuff together," Gramma said firmly. "We're going home."

No one argued for a moment, although we didn't move to comply, either. Gummie responded, finally, her voice equally firm, "No, Hester. I'm not going anywhere. I have a job to do here, and I'm going to do it."

"What job?" Gramma practically sneered. "There's plenty of reporters, Mother. The news will be covered whether you're here or not."

Gummie shook her head. "That's not the job I'm talking about. My job is to witness these acts. My job is to stand side by side with my black sisters and brothers and attempt to offset the hatred being showered on them. My job is to stand in support with those who have no choice but to receive this hatred."

Mom nodded faintly, but Gramma shouted, "Your *job* is going to get you and your family killed!"

Gummie shook her head and answered, "You can go home, Hester. You, too," she looked at Mom and me.

"I'm not going!" I protested, stepping to Gummie's side.

"This is no time to get fresh, young lady," Gramma snapped, then turned her anger toward Mom. "Jane?"

"Just listen for a minute," Gummie interrupted, holding a hand up. "We *believe* everyone in this country should have equal access to all of the rights our constitution guarantees us. We know, however, that that doesn't happen. We all know it. We have an opportunity, here, to insist things change. To insist on justice.

"We can go home, where we're safe, to sputter about how things should be different. While we're doing that, where do these black people go? Can they 'go home and be safe?' They have no choice. How can we expect them to put their lives on the line—just by existing, let alone by demonstrating—and then say we're not going to put *our* lives in jeopardy because *we have a choice?*"

No one said anything for a moment, then Gramma mumbled, "You're going to get us all killed."

"Maybe so," Gummie agreed, putting her arm around me, "but I don't want to die. Or for any of us to. But Hester? I don't want *anyone* to die. If we don't take a stand against this, aren't we almost as bad as those who are throwing the rocks?"

There was no more discussion. We were staying.

Mom and I went to the church to help with first aid. The mood was as dark as the sky outside, people mumbling and moaning. A group of leaders were huddled together in a corner when suddenly the doors of the church flew open and a group of obvious outsiders, black and white people, stood there. A collective flinch seemed to race through the room. One person from this new group stepped forward, hands out in seeming supplication, and said, "We're from New Jersey. We saw the attacks on TV, and we chartered a plane. We're here to share with you your struggle." After a stunned moment's silence, the room broke into a babble of excited voices.

It was the first of a wave of response. Journalists and supporters poured into Selma all day and night. News of the horrific events of "Bloody Sunday" was spreading across the nation. A TV reporter interviewed Gummie, having been told she was the oldest white person there. We stood around her as she spoke eloquently about justice and responsibility and solidarity and revolution. Some of the abomination of the morning subsided with the excitement of thinking my friends back home might see me and my family on TV.

Rumors of deaths and planned attacks on our camp and the impending arrival of federal troops swirled about us all day. In the evening, one Civil Rights luminary after another spoke to us from the pulpit of the overflowing Brown's Chapel.

They talked of dreams and courage and vision. Of the past and the future. They talked about people getting hurt and people's hurt spirits. They talked, with a compassion I couldn't understand, of the haters who, they insisted, hurt themselves more than they could ever hurt us. They talked of nonviolent resistance, insisting we repledge ourselves to that concept. They talked of Jimmie Lee Jackson and all the others who'd been hurt and jailed, in the past as well as that very morning, and how it was our responsibility to properly memorialize all the pain and loss by continuing the struggle. The various voices were low and melodic as well as strident and insistent, all filled with sadness and pain and exhortation, but surprisingly little anger.

Men and women in the mostly black audience nodded and hummed and agreed, calling out, "You tell them, sister!" and "Amen!" and "That's the truth, brother!" I was amazed at this strong verbal support, being used to meetings and demonstrations where no one said anything unless it was their turn to speak. I felt safe in the enveloping solidarity of these folks, with their visible and adamant unity.

We outsiders were "let off the hook." We were told to go home if we wanted to be certain of safety but never to forget, "Injustice anywhere is a threat to justice everywhere." Flagging spirits were raised once again. Gummie and Gramma went to bed early, but Mom and I lingered with others around the church. Gloria found us there.

"What are you doing here?" Mom asked stupidly, as the two of them hugged.

"Oh, they can just fire me if they want," Gloria insisted. "When the news reached us back home, I knew I had to come."

"How did you get here so soon?"

"I drove to the airport, in search of any flight bringing me close to Selma. You wouldn't believe it! Right away, I ran into a friend from the University with a group who had chartered a plane to Montgomery, so I joined them. We intended to rent a car, but people were pouring in from all over the country, so buses were being provided to transport us. Let me tell you, those Southern Christian Leadership Conference people really know their stuff. They are so organized, it's amazing!"

We were jubilant at Gloria's arrival—I even forgot about having to sleep on the floor of the bus—and went back to wake Gummie and Gramma. Gloria put her arm around me and said, "Maddie? Annie stopped by my classroom today and asked me if I'd give you a message when I talked to your mom. I told her I was coming down here, so she said Jack misses you but is doing fine. She made me promise to give you this." She pressed a coin into my hand, and I knew it was the silver dollar Annie'd been given by her beloved grandfather. She thought of it as her lucky talisman. I pressed it against my chest, tears swamping my eyes, and thanked Gloria. It was hard to imagine Riverton just then— remote and cold, its residents maybe as much so as its climate.

Our ranks had swollen to about 1,500 by Tuesday, March 9, when we started out, once more, for the Edmund Pettus Bridge.

Although we sang songs and chanted with gusto, there was an undercurrent of tension moving through the crowd. On this day, Martin Luther King—who had not been present on Sunday—walked at the front of the march and asked for others to join him. Black and white ministers, arriving the day and night before, joined King.

The streets, more than on Bloody Sunday, were crowded with hooting and jeering crowds. The threatening line of state troopers was waiting for us, again, at the bridge. When they asked us to turn back, King led us all in singing "We Shall Overcome." Then he kneeled on the bed of the bridge, and Reverend Ralph Abernathy led the demonstrators in prayer. After that, much to most people's surprise, we simply turned around and walked back, peaceably giving way. Many were angry and disappointed, feeling that King had betrayed us, including Gummie.

Gramma snorted. "He did what he thought was best. He put safety first." Gummie did not argue back.

That night, we were informed the march was being postponed for a few days, when we'd have the protection of federal troops. At least that was the hope. King requested the ministers who'd been arriving from all over the country to stay for a few more days, and as many of the rest of us who could. Gloria and Mom flew home the next day, to return to their jobs. Gummie insisted on staying, and Gramma stayed with her. I prevailed on Mom to let me stay, too.

"This is an education I'm never going to get sitting in a classroom, Mom. Or even watching TV or reading the newspapers. This is *our* times, and I need to be a part of it." Gummie nodded, her eyes shining, and even Gramma didn't object.

Mom looked stricken, imagining—I was sure—all the things that might happen to me. Then, her face cleared, and she laughed, hugging me. "You know, Maddie, sometimes I think we've taught you too well." I knew I'd convinced her.

We didn't know, until after Mom and Gloria were gone, that a white, Unitarian minister from Boston had been murdered the night before. The police cordoned off the area around Brown's Chapel to pen us in and, supposedly, to keep hostile whites out. We all chafed under this enforced imprisonment, and people kept "escaping" until finally the barriers were removed.

I spent the next weeks doing schoolwork that Mom sent down to me, reading borrowed books, working on a long essay I was writing for extra credit, and talking to lots of people, both black and white.

I got to be especially fond of a little girl who lived in the area. Her mother addressed her by her entire name. "Janie Louise Martin! It's way past your bedtime! Y'all come on home."

"Janie Louise Martin! Y'all come on home to dinner right this very instant!"

"Janie Louise Martin! Y'all stop pestering these nice folk."

"Y'all can jest call me Janie," she told me the first time her mother had come looking for her and insisted, "Janie Louise Martin! Y'all get on home and 'tend to your homework."

"Mama's the only one calls me Janie Louise," she'd said. "Everyone else calls me jest Janie. Janie's 'nuff."

Janie was two years younger than I, not quite eleven, but seemed to be eons older. At least to me. She taught me what it is to be ten years old and black in the United States. She'd already gotten arrested, twice, for demonstrating after lots of grown-ups—some of them her teachers—had gotten arrested for just trying to register. Her daddy wasn't active in Civil Rights, she told me, because he was afraid of losing his job—he worked for the city-owned bus company; they needed his income to feed the six of them plus to put enough by to send all four of the kids—Janie and her three brothers—to college. She told me how her mother worked for a white woman, taking care of the woman's house and food and kids, but did demonstrations anyway.

"Her employer doesn't mind?" I wondered.

"Not the lady. Not so long as Mama gets all her work done. She kind of encourages Mama even, but real quiet like, because the man? He's in one of those groups—not the KKK, one of the other ones for the men who wear suits and ties. Those boys like to pretend they're *good men* working to do right for us all. They think they're better because they're above the hate tactics of those KKK boys, but we all know jest the same—we sure do—they merely be the KKK without the sheets."

I always felt amazed at the things she knew and talked about. "My oldest brother? Leon?" she told me one day, "He was pals with Jimmie Lee Jackson. You know who he is?" I nodded. "You know what happened to Jimmie Lee?"

"He got killed," I answered. "Murdered by the police, I guess."

She nodded, adding, "He was active in the movement, real good at getting people whipped up 'bout registering. The cops knew him, already hated him. The night he got killed? He was at a demonstration. Whole lot of folks there. The police and a lot of white folk broke it up—swinging bats and nightsticks and chains and stuff—even though everyone, by then, was jest trying to go home. Jimmie Lee hustled his mama and granddaddy into a cafe. The police followed them and started hitting on his old granddaddy. Eighty-two years old, he was, and those cops trying to bust him up. Then they started working over Jimmie Lee's mama. Jimmie Lee tried to stop them. 'Course he'd try to stop them. Who wouldn't? And they jest shot him. Shot him in the belly. Shot him dead."

We sat quietly, side by side, on the steps of the Brown's Chapel, contemplating the images this story created in our minds. Finally, I broke the silence and said, "Your brother must've been awful sad."

"Mmm-hmm," she agreed. "Sad, yes. But mad, too. He jest wanted to smash things. Even tho' he's committed to nonviolence, like the rest of us. Hard to know what to do with all that fury."

After another moment's silence, I asked, "How can you stand it?" I thought of the little bit of hatefulness I'd witnessed and couldn't imagine a lifetime of having that heaped on me. What I had experienced back home—regarding my lineage and elders' choices—seemed inconsequential compared to what it meant to be black.

She shrugged, got up and skipped down the stairs, placing her feet next to each other at the start of the hopscotch board we'd scratched into the sidewalk earlier. Hop-hop-two feet down-hop-hop-teeter-two feet down. "Don't have no choice." Hop-turn-two feet down-hop-hop . . . I knew, a little, what she was saying. She looked up at me then, her eyes calm and clear, and solemnly intoned, "Life's life. Whatever is yours, that's that."

She noticed, right away, that I liked books and brought me some to read. Richard Wright's *Native Son* and *The Street* by Ann Petry. When I'd devoured them, she next brought me *Invisible Man* by Ralph Ellison and James Baldwin's *Go Tell It on the Mountain*. Books that led me to other books I might never have thought of reading, books that ended up changing my life as much as being in Selma that spring. They were not books I could imagine a little girl reading, and yet, she'd read them. And I did, too. And wanted more.

They taught me of lives led, injustice meted out beyond my envisioning. They made me look at my own life in startling new ways. Growing up in a family who made working for justice a religion, I'd never realized how little I really knew. Or had experienced. I'd certainly never thought of myself as "white."

I tried explaining this to Annie when I returned home, "When you're white, you're just *normal*. You never have to think about being a color. You're just the *normal* color, but black people can never stop thinking about their color. Because they're *not* normal. At least, that's what we believe, without even thinking about it. We're normal, and they're different." My reality was shifting.

We bought all our food at grocery stores in the black community, our accents preventing us from getting goods elsewhere. Southerners volunteered to get what we needed. As long as they had a southern accent, they could buy anywhere because they were still considered part of the community. The rest of us were "those outside commie agitators and anarchists," and none of us ventured far from the camp or the black end of town. We were keenly aware of the murder of other Civil Rights workers.

Most nights, some black preacher held church services, and Gramma and I attended. Having never been to church regularly, I didn't know what was routine, but I was mesmerized and moved by the pastors' passionate and musical oratory and the vocal response from the black crowd. I could understand why some people would turn to religion, listening to these spellbinding speakers. Gramma and I speculated on whether or not black churches in the North were as intensely emotional as these ones while Gummie and I argued about the depth of spirituality involved.

"It's just a show," Gummie insisted. "These ministers are like entertainers. Dazzling their audiences. Doesn't mean they believe half of what they say."

I'd frown and retort, angrily, "How can you say that? You don't even go! I think you're wrong, Gummie. These preachers—and most of their audiences, too—fervently believe in *something*. It doesn't matter whether we believe in it or not, or even believe in their belief. They've still got it." I paused, a little surprised at my own temerity, adding, "Actually, I envy them. What they have— well, it shines through their eyes. Like they've got suns inside them. And all that singing! It just makes you *feel good*, Gummie. What could be wrong about that?"

"Amen," Gramma chorused, breaking the tension building between Gummie and me.

Gummie was afraid I was going to be converted, I think. Conversion wasn't it, though. In a way, I *did* want to be a part of it. I liked the feeling of elation and well-being that washed over me—listening to ministers and congregants incite and commit, watching the blue-and-gold-gowned choirs sway and clap and stamp their feet to the music, being swamped in a sea of harmonious and zealous singing. At the same time, even in the midst of my euphoria, I knew I was an outsider, an observer.

It made all of us furious that the murder of a white man, the minister from Boston, had finally awakened the nation to the horrendous events being played out in the South. The second, aborted march was referred to as "Turnaround Tuesday," because the marchers had turned back but also because public opinion was turned around by the minister's murder. Still, we couldn't help but be elated when we heard President Johnson announced to Congress, on March 15, that he was sending a voting rights registration bill to them.

I asked Janie what her family thought. She answered, "Mama put her apron to her face and wept while Daddy patted her arm and jest said it was a 'fine thing,' the president taking up for us like that." She paused then, smiling. "But my brother, Leon? He was not so easily impressed. 'We'll see. Nothing's changed yet,' was his reaction. My daddy shushed him, warning him not to 'disrespect the President of the United States that way,' and Leon just shot back, 'Daddy why you wanna give that man credit for jest doing what's right?' Daddy wouldn't back down, though, warning Leon to have a little faith and patience. Leon mumbled, 'Lot of good that's done us all these hundred years,' but he said it real low as he was walking out the door so as not to further upset Daddy."

Leon was right. The next night, demonstrators in Montgomery were attacked by police on horseback with nightsticks, cattle prods, whips, and ropes. The South had not changed its mind about registration. That same night, we finally heard an Alabama judge had ruled on our legal and constitutional right to march from Selma to Montgomery. We celebrated late into the night with songs and talk and prayer.

When the march was rescheduled, Mom flew back down. Alabama's Governor George Wallace refused to provide protection, insisting we couldn't *be* protected, so President Johnson nationalized the 1,800-member Alabama National Guard plus sent 2,000 Army troops and 100 FBI agents and 100 federal marshalls, all dispatched to escort and protect us throughout the five-day walk from Selma to Montgomery.

On the morning of March 21, Martin Luther King led us across the Edmund Pettus Bridge with fellow Nobel Peace Prize-winner Ralph Bunche and Rabbi Abraham Herschel at his side. Throughout the entire five days, bellicose and angry segregationists lined the route, as usual, taunting us and holding signs like "Yankee Trash—Go Home," but there were no attacks.

Gummie and I, sometimes joined by Gramma or Mom, traversed the entire route. Occasionally, Janie walked with us, other times she stayed with friends or family. Gramma and Mom used the bus to transport food and water and other supplies to the marchers from the volunteer headquarters in Selma. At night, then, the bus was a place for us to sleep; most nights though, other folks slept in our bus with Gummie while Gramma and Mom and I slept outside under the stars, giving our beds to older or disabled people.

I remember no one complaining, no one faltering. There were others, besides Gummie, in wheelchairs. Still others were hobbling along on crutches or with canes. The pace was slow to accommodate everyone's needs. The mood was ebullient. I think the continually growing number of marchers—reaching 25,000 by the time we entered Montgomery—knew we were making history.

In Montgomery, Rosa Parks and Roy Wilkins and Whitney Young and John Lewis and many others regaled us with speeches about faith and hope and goodness and justice and dreams. Martin Luther King gave his usual stirring talk, peppered throughout with the phrase, "How long? Not long!" until some 25,000 voices reacted to his "How long?" by shouting in response, "Not long!" Almost everyone had tears streaming down their cheeks, smiles splitting their faces, hugs and squeezes for their neighbors.

With many others, we parked in a lot adjoining the Dexter Avenue Baptist Church—King's congregation during the Montgomery bus boycott. I tried to find Janie to say good-bye, but the crowd had gotten too large. We intended to start for home the next morning. During the night, however, we were awakened and encouraged to leave right away. A white woman, in a car with Michigan plates who'd been driving marchers back to Selma, had been murdered by four Klansmen. All of us with plates from northern states were being warned.

It was a tragic and somber finish to a triumphant march; nonetheless, the real triumph came later that year when President Johnson's Voting Rights Bill passed both houses.

Gummie's series of passionate articles in *The Prairie Voice* garnered her a Pulitzer Prize. I was proud to be, even in such a small way, a part of the movement. Janie and I remained pen pals for years afterward. I never forgot the faces of those opposing us, never really forgot what I learned that first day: human beings are capable of the most vicious hatred. More important, however, I never forgot the flip side of this lesson, either. I cherish the clear memory of the care and concern everyone had for everyone else,

Janie Louise Martin's childlike ways ruptured by the somber rendering of the hideous facts of her life and her serene acceptance of that reality, the warmth and love that passed from body to body as we leaned into one another at church services or slipped our arms into our neighbors' arms while we walked, the thrumming sound of many voices floating up into the sky, splitting it open to give us a glimpse of other possibilities.

25

A Good Night's Sleep

"Gummie?" We were walking home from the paper. It was late fall, all the leaves were off the trees and mostly raked and burned, too. There was a bleak look to the naked trees, one that would be rectified as soon as we got our first snow. It was cold—making our nostrils pinch and feel crunchy, our breath hang in the air by our mouths like puffs of smoke, and our skin tingle inside our mittens. Sullen clouds hid the sun. "How come Mom never dates anyone?" I was thirteen and finally had gotten up the courage to probe a little more into my family's sexual habits.

"What?" Gummie looked startled, and my ears perked up because I knew she was *never* vague unless she was trying to avoid a conversation.

"How come Mom never dates anyone?" I repeated firmly. "You know, goes out with men. Dates. You *know*."

"Well, I . . ." she looked at me sharply, like maybe she wanted to make sure I wasn't teasing her. "You don't know?"

It was my turn to look at her curiously. "Know? Know what?"

Gummie shook her head a little, and we walked, wordlessly, for about a block before she said, "I think you'd better have this talk with your mother."

I was instantly intrigued. And a little wary. Why would Gummie be fobbing me off like this? Why didn't she just answer me? This evasion on her part so puzzled me—and unnerved me, too—that I didn't say anything to Mom for a couple of weeks. I was waiting for the right moment, I told myself, but I knew—in my heart of hearts—I knew that I was just a little chicken. I was about to learn something, I was certain, from Gummie's response. But what? And whatever it was, did I want to know? I didn't even talk it over with Annie, I felt that uneasy.

Then one brittle evening as we walked in the early darkness of late autumn, I cleared my throat self-consciously and inquired, "Mom? How come you never go on dates?"

Mom shot a surprised look my way, then asked, "Where did *this* question come from?"

I looked a little askance at her, frowning. "My brain, where else?"

"I mean, Miss Smarty Pants, is there some particular reason you're asking this question at this time. Did someone say something to you . . . or . . . something?"

"Like what?"

"I don't know. I'm asking you."

"No, no one said something." I thought about that man who was my father saying, ". . . those Jordan girls never did want anything to do with sex," but I didn't think I'd mention that. "I . . . you know, I just wondered. I mean, it's not like you're ugly or mean or stupid or anything. And yet, you *never* date. Ever. How come?"

She was silent for a long time, and I wasn't sure how to read that silence. I was used to Gummie's silences, knew she would always come back to the conversation. And even more used to Gramma's silences, which were more frequent, wherein I knew she would never come back unless I prodded her. But Mom, she was not in the habit of long silences with me, so I didn't know how to handle it. I wondered if I was supposed to push her further or just drop the matter or what?

Finally, while I was trying to decide what to do next, she said, "Well, Maddie, I guess it's time to tell you. I guess you are old enough."

Oh no, I thought, *what does this mean?* And I felt a shock of jangled nerves hopping through my body. Did she have a dread disease? Something that was going to kill her? Or me? What could be this ominous? Maybe I didn't want to know. Maybe I *wasn't* old enough.

"I love women."

I frowned, then shrugged. "Yeah, but . . . well, so do I. I mean . . ."

She snuck a look at me, then immediately shifted her eyes straight ahead. "Maddie. I'm a lesbian."

A lesbian? I thought, feeling some relief that she wasn't dying. But . . . *a lesbian? A queer? Don't wear green and yellow on Thursday because it means you're a fairy.* My *mother wore green and yellow on Thursday?* My *mother was a pervert?* I felt as though someone had kicked me in the stomach.

"Maddie?" she asked. "Are you okay?"

With what? I thought. *With being the daughter of a homosexual? A queer? Oh no!* Another thought popped into my head. *Gloria! She must be it! Who else could it be? Was it her fault? Did she make Mom a lesbian?* "I don't know. I mean, what mom tells her daughter she's a lesbian?"

"The one who is, I guess."

"Gloria . . . ?"

"That's right. Gloria's my sweetheart. Has been for years, of course. Tell me what you're feeling, honey. Please?"

"That means Gloria's a . . ." Queer?

"A lesbian? Well, I certainly hope so!" And her bell-like laughter pealed out as sweet and clear as ever. As if nothing had changed. And yet, everything had changed. Hadn't it?

"Honey . . . ?"

"I don't *know* how I feel, Mom." I knew the tone of my voice sounded peeved. I tried to soften it. "Confused, I guess. I mean, well, everyone talks like homos are—you know—sick or something. But you and Gloria . . ."

"We're not sick, Maddie. You can see that for yourself, can't you?" I nodded slowly. "We're just different. But Maddie, and this is the important part," she sounded just like Gummie at that moment, "it's about love. Gloria and I love each other, deeply and wonderfully. How could something about love be *anything* but good?"

That did make sense. Still . . . "So Gummie and Gramma know already, don't they?"

"Sure. We're not ashamed, Maddie. We're happy together. And want to share that happiness with other people we love. We just can't tell everyone because . . .," here she faltered, not sounding quite as sure of herself, "because we'd probably lose our jobs if we did."

"You would?" I asked, glad for this distraction from the picture I was conjuring of Mom and Gloria together.

"Almost for certain. Both of us work with children, especially Gloria, and people just have some weird ideas about 'homos' being around their kids. Like it might be catching or something. Or, even worse, like we might try to hurt them, touch them inappropriately. And that's absurd. But that's the way the world is, unfortunately."

"So you didn't tell me sooner because . . ."

When I didn't continue, she filled in. "Well, mostly because I didn't think you were old enough. And when you weren't old enough, you wouldn't know how to be discreet. It's not that I want you to keep it a secret, like it's a bad thing, it's just that we do have to keep it private. Because of our jobs. And you're old enough to understand that now. Does this make sense to you?"

"Is it okay if I tell Annie?"

She paused, then said, "Sure. I wouldn't want you to keep something like this from your best friend. Only . . ."

When her hesitation stretched longer, I asked, "Only what?"

"Well, I guess you need to know that if you tell someone, it might alter your relationship with that person."

I thought this over. "Annie's not like that."

"No," she was speaking slowly, carefully. "It's just . . . well, she might tell her parents. And her parents might . . . Well, maybe nothing would happen. You just have to be prepared for the worst, Maddie. You have to understand the risks of telling anyone."

I nodded, picking at my lip, wondering how I was going to tell Annie. Or *if* I was. "So, Mom, how did you—you know—how did you find out that you were a . . . like this?"

Mom laughed again. "You can say it, Maddie. Lesbian. It's not going to bite you."

I curled my lip but blurted out, "*Lesbian.* So big deal."

Mom flicked her eyes at me, then said, "I guess I knew, since I was little, that I was different. I went out with boys in high school, but mostly I just wanted to spend time with my girlfriends." I felt that way about Annie. I couldn't imagine some dumb boy meaning more to me than she did. Did that mean *I* was a lesbian? "I had crushes on some of my teachers, women teachers, but didn't really think all that much about it. It wasn't as if I knew I could be anything but heterosexual. It's not as if people talk about this as some kind of option or something."

"Except Gummie," I inserted, thinking of the times she'd told me there were lots of ways to live your private life—with a man, with another woman, alone, with a group of people. I'd never really thought much about it before, but it suddenly made a kind of sense I'd heretofore not perceived.

"Yes," Mom agreed, "Gummie's a wise woman. She's the one who, actually, helped me figure it out for myself." She laughed suddenly. "Everyone else gets to hear about the 'birds and the bees.' I think Gummie might be the only one to give the birds-and-the-birds version." She laughed again, and I tried to smile. She noticed my struggle and continued. "Gummie pays attention. I think because Gummie is open to the world, wants to experience everything, observe everything, know about everything . . . Mom, well, I definitely wouldn't say she's closed—she's just more cautious and less adventurous. And wants to feel safe in a way that Gummie never even contemplates.

"So Gummie noticed I didn't seem much interested in boys. As I said, I'd gone out with some in high school, then chose the man to help me make you. After that, I pretty much dropped the idea of men altogether. Of course, I had you, and I was in school, and so it was easy to just ignore the fact that I wasn't dating or anything. I was busy. Most men, anyway, seemed to want to go out with me because they figured I'd be an 'easy lay.' I had a baby, after all, was their thinking, so there was nothing to protect." She looked at me. "You know what I'm saying?"

I curled my lip again and intoned, sarcastically, "Yes, Mom, I know what you're saying."

She ignored my tone. "One day, in that blunt way of hers, Gummie just blurted out, 'So, Jane, is it that you prefer women?'

I was maybe twenty-one at the time, and I don't think I really knew yet, myself. Or maybe wasn't letting myself know. But when she asked, I blushed a dozen shades of red. That was a pretty big tip-off, I can tell you." She laughed again, and I smiled a little, feeling more embarrassment than merriment, but also being embarrassed at my embarrassment. I mean, no one else in my family seemed to have any problem with this.

"Anyway, she talked to me about it some, steered me toward some books that might give me a bit to think about, and it's just as if—once I had permission—I opened up to the possibility. And when Gloria came here to teach—you were about four by then, and I was just starting graduate school for library science—we became friends, first, and eventually fell in love. It was wonderful, and it still is."

I knew that. I knew that Mom and Gloria loved each other and took great pleasure in each other's company. I'd grown up knowing that. I'd just never thought . . . It probably wasn't any worse than thinking about men and women doing "it." I mean, when you first hear about that, you just want to barf. Yeee-uck! Annie and I talked about it frequently and, truly, although it was kind of thrilling in some ways to imagine, mostly we just gagged and cringed at the thought of any of the boys *we* knew putting their tongues in our mouths or their hands on our bodies or their penises inside us. I mean, major gross-out!

Then Annie might say, "Well, maybe I would let Steve McQueen do that stuff. He's sooo cute!"

"Yeah, but Annie? *His tongue in your mouth?*"

She'd raise her eyebrows and answer, "Maybe not that, but . . . There must be something here that we don't know, Maddie. Grown-ups seem to *love* that stuff. Remember before Robin got married?" Robin was her older sister. Annie leaned toward me in obvious partnership. "Remember how we'd spy on them? And he

215

would be sticking his tongue in her, and she'd be moaning and writhing . . ."

"Geez, Annie," I objected. "You sound like one of those stupid romance books." And I'd grimace, wondering if I, one of "those Jordan girls" after all, was not going to want sex. But then, I guess my father wasn't right about my mother not liking sex. Or, more likely, he just thought of sex as something that occurred between men and women.

So how could sex between two women be any worse than between a woman and a man? But then, how could two women *have* sex? I mean . . . This was a disquieting thought. I read a lot and consequently had some vague notion of tongues being placed in other orifices besides mouths, but this was so incredibly repugnant to me that French kissing looked almost good by comparison.

A few days later, I was hanging out in the kitchen, cadging lumps of dough from the chocolate chip cookies Gramma was making. "So, Gramma," I broached casually, "Mom told me about her and Gloria."

"Mm-mmm," she responded, darting a look at me. "And how do you feel about it?" She was so calm and relaxed, I was pretty sure Mom had told her already.

"I don't know," I maintained my nonchalance. "How do *you* feel?"

She stopped mixing for a minute, looking out the back window at my lonely tree house huddling in the naked maple—waiting for snow, I thought. "You know, Maddie, what I imagined, what I wanted for my daughter—when she was growing up—was that she find and love a good man, get married, have a passel of kids, and be happy. You know what the most important part of that picture was?"

I took advantage of her inattention and dipped my finger in the dough again. "Being happy?"

"Exactly," she agreed, halfheartedly tapping my hand with her wooden spoon and attending once more to her baking. "And she's sure got that. So the rest of my fantasy? That was my dream, not hers. She found and loved a good woman, had the child she wanted and chose, and is very happy. This makes me happy."

I wasn't quite sure why at the time, but I felt a great rising of love for Gramma and wrapped my arms around her ample middle and squeezed. "I love you, Gramma."

She pressed her lips against my forehead and said, "I love you, too, Madelaine Iris, and bless the day you graced us with your presence."

And one night, when I was in my flannel nightgown, rosy warm from my bath, I poked my head into Gummie's room. She was propped up in her bed, reading. "Got a moment, Gummie?"

"For you, Maddie?" she laid her book down. "Always."

I plopped myself on the corner of her old bed, whose springs moaned in protest, and said, "I talked to Mom. You know, about dating."

"Uh-huh."

"So," I was idly picking at the fuzz on the chenille bedspread, not making eye contact with Gummie, "she told me."

"That's good. How do you feel about it?"

"I don't know." *Like I wish everyone would stop asking me how I feel,* I thought, but didn't express. "You're all so . . . okay about it. I mean, I like Gloria lots. I guess I even love her. She's been a part of my life since I was little. And I certainly love Mom, but . . ."

"But?"

"Well, everyone out there," I gestured toward the window. "They're not so 'okay' about it."

"That's true. But Maddie, if you live your life to please 'everyone out there,' you're not going to please yourself much. And nothing ever changes. People have to take risks and do things differently to get other people used to the idea that there *are* different ways of being in the world, different ways of doing things. Your mother, Maddie, is strong and courageous. She does what's right for her, no matter what. You could never have a better role model than she is."

I turned this over in my head for a few minutes. "Yeah, well . . ." I hesitated. "Sometimes, Gummie, I just get tired. Can you understand this? Can any of you?" I realized my voice was almost cracking, and I suddenly got worked up in a way I hadn't let myself since my mother first said those fateful words: *I'm a lesbian.* "I just get tired having to be strong and courageous and tough and better than everyone else all the time. You know? It seems to me that you all made these decisions—or had this happen to you, I don't know. I mean I guess Gramma didn't *decide* for that odious man to leave— but you know what I mean? These things happened to you and Gramma and Mom, and some of them you decided, and *I* get to pay the price. *I'm* the one who has to be strong and not care what people say because I was born out of wedlock and Gramma was abandoned and you're an atheist and probably a commie, too, and now Mom's a fairy . . ." And I surprised myself by starting to cry.

And Gummie, whom I would have expected to lecture me on how lucky I was and how much character I was developing and how good it was that we were all so "different," surprised me even more by saying, in a soft voice, "Come here, Madelaine," and I curled next to her in the bed while she wrapped her arms around me—something we hadn't done for years—and I cried and cried and cried until I fell asleep.

In the morning, when I woke up in my own bed, having no memory of how I'd gotten there, the world seemed much more manageable, just as Gramma always predicted it would. I could hear her in my head, "Go get a good night's sleep, Maddie. The world will be more manageable come morning." And I think that might have been the first time I realized that I was going to be carrying Gummie's and Gramma's and Mom's voices around in my head for the rest of my life.

26

The Most Interesting Family

I did tell Annie, of course. I needed *someone* to talk this over with, someone who would truly understand what it was like for me, what it was like to be a part of the world, not just living that almost insular life of one of those Jordan girls.

Annie's response was "pure Annie." "Wow! Your family has got to be the most interesting family in Riverton. Maybe in all of Minnesota."

"Whoopee," I said, with no enthusiasm whatsoever. "Who wants to be part of such an *interesting* family? I'd settle for just ordinary."

Annie furrowed her brow, then shook her head. "No, you wouldn't, Maddie."

"I would, too," I insisted angrily.

Annie just shook her head again. "Look at you, Maddie. There's nothing *ordinary* about you. There's nothing about you that *wants* to be ordinary. It's never been in the cards for you."

"That's the whole point, Annie. It's never been 'in the cards' for me because *they* all determined everything before I was even born. You know I love Gummie and Gramma and Mom. I admire them a lot, too. You're right—they *are* interesting women. I just wish, sometimes, they were someone *else's* interesting family, and I could just admire them without having to *be* one of them. Does that make sense?"

"Sure, it makes sense, but Maddie, I don't think it's really true." She put up her hand to ward off my intended objection. "Just listen a minute, will you? It's hard to be in a family so different. I understand. It's hard to have people judge you by things you had nothing to do with and to have people whisper or shake their heads or keep their distance. I get all of that, too. Really. But Maddie, *this is your family*. It's what's normal for you. Even though you protest, part of you also loves it, eats it up.

"You could've taken the route your grandma took when she was younger: making yourself as conventional and unnoticeable as possible. You've never really done that, have you? Look at you! You wear weird clothing, speak your mind even when you know you'll get in trouble, fight with anyone who needs to be set straight. You have never—as long as I've known you—NEVER shrunk from being part of your remarkable family. It may be hard sometimes, and you may wish it different sometimes, but Maddie—it's obvious you are *proud* to be one of those Jordan girls."

My frown deepened as I stared at her. Annie had a mind as keen and honed as my own, but she was not given to long monologues. Finally, I said, "About now, Gummie would probably be saying— 'out of the mouths of babes'—or some such thing," and we grinned at each other while a flush of pleasure spread across her face like a rosy sunset. "So *okay*, I'm a Jordan girl, and I don't exactly hate it. But a lesbian, Annie?" I shook my head dolefully.

"Doesn't that take the cake?"

"Is it really a complete surprise to you?"

I brought my eyebrows together. "Yes. Why? Isn't it to you?"

She shook her head slowly. "No. I mean, your mom is reasonably young and everything, so it doesn't make sense she wouldn't be dating. Plus Gloria's always at your house. Or they're always going somewhere together. Or . . . I don't know. Maybe I wouldn't have thought of them as lesbians, just friends, except . . ."

"Except what?"

She shrugged. "I once heard one of those stupid boys, probably Randy Eastlund, say something about how you were undoubtedly going to turn out to be a fairy like your mom."

"You did?! You actually heard something like that, and you didn't tell me?" I was shouting.

"Come on, Maddie. It was right after Liza Dowling had gone off on you for being in a family of commie spies and, you know, 'nigger' lovers. I figured you didn't need any more crap right then. Anyway, I thought probably you already knew and didn't want to talk about it, so . . ."

"What do you mean, I 'already knew'? You mean, when Eastlund said that, you just accepted it as truth?"

She shrugged and smiled a little. "I did beat the crap out of him for saying it first. Not exactly, but I did slug him."

I stared at her in amazement and reproach for a moment. Then, I grinned. "Is that when he had the black eye and bragged he'd gotten drunk on his uncle's hooch and run into a tree, and we all figured he'd actually been popped by his dad for smarting off?"

She pursed her lips, as though she were thinking it over, and said, "Yeah, that might've been about the time," at which point we both hooted.

"Really, Annie, you just believed him?"

She shrugged. "No, but I thought about it and watched your

mom and Gloria and put two and two together . . . You all seemed so comfortable about it, I just figured you knew and chose not to talk about it."

"Annie!" I wailed. "You're my best friend, my own true blood sister. I don't keep secrets from you."

She hugged me but said, "I know. I just thought—you'd talk about it when you were ready."

We examined what it meant to have a mom who was a lesbian. We wondered if it meant I was, too. We wondered if that man who was my father knew and if that was why he'd said that thing about "those Jordan girls." Mostly, we speculated about how they "did it."

"Fingers," Annie said confidently. I looked askance at her. "No really, Maddie. Even when you do it with a guy, you use fingers a lot. And . . ." Here her voice dropped to a whisper, even though we were in my bedroom with the door closed, and no one would overhear her, ". . . tongues."

"But . . . I mean . . . down there?" I hissed back at her. She nodded firmly. "Yee-uck! How can you be so sure?"

She looked exasperated. "Don't you retain *anything* you read?" *Not this kind of stuff*, I thought, but didn't say. "Remember when we found Gary's stash of girlie magazines?" Gary was her high school brother—a guy who sort of strutted and puffed and whom I mostly found unbearably obnoxious, but—at the same time—I felt a kind of tingle around him that was both thrilling and disgusting. I felt a guilty stab because I'd just assured Annie that I kept no secrets from her when I would *never* have told her about this strange and despicable attraction I felt toward her brother. "Those mags had all sorts of stuff about—" again her voice dropped a register or two, "licking one another. There must be lots of things we don't know, Maddie."

I felt a sudden, inexplicable dampness and tightness "down

there." Although it made me uneasy, I was aware that it was not exactly unpleasant. I wondered if Annie felt a similar sensation, too, and wanted to ask her, but it seemed so perverted—and I was worried enough about perversion in those days—I didn't dare. We knew nothing about the clitoris, had never even heard the word, so—in spite of our certainty regarding our advanced sexual knowledge—there *was* much for us to learn.

I never did talk about my mother to anyone else. At least not for years. I watched more carefully and was astonished to discover that all the evidence was right there in front of me all my life, and I'd never picked up on it. Annie and I talked about this, too.

"I guess when you're so close to people, you don't really notice things so much."

"Sure," Annie agreed, "plus you grew up with this stuff so . . . It seemed perfectly normal to you, ordinary even. You wouldn't notice something just *there,* you know?"

I nodded my agreement. "Annie, do you think everyone else notices?"

"Naw. You know, most people don't even think about things like this. I mean, imagine Miss Sommers thinking about lesbians." We snorted in unison. Miss Sommers was our ditzy home ec teacher who blushed when she had to do a unit on sex education and who didn't seem to know as much as most of us eighth graders.

Lately, we'd been going through all the grown-ups we knew— teachers, storekeepers, parents, and friends' parents—trying to imagine who would have sex and who wouldn't. We weren't old enough, yet, to realize how wrong we were or how little we understood about people and sexuality. "Still, you know, I think probably more people know than would ever let on. Maybe even to themselves."

"You do?" I tensed at this thought—more for people to talk

about, to hate us Jordan girls for.

"Yeah, but Maddie? It's okay. I think the people who know are mostly the ones who just accept it or, basically, ignore it. As long as your mom and Gloria don't do anything too noticeable, people are probably pretty tolerant." This was prior to Stonewall or the women's liberation movement, and we couldn't even imagine lesbians being open about their relationships in the ways they were going to start being in a scant ten or so years.

Mom and Gloria were clearly attached to one another in ways I'd always taken for granted and, consequently, not really noted. There were dozens of endearments passing between them, sometimes heart-wrenchingly so, I thought, in my dreamy adolescent romanticism. Without thinking about it, I was beginning to concentrate on the lovingness of their connection, rather than on the perversity of it.

One would touch the other when talking—on the arm or shoulder, sometimes on the hand. Occasionally, Gloria would briefly touch her finger to Mom's cheek and Mom would push Gloria's hair behind her ear. Once, Mom stumbled, and Gloria, reflexively, put her hand under Mom's elbow to steady her. I also, once or twice, caught them gazing at each other with a kind of look that I realized I never saw around this household of spinsters—a look that seemed to *drink* them into each other's eyes.

Gradually, by becoming more aware of how they communicated with each other, I also became more aware—as Annie already had—of the fact many other people seemed to know about them. I became aware of a kind of adult code used in their presence, a code that communicated something like, "We know who you are, and we won't say anything, but we want you to know it's okay with us."

And that's how it came to be with me, too. Okay.

27

A War of Words

I began school in 1957, and for a few years following my entry, I spent some time curled up under my desk while air-raid sirens wailed. This was the heritage, I was to learn, of our own nation's decision to drop A-bombs on Japan and the subsequent Cold War that developed between us and the Soviet Union, both creating a kind of national paranoia.

What we were told in school was that Russia was determined to rule the world, and we were the major proponent of peace, thereby making us targets for Soviet attack. Why we thought a small river town on the cusp of forest and prairie might have bombs dropped on it escaped me—and still escapes me. If any of us asked such impertinent questions, we were apprised of large missile silos buried deep in North Dakota's prairies, explaining the possibility of Soviet bombings.

Since North Dakota was some distance from us, our preparatory strategies were still baffling. We would crouch under our desks, faces nested in encircling arms, knees pulled snugly under our bodies, waiting for the all-clear signal. Did we really believe we could protect our frail bones, our chubby flesh from buildings falling on us? Did we really believe our arms shielding our unprotected faces would be sufficient to save us from nuclear fallout?

Sometimes, while cramped in this absurd position, I would imagine no all-clear signal coming. We would hear—instead—the drone of approaching airplanes, the dreaded whistle of falling bombs, the subsequent yowling of steel being wrenched loose from brick as buildings disintegrated all around us. A part of me was intoxicated with the thrill of such an occurrence, always imagining myself in the position of super-hero—rescuing teachers and friends from the rubble of our devastated school building. I never imagined death, mine or anyone else's, with the possible exception of a handful of students I quite despised. Maybe Randy Eastlund—the bully who'd bloodied Annie's nose, for instance, would be pinned under a steel beam and writhing in agony, crying piteously for help. Unfortunately, I would not have time to save him.

I never told anyone about these fantasies of mine, not even Annie. It seemed too awfully macabre that I would indulge, even momentarily, in such destruction—exploiting it to re-create myself as a kind of savior. Many of the boys in my classes would actually describe such scenes, their voices full of bravado and swagger; my unspoken variations of the same stories disturbed me even more, then.

Forever after, people talked about how the baby boomers, my generation, grew up in the long, debilitating shadow of nuclear war, and how it indelibly marked us. I try to remember if I ever felt frightened, hounded, or hopeless—all words applied to us as the signs of our despair. It always seemed like a textbook description rather than an actual depiction of my childhood.

I might be wrong or maybe my own family was successful in teaching me the other side of the story and, basically, just dismissed the notion that we were in any kind of imminent danger. However, when I think about it, most of my classmates came from families who also dismissed what they viewed as a kind of "city" hysteria about impending disaster. Midwesterners, in general, are stable people, not much attracted to drama. Later, I wondered if this idea of the baby boomers being touched by twentieth century despondency wasn't just conjured by some writers and philosophers as an excuse for lives of unbridled debauchery or unchecked depression.

For most of us kids, huddling under our desks a few times a year was just one of those things you did, like going to school every day. It was ordinary and routine, so not particularly noteworthy. For some of us, it was fertile ground for grandiose dreams—spoken or unspoken. Few of us took the air raids seriously, I suspect, because we were children who lived rather commonplace and protected lives, more often than not our only encounter with violent death or war coming on Saturday afternoons when we got to go to the matinee at the local movie house.

For me, the issue was further complicated—and perhaps clarified—by the rather less-than-ordinary atmosphere in which I was growing up. I was taught—and believed—the air raid drills were preposterous and the result of a clever campaign to whip up public sentiment against communism or anything being lumped in with communism.

"By making someone else the enemy, by focusing our attention on the Soviet Union and its activities, we then succeed in keeping people's minds off their own dissatisfactions. If someone *does* notice an injustice in one's own life and makes some move to organize others to change this injustice, then we can label it communism and make it part of the 'inside plot' to take over our country. It's a very cunning technique to disallow any meaningful and essential progress," Gummie would explain to me.

As I grew older, it wasn't hard to see exactly what she was talking about as one after another Civil Rights organization—or the leaders, like Martin Luther King, Jr.—were labeled pawns of the communist conspiracy. Then the same slurs were hurled at those who began to oppose the Vietnam War.

The five of us—Mom and Gloria and Gramma and Gummie and I—drove to the Cities and participated in marches and demonstrations against the war-that-wasn't-a-war. Compared to "Bloody Sunday," these were quiet events—tantamount to evening strolls. There were always some hecklers on the sidelines, often men dressed in their uniforms from the more "popular" wars—I and II, and sometimes they even threw a rock or two at us, but mostly they just flung words. It was pretty easy to ignore them.

Once, on the ride back to Riverton, I asked Gummie, "Were all those other wars really so popular? No one ever objected to them?"

Gummie snorted. "Hell no, Maddie. We've not had a popular war this century." I knew, right away, I could settle in as she began the expansion of my education. "We only got into WWI at the end, and it took that long because so many of us opposed any involvement at all. When a government declares war against another government, it needs the support of its constituents, so we ended up fighting several battles inside our own country over specious issues like loyalty.

"In Minnesota—as well as other places—all the progressive movements ground to a halt because people were taking opposite sides regarding our involvement in the war. For the most part, progressive folks were at least neutralists, at best pacifists. Instead of being allowed the luxury—and absolute right, I might add—of having our own opinion, the pro-war machine whipped up popular sentiment about protecting America from the encroachment of foreign interests and, to still the opposing voices, labeled those of us who opposed war as unpatriotic or disloyal. Centuries ago, this same tactic was used to create a European-wide allegiance to Christianity."

This digression, as usual, snagged me. "I don't understand, Gummie. What do you mean?"

"In the centuries following Jesus' execution, the Christian church began forcing itself on other countries. Christians still do this through their missionary work, although usually not by force now. Northern Europe—the Celts, the Saxons, the Vikings—had their own forms of spirituality. It was a land-based spirituality, rather similar to American Indian spirituality. The point is—it was *their* spirituality, *their* culture. The Roman-influenced Christian countries, notably Italy and then France, conquered these other countries and superimposed their beliefs and culture over the indigenous peoples, most often by military force.

"Military force can make people comply, but it can't change people's hearts. So the more insidious methods employed were simply spreading lies about the 'old ways,' labeling the original forms of spirituality as heathen, demonic, witchery. They were discredited in every manner they could be until people started finding anything that was non-Christian suspect."

"What about the people who continued to believe in these religions? What about the practitioners?"

"They were forced underground or killed. This went on for centuries, Maddie. The Crusades and the great witch hunts of the Middle Ages were part of the final cleansing process led by the new religion—Christianity."

I turned all this over in my head, having immediate faith that it was going to make perfect sense when I applied it to actual situations. "So those were the same techniques used during WWI to whip up support for the war?"

"That's right. Guilt by inference. Discredit everyone who isn't gung ho war. Being pro-war became synonymous with being a patriot. Being anti-war—not implying, in any way, you love'd your country any less—became synonymous with being a traitor—or at best, disloyal. It was very effective. These methods were ostensibly created to ensure support for the war, but the most damaging result was the dismantling of essential organizations, which could've made a difference."

"Tell her about your newspaper friend in Alexandria, Minnesota," Gramma inserted.

"You mean Carl Wold," Gummie responded, "of the *Park Region Echo.* He was a staunch believer that personal opinion had nothing to do with patriotism and even went so far as to place his paper at the disposal of the Nonpartisan League. An angry, so-called patriotic mob beat him and wrecked his presses. That was only one such incident. Some objectors were actually tarred and feathered. Others were beaten, then 'deported' to Iowa or one of the Dakotas."

"Did anything like that ever happen to you?" I wondered how many stories I still hadn't heard. I looked at her as her jaw tightened. I was sitting in the backseat, between Gramma and her, while Mom drove. Gloria sat up front with Mom but was twisted around in her seat, listening to Gummie, too.

Gummie shook her head shortly. "No. I never got beaten. Maybe just because I was a woman." She barked something resembling a laugh. "An odd plus. A couple of bricks, at different times, were thrown through the office windows, and once a fire was set, but we were lucky—it was discovered immediately and extinguished before much damage was done. Lots of newspapers went out of business or were harassed into quitting during that period.

"It was almost worse after the war. Then we had the Americans First and other organizations that were created, basically, to subvert the subversives."

"What does that mean?"

"A lot of men came home from the war, Maddie, dispirited and angry. Naturally. Instead of blaming their own government for sending them over there, they blamed 'those damn foreigners.' So they wanted, now, for the country to become isolationist—not allowing any more immigrants to come to 'steal their jobs away,' and instituting discriminatory hiring practices so 'Americans' were hired first—and they got to define *American*: white, more than first-generation, men.

"The next twenty years resulted in a withdrawal, to some extent, from reform politics. A retrenchment. People wanted to just play turtle. When WWII started, we ended up with the odd bedfellows—those isolationists and the left-wing pacifists all not wanting us to go to war.

"Now this was a whole different situation, Maddie. We were in the worst depression the U.S. had ever known. People were starving, crime was up, people lived in tents and shanties and vehicles across the country. FDR had been combatting the Depression, in one way or another and not very successfully, for nearly a decade by 1941. He and his advisors were not dummies. They knew war would 'save the day'—both economically and by refocusing our attention. The American public, on the right and the left, were not in the mood for war. The devastations of WWI were still too clear in our minds, and the Depression had sapped our energy.

"So, the question became: how to mobilize public sentiment in favor of war, which would stimulate the economy and make Roosevelt look like he'd actually pulled us out of the Depression?

It turned out to be easier than they thought. When word came that a Japanese warship was moving toward Honolulu with the intention of bombing the ships in Pearl Harbor, our government chose to ignore this information and simply let it happen. They reasoned, if we were attacked first, the American public would be so outraged, war would be a given. They reasoned correctly."

"I never heard that before," Gloria interposed. "Thousands of men died at Pearl Harbor! What you're saying is we could've prevented those deaths! That's terrible!"

Gummie nodded grimly, and I repeated, "Roosevelt actually knew before it happened?"

"Oh yes," Gummie nodded affirmatively. "Of course, we didn't know the facts for years, and even now, no one wants to admit the truth. They still don't teach it in school. 'Roosevelt saved us from the Depression, and we saved the world for democracy!' These are the things people want to believe. There were lots of draft dodgers in that war, Maddie, lots of demonstrations against the war, lots of boys going AWOL, lots of objections. Now, all anyone wants to remember is it was a *just* war, a *necessary* war. Especially after we discovered what was happening to the Jews and other outsiders in Germany and its occupied countries."

"What they did to the Jews *was* horrible, Gummie. Didn't we have to stop them?"

"Maybe, Maddie, maybe we did. The truth is, however, that's not why we went to war. Mostly, we didn't even know what was happening until afterward. We went to war for the same reason countries almost always go to war—economics. If we think we should've stopped the Nazis, then why didn't we stop the Belgians from butchering the Africans in the Belgian Congo?"

"Well," I hesitated because I knew nothing of this event, "was it as bad as the Holocaust?"

"Probably worse, Maddie. Best guess estimate—ten million

Africans died vicious and unnecessary deaths at the hands of the Belgians, ordered so by King Leopold II of Belgium himself."

"When was this?" Gloria asked.

"Turn of the century. The unspeakable atrocities committed in the Congo resulted in the first large-scale, international human rights movement. Not only was there genocide, there was also forced slave labor and brutal mutilation of the native Africans. Yet now, a scant sixty years later, no one even remembers—or knows about it. You didn't know, did you, Maddie? Gloria?" We both shook our heads. "The main reason why the hue and cry was never as loud as the ensuing ruckus regarding the Holocaust was that, one, the Congo wasn't economically important to us; and two, Leopold was just slaughtering *blacks* while Hitler was slaughtering *whites.*"

None of us said anything for a couple of minutes. I felt stunned by the scale of what Gummie'd just imparted and, as always, by how inaccurate or, at best, incomplete history in school was. How could I *not* know about this?

Gloria finally broke the silence. "What about Korea?"

"Same thing but maybe a little less. By then, the propaganda against communism was so thorough, so damaging, a lot of us thought we really had to fight communism *over there* to prevent it from happening *over here.*"

"Us? Did *you* think that?"

"No. I'm a pacifist, Maddie. I don't believe in war under any circumstances."

"None? If they were here and putting your friends to death, you wouldn't fight back?"

"Who's 'they,' Maddie? We *are* here, and we *are* putting my friends to death. We did it in the twenties when we executed Sacco and Vanzetti and in the fifties again when we executed the Rosenbergs. How about the blacks and other Civil Rights workers? The Native Americans who were massacred because—imagine!—they just wanted to live on the land of their ancestors in their own way? The ones, more recently, who've been murdered because they're now demanding we honor our treaties with them? How many others have been imprisoned or executed that we don't know about? Now, we're drafting our boys and sending them over to die in a "police action" in a country in which we have no business meddling. War begets more war, violence just more violence. The only war I want to wage is a war of words."

At some point, I think I fell asleep. Maybe Gummie had said it all first or maybe it still lodged in my brain, through the dull haze of slumber. I only remember thinking how much there was to learn.

28

Just Practice

I will never forget the first time I beat Gummie at Scrabble. It was raining. It was pouring, actually. It had been raining for four days. Not the kind of soaker making a thirsty soil open up in glad welcome, but the kind of steady drencher making the earth—and everyone on it—want to curl up in a defensive ball.

It had been a scorching summer, weeks without rain, day after day of sweltering humidity and high temperatures, resulting in sullenness and prickly heat rashes and depleted energy. The kind of oppressive heat that made children march resolutely to unfinished attics hot enough to bake a cake, sit motionless up there while counting slowly to a hundred—"one-thousand-one, one-thousand-two"—while ignoring the rivulets of sweat streaming down every inch of their bodies, then tumble gleefully to the first floor where the temperature suddenly seemed bearable in comparison. The kind of heat that pressed down on you, heavy and menacing, forcing you to search the sky for a puff of cloud every morning, the leaves in trees for any indication of a breeze that might stir the air enough to make it feel breathable again. The kind of heat that caused fully dressed adults to join children running through sprinklers. The kind of weighty, implacable heat that lingered in houses long after the sun gratefully escaped, while folks moved restlessly in their beds, trying to find a cool spot on damp sheets. Some days, it was so hot that Gramma put our sheets in the freezer; we would make our beds right before we retired, giving us—if we were lucky—enough coolness to get to sleep.

The first day of steady downpour, naturally, was heavenly release, inducing everyone to want to go outside and open their mouths like baby birds to receive the blessing of moisture not produced by their own bodies. Most people moved through the second day of rain with a shared sense of welcome relief. "Isn't this rain a godsend?" they'd say to one another at the post office or hesitating at the door of their workplaces before dashing to their cars.

On the third day of rain, many people started to forget the long spell of blistering drought and began asking querulously, "When do you think this rain is going to let up?"

All the old stories started surfacing, like branches in the river—bobbing up. "Remember the rains of '54?"

"My lord, you don't think this'll get that bad, do you?"

"Maybe. Looks bad, don't it?"

"Remember the floods?"

"God, yes! The river rose right up to the floor of the bridge out on thirty-seven."

"And all the houses in the bottom were clean swept away." By the fourth day, almost everyone was resentful.

"Gummie," I began while we were playing Scrabble at the

kitchen table, "how did you get to be so confident?" The raindrops plopped down into puddles perched on soil too soaked to accept more liquid, filling the kitchen with splashing sounds, which might've been pleasant but weren't. Jack stirred under the table. The intermittent murmur of thunder disturbed her.

The line between Gummie's eyes deepened as she thought about my question. "I don't know exactly. I just always was, it seems. I'm sitting here trying to figure out if people are born that way or learn it. What do you think?" She played "crabby"—*yep, I am,* I thought—on a triple word score and got fifty-four points— *and I'm not sure having a ninety-three-year-old whomp me at Scrabble is going to help my state of mind all that much.*

I scrunched up my own brow and worried about answering "right." Finally, I said, "I think maybe they're born that way, first, and then they probably learn it some more. Or sometimes, unlearn it."

"Mmm-humph," Gummie snorted. I didn't know if she thought I was right or not. Her eyes were on her new letters as she waited for me to play. After a minute, she said, "You know, Maddie, I think you're right."

"You do?"

"Mm-hmm. All of us girls had the same parents, the same upbringing, but we were all different. Violet and I were probably the most sure of ourselves, Dolly a little less so, and Pansy hardly at all. Yet, all of us were more confident than most girls we knew. I think that was because we were all taught to be independent. I also believe Vi and I were probably the *most* certain because we were just born that way."

I turned all this information over in my head, the way she'd taught me to do before "jumping into words." I played "mocking," the "m" on Gummie's "y." Because I used all seven of my letters, I got an extra fifty points, resulting in a total of eighty-seven points. I screeched, popped my head into the living room to tell Mom and Gramma, and smirked at Gummie. She said, "Huh. You're getting too good, or I'm getting too old. Probably both."

"Right," I sneered, picking seven new letters and groaning to discover that five of them were vowels. "Like this means I'm going to win or something."

"You might," Gummie encouraged.

"It makes sense—what you said about your sisters and you." After a pause, I added sadly, "So I guess if I'm not so confident yet, I probably never will be."

Gummie's eyes left her letters to stare at me. After an uncomfortable silence (at least uncomfortable for *me* because of her dreaded look), she said, "Madelaine Iris, what are most girls your age wearing these days?"

It was 1966. I frowned at her question but answered with a shrug. "I don't know. Miniskirts. Bell-bottomed jeans. Pleated skirts. Stuff like that."

"Mmm-hmm," she said, nodding her head slightly, saying no more.

Finally, I couldn't stand it and demanded, "What?"

She glanced up at me, let a lazy grin spread across her face as she drawled, "Well, Maddie, look at your clothing."

I scanned myself: I was wearing a forget-me-not-sprigged frock and clunky boots. The soft cotton dress I'd pulled out of one of the old trunks in the attic, and the boots came from the Thrift Shop downtown. The dress had a crumpled round collar, buttons marching primly to a hem that swirled outward below my knees, tickling the tops of my boots. I shrugged. "So? I'm not exactly stylish."

"*Not exactly stylish?*" Gummie echoed. "How old are you? Twelve? Thirteen?"

"Fourteen," I glowered at her.

"Mmm-hmm. Fourteen and 'not exactly stylish.'" She placed an "a" and an "r" in front of "my" for "army" and got a mere nine points. I raised my eyebrows, and she shrugged, "Crummy letters." Then she added, "You don't think it takes confidence to be not-exactly-stylish?"

I should have seen that one coming. "Oh," I hardly knew how to react. "I don't know . . ." I floundered, thinking about Annie, who loved the way I dressed in '30s and '40s castoffs—whatever kind of outlandish getups I could put together—and who adamantly declared that she'd *never* have the courage to dress "so different" like I did, but she was sure glad to be around me. "Maybe I'm just kind of silly."

"Silly?" Gummie was immediately alert. "What do you mean?"

"I don't know . . ."

Gummie interrupted me, almost snapping, "Quit saying 'I don't know,' Maddie. It makes you sound stupid and tentative."

I feel stupid and tentative, I thought. I wasn't quite gutsy enough to snap back at her, but I had begun arguing with her in my head. I took a deep breath. "I guess I mean maybe I'm being silly because I just want attention. So, I wear clothing no one else would wear. I mean, I like the stuff I wear, but I also know it will make me . . ." I almost said 'you know,' catching myself because Gummie hated that phrase as much as 'I don't know,' "it will make me more noticeable." I added to myself, *Everyone knows I'm the offspring of commies/atheists/abandoned wives/unwed mothers/lesbians anyway, so I might as well go for broke.*

"Does it?"

I shrugged and then nodded. "Yeah. Not always favorably."

We concentrated on the game for a few minutes, Gummie playing "wave," getting eighteen points and me playing "quays" on "wave"—the "q" hitting a double letter and the whole word on a double score, resulting in sixty-five points. I yelped and dashed into the living room again to share with Mom and Gramma. Jack was jubilant, too, mostly for an excuse to chase after me, barking.

When I returned to the kitchen and settled back down, Gummie asked, "So tell me, Maddie, what is it you think confidence is, anyway?"

Not what I have, I thought. Aloud I said, "I guess it's being sure of yourself. Being courageous and unafraid, even in opposition to other people. It's not," here I started meting my words out carefully, paying more attention to them myself, "it's not caring what other people think. Huh." She said nothing more. After a moment, I protested, "But, Gummie, I don't *feel* all that confident."

She laughed, that roaring rumble of hers, echoed by actual thunder outside. "I'll let you in on a little secret, Maddie. *None of us* feel all that confident."

I looked at her with astonishment and disbelief. "*You do*, Gummie. You can't possibly mean you don't!" I moved to Gummie's "c" at the top of the board to play "ionic," getting rid of three of my vowels but garnering only eight points.

Gummie waved her hand airily, "Oh sure, most of the time, but I'm old, Maddie. I've had a lot of practice. Sometimes I don't feel as confident as I appear, but you'd never notice the difference from when I do. Confidence is half bluff and half certainty, sometimes swinging a bit more one way or the other." She moved to the other side of the board to play "joints" on another word, gaining forty-two points. "Tell me this, when you wear an unstylish outfit to school, do you feel absolutely, one hundred percent comfortable?"

"No."

"How do you act?"

The lights started going on in my head. I grinned and said, "I act as if *I'm* the one who's stylish, and the rest of them are the weirdos."

"Exactly. Half bluff, half certainty. Because surely you do believe, at least to some degree, that your manner of dressing *is* more superior, yes?"

I grimaced, responding, "I don't know about *superior*. Certainly more interesting." After a small pause, in which I avoided Gummie's baleful stare, I agreed. "Yeah, okay, maybe even superior." We beamed at each other in our usual complicity.

"Do you see what I'm trying to say?"

"I guess," I conceded. "Still, you must have been far more confident at my age than I am."

"If you're asking whether I appeared to be confident, absolutely. I most certainly did. Was I as confident as I appeared? Absolutely not! I never would've admitted that at your age, or maybe for many, many ages afterward, but underneath all my bravado was often a really scared girl. She's still there, in fact, more than you'd believe, but you bluster through—" like I did, I realized, when I was in intimidating situations—"and all that bluster, without you even knowing it, becomes practice for the 'real' thing, and gradually, you actually become almost as confident as you appear to be to others."

My next play gave me thirty-seven points. I wondered what it would be like, as I often did, to have siblings, to grow up with other kids who were different from me. If I had someone else who was experiencing the same environment I was, would I be better able to gauge things like my own confidence level? It was hard to measure against Gummie's—or even Gramma's or Mom's—when theirs seemed infinitesimally larger than mine could ever be. If Gummie was right—and after all, she usually was—then maybe they weren't always so sure of themselves.

"How about Gramma and Mom, Gummie? Were they born with it or did they learn it, do you think?"

She said, "I think your Gramma was born with an adequate

amount of confidence. We probably all are, but some of us—like Violet and me—are born with a personality larger than life, which radiates an illusion of confidence. That was not the case with your grandmother."

Gummie's personality was larger than life, all right. Gummie never hesitated to give anyone her opinion, never seemed to wonder whether she was right or wrong, always just sailed into every situation as if she were the Mother Ship. I really wanted her kind of audacity, but I was pretty sure my personality, my presence was never going to be as commanding as hers.

Gummie was still talking about Gramma. "Her personality did not quite . . .," she hesitated here, ". . . boom, I guess. Then there was the problem of having me for a mother."

"Problem?" I thought I probably knew what she was talking about but wanted to hear how she'd word it.

"You know, Maddie, I cast an enormous shadow. It's easy for someone to get lost in that murkiness." I was on the right track. "I was so busy running the newspaper and trying to fix the world and loving Hubert, I think sometimes I just didn't pay enough attention to Hester. Plus, it's hard to be sure of yourself when your mother . . .," she hesitated again, looking kind of sad, ". . . when your mother is always telling you you're wrong. Or else telling you what's right."

"She seems pretty confident, now," I contradicted.

"I think you're right, Maddie, absolutely right. Even so, she *grew* into confidence. See," she leaned toward me, as she usually did when she was going to impart some wise nugget, "I don't believe Hester would've ever married that odious man if she'd been more confident, more sure of herself. She didn't really know who she was, just saw herself reflected in my eyes and had to resist, so . . ." She paused for a minute, her body resting back into her chair. "She found someone else to give her a different reflection."

After a moment of perusing her letters and the board, she added, "I will never forgive that man for hurting my Hester and Jane the way he did, but Maddie? Just between you and me," she leaned forward again, "he did Hester a big favor."

"He did?"

"Oh yes," she stated unequivocally, "oh yes. He gave her Jane and you, for one thing, but even more. Once he was gone, I encouraged Hester to move back in with us—Hubert and me—and let us support one another while Jane was growing up. You know, Hester was smarter than me. She sure was. She refused to comply, probably knew—maybe without knowing she knew—that once back in my orbit, she would just become another rotating planet, losing all sense of separate self, independence.

"She didn't move back. Instead, she turned this house into a boarding house and got herself a nursing job. She created a life independent of anyone else and in which she was no longer a wispy figure in the mirror of someone else's eyes, fully becoming her own self."

My eyes, I knew, were shining with this altered version of my Gramma's life. I felt—I didn't know exactly how to put it in words or even identify the feeling—like I was bursting with pride for these strong, courageous women who were my elders. "Did you ever *tell* Gramma all this?" I queried.

Gummie frowned at me, then said, "Not in so many words. I'm sure Hester knows how proud I am of her . . ."

I shook my head vigorously. "*I'm* not so sure, Gummie. Who is it, anyway, who always tells me—'Be clear, be clear'? I think you should tell her!"

She directed her X-ray stare toward me momentarily, then her eyes softened as she shook her head. "I swear, Maddie, sometimes I think all the collected wisdom of this family has come to reside in you. You might be right. I probably should tell her." She smiled, lost in reverie. "She did a fine job, Maddie, an exceptionally fine job with her life. Raised Jane to be a spectacular woman," I squirmed regarding this compliment to my mother. "You, too. She never, ever had to rely on Hubert and me for any help financially. She did fine, just fine. In the process, she came into her own—learned to trust herself, believe in herself, be confident. She might be quieter than her infamous mother," she barked a half laugh, half snort at this utterance, "but she knows who she is all right and rests comfortably in that knowledge."

"See, Gummie," this time *I* leaned toward *her*, "I think you're really good at letting Mom and me know how special you think we are. Not so much with Gramma, though. It's as though you just take her for granted or something. Or worse—like you dismiss her, like she doesn't really count in this family. Like you and Mom and me—we're the *real* Jordans, and she's just—I don't know, someone on the edge." New thoughts were swirling through my head. "Gummie? Imagine what that might feel like to her! Especially because she's adopted, not your *real* child, you know."

Gummie remonstrated violently to this statement and roared, "She *is* my real child! Don't be absurd! 'Realness' is not about blood!"

"I know, Gummie, but does Gramma know? I think you have to tell her how well you think she's done and everything else, especially the part about her being smarter than you." I turned my head a little, as if to look out the rain-streaked window, peeking back at her out of the corner of my eye. She was doing her horrid stare again.

Suddenly, she laughed loudly and said, "Out of the mouths of babes. Indeed, indeed. I'll just have to see, won't I?" I nodded encouragement. "You know the rest, don't you? Jane came along, in some ways the quietest of us all, the most introverted. And yet—probably the most individualistic, too. In her quiet way, she's cut a swathe as wide as a country road for herself. Then you . . ."

When she hesitated, I finished, "Probably the least confident of us all."

Gummie shook her head. "No, I don't think so. I think what you've done is absorb the best of all of us. Equal measures of thoughtfulness and confidence, enough bluster to get by with and enough quietness to figure things out, too. Remember? We started this conversation with your question about how one gets so confident? Practice, Maddie, pure and simple. Just practice."

Like Scrabble, I thought, as I played my last letters—t-a-x-i for thirty-seven points—and actually beat Gummie, 318 to 301.

29

"Are You a Communist?"

"So, Gummie, is it true? *Are* you a communist?" I was fifteen or sixteen before I accrued enough courage to ask this question. In some ways, it was anticlimactic by then because it didn't matter as much as it did when I was younger, which is probably why I didn't ask the question earlier. Like most people, I'd always assumed she was, and because I lived in a time fraught with almost hysterical anti-communism, I hardly wanted to confirm my worst fears. Nevertheless, I'd also been taught to believe that communism was positive, a way of organizing a society so it was good for everyone rather than a lucky few. Accepting this, I was no longer certain I really minded if she were indeed a communist.

Gummie looked up from her reading, a glimmer of surprise in her eyes. We were both at the kitchen table, my social studies homework spread around me and various newspapers spread around her. "A communist," she said slowly, as if maybe she were considering it for the first time. She didn't drop her eyes back to her paper but continued to let them bore into me. "What exactly are you asking, Maddie? Do you want to know if I believe in communism, or if I am a member of the Communist Party?"

It was my turn to be surprised. I stuttered a little in response. "Uh . . . uh, I guess I always thought they were the same. At least for you. I mean—*are* you a member?"

"No," she answered without hesitation, and my surprise deepened.

"No? I always thought you were."

"You certainly wouldn't be alone," she leaned back in her chair, sighing, her eyes far away. "It was something of a problem for Hubert and me. It's true, I'm a great advocate of communism, definitely a philosophy to admire. Just as there is much in Christianity I admire."

"*There is?*" I hardly expected *this* remark to come from my staunchly atheistic great-grandmother.

"Absolutely. Maddie, the philosophy of Christianity is mostly good. Did you know early Christians lived in communal arrangements?" I shook my head, thinking about hippies who acted as if they'd created the concept, and how I'd assumed they had. "It's *people* who mess it all up, in both communism and Christianity. These two philosophies have a great deal more in common— good and bad—than their various proponents would ever want to admit. In fact, most of the followers from either side would shudder to hear such a statement. When you fervently believe you have ALL the answers, Maddie, all the *right* answers, you have a license to steal. Both groups endlessly justify their horrendous actions by believing they *can* because they know what's *right* for others."

The wind whipped around the corners of our solid old house, prying with icy fingers to find ingress, sighing and whistling in disappointment when it couldn't, then scooping up snow and flinging it at our windows in hostile protest. The snow glowed surreally, resulting in an eerie brightness on an otherwise inky winter evening. Gummie and I stared out the kitchen window for a couple of minutes before she continued.

"Awful things have been done over the centuries in the name of Christianity: invasions, conquests, subjugating other cultures, erasing or diminishing those same cultures, wholesale murder in the name of all that's holy—the Crusades, the witch hunts, war, colonialism, resulting in extreme abominations like the mass mutilation and slaughter of millions of natives in the Congo under the 'benevolence' of the Belgians and the vile torture and murder of millions of Jews by the Nazis. That kind of wholesale genocide? It's happened lots of places and in lots of ways over the centuries. Not just by *others*, either, Maddie. The U.S. has done its part by funding revolutions, ordering assassinations, backing murderous regimes with arms and money, like we're doing with Mobutu in the Congo right now.

"Then communism? It rejects Christianity or any organized religion but echoes these philosophies by invading, conquering, subjugating, erasing or diminishing, murdering, relying heavily on military *force*—and is, interestingly enough, also anti-Semitic. At least in the Soviet Union." She shook her head. "In the name of communism, Maddie, during Stalin's reign of terror in the U.S.S.R, millions of peasants were exiled to labor camps or executed or starved to death for opposing his collectivization of agriculture. Millions! How is that different from what Hitler did to the Jews?"

I stared at her for a moment, feeling my usual amazement at how much gets left out of the history we get at school. "It's—it's not, is it?"

She shook her head. "No, it's not. It always comes down to the same thing—whether it's religion or Nazism or communism—power. Or, probably more accurately, the corruption of power. In and of itself, power is not a bad thing. It's about being effective, about acting rather than reacting. All too often, however, it gets transformed into power *over* others—might, force, control. We always justify this kind of power, this misuse and abuse of power, by insisting we KNOW what is best.

"So, Christians know what is best and right and go about the world insisting everyone else would be better if they, too, were Christians. Sometimes they do this with military force and a government backing them up, sometimes with just a church behind them, but all too often a *very powerful* church. Then communism comes along, eschews Chrisitianity, and goes about the world insisting everyone else would be better off if they, too, were Communists."

She told me how, at the turn of the century, she and Hubert had read *The Communist Manifesto* and *Das Kapital*, then argued with friends about these issues, coming to believe that class struggles were at the heart of the planet's economic problems. Embracing Marxism heightened their labor-agrarian activism. When the Russian Revolution occurred in 1917, both were excited about the possibilities of worldwide revolution where the workers would end up in charge of their own destiny, and everyone would share in the abundance, rather than a handful prospering at the expense of all the others.

"Somehow things got a little derailed about then," Gummie said, shaking her head slowly.

She and Hubert started to fight.

"You see, Maddie, somehow we had shifted, just slightly, from worker-owned-and-operated enterprise to state-owned-and-operated enterprise. That slight swerve resulted in a dictatorship, which required workers to trust some man or group of men in charge who were suddenly doing whatever they deemed necessary to ensure *their* absolute power, *their* absolute authority, *their* absolute control—because these leaders *knew* what was right for everyone else. Guess who everyone else was?" She didn't wait for me to answer. "Those pesky workers, the very ones who were *supposed* to end up in charge of their own destiny and who, suddenly, just weren't smart enough to make good decisions for themselves. The state had to make those decisions." Sarcasm and anger were equal weights in her voice.

"Iris," Hubert would argue when she voiced skepticism about Lenin, "you have to be patient. Change doesn't happen overnight, you know."

"Oh, Hubert," she'd retort, "how does that differ from others who've resisted change over the centuries?"

"You're being so negative!"

"And you're putting your head in the sand!"

After relating this to me, she'd say, "But really, I hoped he was right. I truly hoped this time I was wrong. When the American Communist Party was formed in 1919, Guppie joined. I did not." This led to more problems between them. "He was so idealistic, Maddie, so excited about the promise of a different future. This is what I loved about him, but . . . I couldn't just jump on the bandwagon with him. I felt wary.

"Lenin's goals were good and appropriate: the destruction of free enterprise—privately owned and controlled businesses, resulting in a classless society without the extremes of rich and poor. It was his methods I distrusted. Lenin—and his followers everywhere—believed violent overthrow and bloody revolution

were necessary to reach these goals. Lenin also believed that workers and peasants could not do this alone, would have to be led by
professional revolutionaries—who turned out to be a dictator and
his pals. Surprise, surprise, Lenin was just the dictator for them.
In addition, he believed his goals—the *best* goals, the *right* goals—
could not be met with ANY opposition, and force and terror were
appropriate tools to achieve this utopian society."

"*No* opposition was allowed?"

"None."

"And people believed force and terror would result in a utopian
society?" Gummie nodded. "I don't get it. I thought the czars
were supposed to be so bad."

"The czars *were* bad, Maddie. Don't be misled. I'm talking
about the attempt to dismantle one rotten system by employing
all too similar methods."

"How could Guppie think this was all right?"

"Because I'm wording it so you can see the worst of it, Maddie.
This is the power of communication: how you present something
results in the subtle emphasis on one thing over another. Guppie
would have presented it differently. He *saw* it differently than I
did."

Hubert lectured his wife. "Lenin's reign, Iris, is temporary.
This is just a way to get organized, then there won't be one
person in charge. It will be the rule of the proletariat, workers in
charge of their own lives—all sharing equally and fairly in the
resources of the world. This is a transitional time, a necessary
passage from one failing system to a better one. The glorious
ascendancy of a just society!"

Iris remained skeptical.

More and more reports came out of Russia, making it appear
that Lenin's totalitarian regime was both stultifying to individual

freedom and murderous. Hubert dismissed these reports, insisting, "It's just propaganda, intended to plant doubts in our minds."

"I don't know," Iris refuted. "Some of the information we're getting seems factual. Don't you think we should just wait and watch for a while?"

Hubert flashed a rare streak of anger. "It's propaganda, I tell you! And you're buying it! I expected more of you!"

Iris became uncharacteristically quiet, thinking to herself, "And *I* expected more of *you*."

The frigid wind continued howling as Gummie folded the newspapers in front of her, carefully and methodically, then stared sadly out the window. "It was the biggest crisis of our marriage." She stopped momentarily, as if scrolling through the marriage to see if she really agreed with herself. "I had always been the most verbal, the most vociferously opinionated. Suddenly, Hubert was arguing with me as he'd never done before. He was impatient and frustrated, clearly disappointed. To me, it seemed unnecessary we convince each other or waste time arguing when, in essence, we were on the same side. Of course," she pushed her glasses up to nest in her wispy, white hair and pinched the upper reaches of her nose, "he did have other things on his mind, too." That lugubrious but offhand statement didn't capture my attention, and I was not to know its importance for some years.

Hubert accused Iris of being more conservative than she'd admit, of being a capitalist at heart. He said she ran *The Prairie Voice* as if she owned it, and the workers owning it was just window dressing for her nominal socialism.

Iris railed back. "Who do you think you are? Questioning my credentials? Your slavish devotion to the Party is scary, eerily reminiscent of Christianity's early years when that same kind of singular worship of its tenets was expected! And what did that result in, Hubert? Mmmm? An erasure of individual rights and beliefs around the world, and eventually, a splintering into dozens of watered-down, weakened versions of the Catholic Church in opposition to one-way, one-truth thinking! Is that what you want for the world? Or the Communist Party?"

By 1919, Russia was deep in Civil War.

"Why would the people rise up against Lenin, if he was doing right by them?" Iris would insist.

"They're confused, Iris, and tired. They want everything to change right away. It takes time."

"Let me see if I have this right. Lenin and his pals—*the new ruling class*, Hubert—get to impose their views on the masses with force, with military might?"

He would nod adamantly, saying, "If necessary, Iris, yes. This is temporary. All revolutions go through growing pains. It'll get better. You know that. You believe that. I know you do."

Iris wasn't so sure she *did* believe, though. She thought she could tell by Hubert's voice he wasn't so sure either—though he tenaciously held on to his faith in the Party. She would push what she saw as her advantage and demand to know, "Why are you men so certain violent revolution is the only way? Women have been fighting for seventy-one years to get the vote in this country. *And not one drop of blood has been shed*, even though we still don't have it."

Hubert would ask, angrily, "You want us to wait seventy-one years?"

In response, Gummie would acidly point out, "*We* have, but we don't really count, do we? *We're just women.* Don't worry, the way you and all your buddies talk, it might take seventy years of dictatorship before the workers are *sufficiently ready* to actually rule themselves. How many will be dead by then? How many drops of blood will be shed?"

G ummie continued to me, "When Lenin died and Stalin took over, everything seemed to get worse. The barrage of reports being smuggled out were filled with stories of massive executions and exilings of individuals or groups who opposed the Soviet leaders. Each new nugget of information meant a major disagreement in our household. Hubert and his cronies insisted these disclosures were actually being made by dupes of capitalism, but many of them were coming from respected intellectuals who had been pro-communist before the Revolution. I thought they were being dismissed too handily. Actually, we didn't know the half of it, not until the mid-fifties when Stalin's atrocities were thoroughly exposed by the Soviets themselves. Still, enough info was getting out to convince me—it was disturbing, very disturbing.

"Finally, when Trotsky was exiled by Stalin in 1929, Hubert and many others wavered in their devotion to Mother Russia. Trotsky made it clear how bad things were, and a lot of communists became Trotskyites, not abandoning the party per se, but being part of its first major division. This division grew larger when Trotsky was executed, clearly on Stalin's orders.

"The thirties marked a lot of activity for communism and socialism, mainly in response to the depression devastating most of the world. Political conditions were worse than ever in the Soviet Union, but our focus was elsewhere. On the Spanish Civil War, for instance, where the fascist and communist forces struggled for control. It was tres chic for young, idealistic intellectuals from Great Britain and the U.S. to dabble in communism or at least left-wing politics. Even our darling JFK went to Spain as an observer and vocally supported the Republicans—the communist side, Maddie."

"Really? I never heard anything about that."

"Well, you wouldn't, would you? What with the fervent anti-communism following WWII and Kennedy's grooming for the White House, you can be certain his little foray into left-wing politics was deeply buried."

She stopped for a moment as another smattering of gelid snow smacked against the window. We couldn't tell whether it was coming off the ground or actually falling from the sky, the moaning wind was so erratic.

"Most of us were preoccupied with surviving our own devastating depression here and looking for ways to alleviate the problems through sweeping social legislation, which FDR was pushing through—left and right. Mostly left." I knew this was meant to be a joke, so I dutifully smiled. "We started to believe a socialist government was around the corner.

"Instead, the war came along, and you know a lot of what happened following the war. The world watched, mostly in horror, as the U.S.S.R. gobbled up one neighbor after another and ruled with an iron hand, putting down opposition with immediate and terrible military force. In the U.S., Joe McCarthy and his henchmen created an atmosphere of fear and loathing regarding communism, which swept through the country like a virulent disease.

"Many good, true communists jumped ship, turned tail, 'squealed' on their colleagues, or just quit life altogether. Others of us kept plugging away, trying to capitalize on increased labor unrest and the Civil Rights movement. Doing the only thing we could do: moving forward, no matter how gradually, focusing on what was important, however many barriers were thrown in our way.

Sometimes, as that pendulum came swinging back, we just ducked. As I've told you before, McCarthyism wasn't as bad here in the Midwest as it was on the coasts. We did what we could, your guppie and me, him in the courtroom and me through the paper, combatting the rampant attacks on fine citizens around the country."

"Throughout all of this, you never actually joined the Communist Party?"

She shook her head. "No, but don't confuse these issues, Maddie. I am a communist. I believe in workers owning the means and results of production, a classless society where no one is very rich or very poor, a society in which no one suffers from hunger, a society in which the needier are taken care of by the less needy—children, old people, disabled people, unemployed people—a society where cooperation, not competition and self-interest, is the modus operandi. I believe in free and easy access to education at all levels, medical service available to everyone, and safe, sanitary, and affordable housing.

"What I *don't* believe is the 'end justifies the means'—the main sticking point between Hubert and myself. I don't believe in the violent overthrow of governments nor do I believe in violent methods of maintaining new governments. I don't believe in violence being used to prevent opposition. If there's major opposition, then it's likely—or at least possible—there's something wrong with those in charge. It's what I've told you about the paper, Maddie. If you believe in the system and you believe in people, then you have to trust them to do what's right. If you can't do that, then you're just whistling in the dark, *pretending* you have faith when you don't."

After a pause, in which I struggled to find the words for my next line of questioning, I inquired, "Gummie, in spite of the fact you've never been a Party member, if they came and asked you, say during those McCarthy purges, you would've said you were, wouldn't you?"

"Yes. Yes, Maddie, I would've. And I hope everyone in this household would. When the Nazis took over Denmark, they ordered Jews to wear the Star of David at all times. The King of Denmark—who was not a Jew—immediately responded by pinning a Star of David on his clothing. Soon, all sorts of people were sporting the Star of David. This is a perfect example of nonviolent resistance to injustice!

"So yes, if someone came to this house asking for the communists to step forward, I hope we would all step forward. Just as I would if they came asking if we were lesbians. Or any other persecuted group. The only way to combat persecution is to stand, shoulder to shoulder, with those being persecuted. Oppression doesn't just happen to *some* of us, Maddie, it happens to *all* of us."

"If the persecuted group were Christians?"

"Think you're tough, don't you? Yes, Maddie, even if they were Christians. *All* persecution has to be unacceptable. If we believe in the basic human right of having your own opinion, then we have to support that right wholeheartedly, even when we disagree with that opinion."

"How about Ku Klux Klanners?" I was determined to find holes in her thinking.

She didn't hesitate for a moment. "Not the same thing, Maddie."

"Why not? Don't *they* have the right to believe what they want to believe?"

"Absolutely. To *believe*, yes, but not to terrorize others in the name of those beliefs. The Klan is about hate, Maddie. Christians, communists, lesbians—none of them are about hate. In fact, all of them are about love. At times, they've gone wrong and attempted to force their beliefs on others, using military force or other kinds of armed violence. Except for the lesbians, obviously.

We can't support 'right by might.'

"The Klan's whole philosophy, however, is about hate. Their belief system is about loathsome superiority, and their methodology, being based on this hatred, is always about abrogating others' rights. Violently. You *do* have to have standards about right and wrong, Maddie. For instance, communism is about workers' rights, a good thing. Nazism—another variation of the Klan—is about hating whole groups of people, believing you're superior to them, so they can be annihilated with impunity, a bad thing. Obviously, I'm simplifying, Maddie, but do you understand?"

I nodded my head, then asked, "Even though you aren't a commie, most people think you are. And still . . .," I hesitated, trying to work this out in my mind before saying it. "It's not like people hate you or anything. Actually, most people seem to think you're wonderful."

She laughed. "You make it sound like it's unimaginable! A surprise."

My face flamed. "No, I didn't mean it like that. It's just . . . if they believe you're a communist, and they know you're an atheist, and this is a small town mostly full of church-going, anti-communists and . . . and . . . How come they've never just run you out of town? It's not that, even; it's the opposite. They *like* you, they're *proud* of you, they *respect* you. How did that happen?"

She leaned across the table to me and said, seriously, "I learned, growing up in a small town and returning to one, an important lesson. If you want folks to accept you the way you are, then you've got to accept them the way they are. I don't mean *pretend* to accept them the way they are, people can always see right through that nonsense, and I don't mean *tolerating* them either. Being tolerant of someone just means there's something about them you *have* to tolerate. I mean genuinely accepting them the way they are.

261

"There are people in the world, Maddie, who you just can't stomach. They might be on your 'side,' or they might be on another 'side,' but that's not what's important. You keep people like that at a distance. There's no point wasting your time being around them or putting up with them, but they're the exception. Most people, with all their foibles and despicable qualities, have some good, too. Others, whom you adore for their stupendous amounts of goodness? They also have traits you don't like. Either way, what you have to focus on is their goodness; that's how you accept them. When you accept them, then they do it right back to you. It works."

30

Late Autumn

It was late autumn. The colors were just past their prime—the vivid reds, the sharp yellows, the glorious oranges were fading—all wan facsimiles of their earlier vivacity. The leaves had begun their swan dives in earnest, drifting languidly to the ground, where industrious hands would rake them together in huge piles, allow children to cannonball into them, rake them again, and set fire to them, filling nostrils with the familiar odors of our end-of-summer rituals.

Stragglers of the great flocks of migrating birds—hawks and geese and songbirds—winged across our sky in increasingly fewer numbers. The temperature was cool with a keen nip in the mornings and evenings, the promise of bitterly cold winter days hanging in the sunless air. Gummie and I were making our slow way home from the paper. Jack plodded along with us; at eleven, her pace was finally beginning to slow down enough to match Gummie's. We were arguing.

I was seventeen and in my senior year in high school. I'd just applied to the state college at St. Cloud, near enough to commute. Gummie was not happy with my decision.

"Maddie, you could go anywhere! With your grades and SATs—anywhere! Berkeley, Wellesley, Columbia! Radcliffe or Stanford! If you want to stay close to home, why not my alma mater, Carleton? But St. Cloud State? Pffttt!" She waved her cane in the air, dismissing my choice and almost losing her balance.

I put my hand on her elbow to steady her until she got her cane back on the ground. "What, Gummie? What's 'pffttt?'" I'd mostly gotten over being cowed by her, stood up to her these days. "St. Cloud is *no good* because it's filled with farmers' kids? Huh?"

"Don't you mess with me, Miss Know-It-All." She stopped long enough to shake her cane at me again, this time planting her feet widely so as not to lose her balance.

"Well then, tell me—what's wrong with it?"

"Nothing. Nothing's *wrong* with it. You're smart. You'll get a good education wherever you go. Use those brains to recognize that the best teachers, the most inspired teachers are going to be teaching at schools that will pay them higher wages, schools that will give them the cultural advantages they crave, and colleagues to equal them."

"There are good teachers anywhere," I responded, stubbornly holding my ground.

"You're right, Maddie, there *are* good teachers anywhere, but some places have *more* good teachers. Places where they're not only allowed but encouraged to be free thinkers, to be original researchers, to be creative educators. Places where students benefit from that kind of atmosphere, where students can soak up the heady atmosphere of wide diversity of thinking and backgrounds."

"Gummie," I said patiently but with a definite edge to my voice, "I grew up in that atmosphere. Isn't that enough?"

"No, it's not, Maddie. You need it in a new way—with stimulating and provoking mentors. With questioning, searching peers. You need to go away from home, away from the safe confines of loving nurturance, and *find* yourself. Only then can you come home and burrow in safely."

I sighed. I didn't want to talk to her about her own death. I suspected this reluctance was more for me than for her. Just saying it aloud seemed risky to me. *You and Jack are old, Gummie. You're both gonna die soon. I'm not leaving until you do.* She'd just argue with me, anyway, insist that that was no reason for me to stay around home.

She was ninety-six years old. She walked slower and slower. She was a little more bent over each year. Her nightstand was crowded with medicine bottles: blood thinner, high blood pressure pills, heart pills, aspirin for arthritis, I didn't know what all. She still went to work every day, although now she went in about noon, walking home with me, most days, when I stopped by after school.

"St. Cloud's a fine school, Gummie," I remonstrated.

"You're right," she seemed to capitulate, and I looked askance at her. "No, it is a fine school, Maddie, with many exceptional teachers. I just think you need—and deserve—enormous stimulation. It's not good enough for you."

I stared at her in astonishment. "What a lot of rubbish! I never heard such snobbery! Gummie, I'm ashamed of you!"

"Maddie . . ."

I interrupted her, saying firmly, "Quit arguing with me. It's my life, and I've made my decision."

She stopped and scowled at me, shaking her head and finally smiling. "I swear," she said, and I knew this was high praise indeed, "you're getting more and more like your mother every day."

Then she was gone, her body seeming to deflate as it sank to the pavement. "Gummie!" I shouted, as I grabbed for her, knowing, knowing without wanting to know. "G-u-m-m-m-i-e!" I howled, as if I could somehow call her back to me, banish the inevitable.

She was crumpled in a lifeless heap on the ground, and I was on my knees, gathering her body into my arms. "Help!" I called. "Someone, please! Help! Call an ambulance! Quick!"

I knew she was already dead, knew this lifeless shell had no shred of my gummie left in it. Knew she was never going to say to me again, "Now listen closely, Maddie, this is important." Knew she would no longer wave her cane at me or anyone else. Knew I couldn't possibly go on without her.

"G-u-m-m-i-e!" I threw my head back and shrieked.

M om and I were not able to quit crying after Gummie's death. We were pretty much useless, but Gramma was a rock. She immediately went into action, making certain press releases were sent out to all the newspapers in the state as well as to the major newspapers throughout the country. She also put Gummie's devastated staff to work, sending telegrams to people all over the country and putting together a special issue of the paper honoring her life.

To me, Gummie was just Gummie—an extraordinary woman, to be sure, but still—just my opinionated, cantankerous great-grandmother. I didn't always remember she'd been involved in every major reform movement of the twentieth century, did not even know she had ongoing correspondence with leaders all over the world, was not able to imagine the contacts she maintained in journalism, politics, every endeavor of human effort. Gummie was not Gummie to the world outside of Riverton. She was Iris Jordan—a formidable, brilliant journalist and activist who embodied integrity and dedication to human rights.

The people who rolled into Riverton over the next few days as well as all the telegrams that flooded our house and the newspaper office were testimony to her stature. Iris Hannah Jordan's memorial was held in the high school auditorium. Nothing else in town was big enough. The auditorium was filled, and the overflow crowd were seated in the lunchroom and the gymnasium. The school p.a. system was engaged so everyone could hear the proceedings.

Some said more people came to Gummie's funeral than they did to Eleanor Roosevelt's. I never believed that, but it didn't matter to me, anyway. What mattered was she was gone. Forever.

Gramma managed to get a choir together to sing old movement songs between speeches: "Are You a Wobbly?" "Solidarity Forever!" "We Shall Overcome!" I doubt there was a dry eye to be found. It made me think of our trip to Selma, causing sobs to erupt from me. My mother's or grandmother's hands kept soothing me, patting me, cuddling me.

I felt as if I were moving through molasses that day—each footstep heavier than the last. I was surprised, later on, at how many stories I remembered. There were speeches by people I didn't know, some whom I only knew from pictures in newspapers, and others I'd known all my life—all talking about Gummie's importance in their lives. The stories I remembered best, though, were from the people who came up to me all day and declared, "Your great-grandmother changed my life!"

"I know folks say she was godless, but—so what?—I just don't care. Iris Jordan had a heart of gold! When my Clarence went on strike out to the plant and the strike fund was never enough to stretch and I had just had my Georgie and the kids were just like steps, you know—one-two-three-four years old, why, Iris just right away sent her day worker over to help me till I got back on my feet and Clarence could get back to work. I don't know how we would've managed without her. A heart of gold, I tell you, a heart of gold!"

"Iris saved my job, Maddie . . ."

"If Iris Jordan was an example of what a communist is like, then let me tell you—I want to know where I can sign up! That woman went to bat for me when they let me go at the dairy, even though I'd always kind of bad-mouthed her. What they tried to do to me was not fair, though, and that woman stood for fairness, no matter who was involved. She not only made them take me back, she brought the union to us—making our lives possible."

"I never could have continued working at the paper, Maddie, if she hadn't let me work nights when Jerry was home with the kids. I wanted to keep working, and we needed the money, but I never could have done it if . . ."

"Iris saved my marriage, Maddie . . ."

"Your great-grandmother kept me out of jail. She caught me and a bunch of other boys stealing pumpkins out of Old Man Henderson's garden. If he'd caught us, I know he would've stuck the law on us. She just marched us up to his house with our booty, made us turn it over, and asked Henderson what we could do to make it up to him. I swear, that old geezer 'bout lost it, that surprised he was. Me and my chums weeded his garden the next summer."

"Iris Jordan was the most intelligent person I ever knew. Her political analysis was astute and incisive. Her integrity! My God, nothing would make that woman back down. She was stubborn, that's for sure, but she usually had good reason."

So it went—on and on and on and on. I heard new versions of

stories she'd blessed me with all my life, and ones she'd never shared with me. I didn't even know most of the people talking to me. As the day wore on, I became certain I hadn't heard half of Gummie's tales.

I didn't go to college at all the next year. Jack died a few months after Gummie, and it gave me permission to wander. I put essential belongings—some books, notebooks, a half dozen pens, a handful of clothing—in a backpack and hitchhiked and railed and bussed around Europe, sending postcards home to Gramma and Mom and Annie, who'd entered Duke University. I stood at Marx's grave in Highgate Cemetery in north London—and thought of Gummie and wept. I went to Berlin to see the Wall—and thought of Gummie and wept again. I went to all the places and more, where Gummie'd been sixty-plus years before.

Gramma and Mom and Gloria met me in Paris during Christmas break, and we flew to Israel—a place Gummie had always wanted to see. When they returned stateside, I went on to east Africa and India—thinking about all Gummie'd taught me about colonialism—and then felt like a bloody colonialist myself by having a Singapore sling on the terrace of the Raffles Hotel in Singapore, remembering Somerset Maugham. And Gummie. Back in the U.S., Annie joined me in Los Angeles, and we traveled up the West Coast—especially exploring San Francisco, where Gummie had visited in the early days of the century.

I spent the year thinking about her and Guppie and the Farmers' Alliance and suffrage, temperance and the Wobblies and birth control, the ERA and the Non-Partisan League and the Farmer-Labor Party, labor-agrarian activism and socialism and communism, pacificism and the McCarthy witch hunts and Gummie's faith in people and systems, her tireless activism. And most of all, I tried to remember every word she'd ever imparted to me, remember it and write it down—preserving those times and words, preserving her.

31

One of Those Jordan Girls

After I came home, I enrolled at the University of Minnesota. "Yes, Gummie," I kept talking to her, "I *could* go anywhere, I suppose, but you know what? I want to go here. To my own university in my own state. Close to home, close to Mom and Gramma." I spent the summer before classes commenced at home, thinking a lot about Gummie's stories, about writing a book. My version of Gummie. It was clear to me, Gramma would write Gummie's life differently than I would. So would anybody, I supposed, but my story was the only one I could tell.

While I was traveling, Gloria had moved in with Mom and Gramma. Ostensibly, she was renting a room in our big old house, but I suspected most of Riverton knew what was what. In their usual Midwestern style, however, they simply ignored it. For themselves, Mom and Gloria weren't exactly throwing caution to the winds. After all these years, they just wanted to be together.

Gummie's death reminded them of the transitory nature of our lives. And besides, the house was big and empty without me and Gummie in it.

Gramma surprised everyone by keeping the paper going. She'd been quietly helping out a lot near Gummie's death, much more than any of us had realized. When it came time to vote for a new publisher and managing editor, Gramma insisted they make the city editor the managing editor—the one with the most responsibility and power. The workers readily agreed with her and conveyed the position of publisher on Gramma herself. This job was not particularly demanding, only requiring her presence a day or two a week. I was relieved that I didn't have to be Gummie's heir, happy *The Prairie Voice* was moving in the direction it should move—into others' hands.

Gramma happily filled the rest of her days with her scout troop while creating a program at the high school to teach girls to work with tools—to fix and build things. One night, she knocked lightly on my bedroom door. "Maddie?"

"Come on in, Gramma." I was sitting cross-legged on my bed, just like a kid, with notes spread all around me. I was perusing my diaries and journals, wondering how I might structure a book that would contain a life as big as Gummie's.

Gramma stood in the doorway, a faint smile playing across her lips. "It's nice to have you home, honey." I smiled back. She was a long way from death, I figured, with this family's propensity toward longevity; still, I felt keenly aware of how I was to lose everyone I loved.

She handed me an envelope with my name written on it. The handwriting was Gummie's characteristic scrawl and the familiarity of it created a scrabble of pain in my throat and a stab of tears in my eyes. I looked at Gramma curiously, whose own eyes were noticeably damp.

"Mom gave it to me before she died." She stopped to dab at her eyes and swallow convulsively. "Told me to give it to you when you were all done with college. I don't know why she wanted me to wait that long, but I decided this was long enough. I would've given it to you even sooner, but you know Mom. I'm sure that old bat would've found a way to make my life miserable—even though she didn't believe in any afterlife—if I didn't follow her instructions precisely." A tentative smile touched her lips, and I snorted. "Maddie. Sometimes you sound just like her." Then, after a pause, she added, "I guess she'll get me now."

I smiled again, clutching the envelope to my chest, and said, "Thank you." Gramma patted me on the shoulder, leaving me alone with my gummie.

Dear Maddie, the letter began, and I had to stop to cry, just over those opening words. *She wrote this before she died,* I thought to myself, *she was alive and herself and thinking of her death and me after that death.* I had to wait a long time before I was able to continue reading the letter. I even considered putting it away and reading it in a year or two. Somehow I knew, when I finished reading this letter, Gummie would be truly dead. Even though she'd died almost two years before, this was her last message to me. I saw again, in my mind's eye, her turning toward me that last day, and saying, "I swear, you're getting more and more like your mother every day," and then that slow-motion deflation of her body. I cried some more.

> *Dear Maddie,*
>
> *I know you'll be feeling sad when you read this letter as I'll be gone. I'm sad, too, thinking about it. I've been blessed many times over by the good people in my life—my parents, my sisters yes, even that silly Pansy, Hubert, Hester, Jordie, Jane, you, my*

dear friends, and loyal colleagues. So many, many good people. Take care, Maddie, to surround yourself with good people. Goodness is much underrated in this society. It isn't a very sophisticated concept, I know. Believe me: it will make you happy all the days of your life.

There are things you want to know. I know this. Most of your life, I've tried to tell you the things you wanted to know. Some things you will not know; they're just meant to be a mystery.

I supposed she was talking about her sex life. Damn! She probably knew, all along, what I'd been trying to uncover, even though I thought I'd been so careful.

There's a difference, however, between mystery—usually a matter of privacy, and secrets—usually a matter of shame. I don't wish to take secrets with me, to compound or encourage shame in any way. We all live imperfect lives, making mistakes. Feeling shame and keeping quiet about our mistakes—or others'—does more harm than good. It exaggerates the importance of mistakes, both in our minds but also in the lives of others around us.

So, I want to tell you the only secrets I've kept all these years. You can share them with your mother and grandmother, but I wanted to impart this information to you first. Partly because you're the promise of the future now and partly because you were always so willing to listen to an old lady's stories, ever since you were such a tiny little girl.

As you know, my sister Dolly loved my husband,

Hubert, before I even met him. No one told me, and I would never have gotten involved with him —let alone marry him—had I known. She also loved me and knew I wouldn't knowingly hurt her, and therefore tried to hold no grudge against either of us, but she was unhappy. For some people, there's only one great love in their life. Hubert was that for Dolly.

He fell in love with me, and we got married. She moved away, to go to medical school but also to protect herself from the pain of having to daily witness our happiness. After some years out East, she moved back to Minnesota. It was probably about 1917. She lived and worked in the Cities and came to visit us on occasion. It was wonderful to have her nearby again, and all seemed fine between us.

Nineteen-seventeen. Why did that year ring a bell? I let the question simmer in my mind momentarily. Communism. That was the period of difficulty between Guppie and Gummie, the time they fought so much about communism. I felt a prickling sensation at the edge of my mind.

In 1919, she moved away from Minnesota again, giving none of us any warning or notice.

Or any opportunity to dissuade her. One day, she was simply gone, and then she wrote from Missouri and told us she'd married a man none of us had ever heard of.

Aha! I thought. The mysterious husband!

I was beside myself. I could not believe she would do all this without telling us about him, consulting us, even letting us meet him.

She wrote that he was a doctor, too, and had gotten a job rather suddenly in a hospital in St. Louis. He had to move at once, so they went together. It sounded, in a way, very romantic, but I knew Dolly was just about the most pragmatic person alive, so I wondered what it was really all about.

I especially wondered whether she had gotten pregnant, but it was hard for me to believe she wouldn't have told me if that were the case. She knew I didn't much care whether women were married or not when they had babies, and I did truly believe in what we called "free love" in those days. She was, after all, nearly forty, and perfectly mature and independent enough to make her own decisions.

I stopped reading and gazed out the window, replaying conversations Gummie and I'd had throughout my life. I didn't believe that story, any longer, about Gummie and Guppie never having had sex. I was never to know for sure; it remained one of those *little mysteries* of hers, but when I put the pieces of all our conversations together, including her adamant belief in free love, I just didn't believe it. In fact, I felt pretty certain Guppie was probably not the only man with whom she'd had sex. She was a thoroughly modern woman, in every possible way.

We heard from her once in a while, but the notes were brief and uninformative. I worried a lot and asked her if I couldn't come down to visit her, but she answered that letter immediately—telling me she'd love to have me come visit, but she was busy looking for a job and getting settled and would let me know when it would be more convenient, which she never did.

The year after Dolly so precipitously disappeared, Hubert and I adopted Jordie. He was, as you know, a great surprise rather late in our lives and an inde-scribable joy to us all. Nearly a year later, Dolly came back to Minneapolis. Alone. She was lucky to be reinstated at the hospital in Minneapolis and not much inclined to talk about the mystery hus-band who was no longer in her life.

"He beat me, Iris" she once told me, "and I had to get rid of him." I rather liked that phrase, as it sounded like she'd killed him, even though I knew that was not what she meant. I didn't press her much about this absent husband because, by then, I was pretty sure I knew what had happened. I was never meant to know, but some things just worm their way out.

You see, Maddie, Jordie was Dolly and Hubert's baby.

So much for that theory about Guppie not being able to "get it up" because of disuse. In spite of my sarcastic aside, however, I felt a jolt of surprise at this statement. And dismay. How terrible that must've been for Gummie!

I had already suspected, before Dolly returned, that Jordie was truly Hubert's child. I don't know why I started to think this, exactly. I just intuited it, I guess. Mostly, I would watch Hubert with that baby, and it seemed obvious to me Jordie was his flesh and blood, partly because there was some resemblance but mostly because Hubert doted on this child in a way he never had on Hester. I don't mean to say he didn't adore Hester, which he clearly did. There was just something . . . different. At first, I thought it was because Jordie was a boy, and men often are different with their sons, but . . . I don't know. The thought of Jordie being his child kept niggling away at me.

I hadn't decided, for sure, whether I was going to say something to Hubert when Dolly came home. Then, all the pieces kind of fell together. Dolly had been a good auntie to all of her nieces and nephews, but with Jordie—it was completely different. She went all soft and gooey around him and, at the same time, sort of lit up. It didn't take long for me to intercept a quick glance between Dolly and Hubert from time to time, usually over Jordie's head as one or the other held him or as he displayed his unusual charm for us.

I know you well enough, Maddie, to know that at this point, you'd be asking me—if you could— didn't this hurt you, Gummie? Didn't it make you wild with anger? With jealousy and suspicion?

I smiled because I certainly was entertaining just such questions.

The honest answer to those questions is both yes and no. I did feel hurt and sad and mad and exceedingly suspicious. At first.

"How could they?" I wondered, and—"are they

still?" It was a very difficult time. I was devastated, more than I ever would've admitted at that time, but I buried myself in my work—as I often do, you know. I mulled it over and over. I watched them. I thought about whether or not I'd confront them directly. "What did I want?" I would ask myself, "and how likely was I to get it?"

By then, I think I'd pieced together what must've happened. I was sure there'd never been a husband. I think Dolly made him up so that she could go off and have the baby. It didn't matter if I thought free love was fine, she wasn't quite so "modern" as I was, and it was a very difficult thing for a woman to have a baby and not be married. Besides which, she knew it was my *husband's baby and was afraid I'd figure it out. My guess is she intended to return with the baby sans husband, but Jordie was born with his serious medical problems, and she wanted him to have good care and also a loving family to help him through the surgeries and all.*

So, I think she placed him in that orphanage where Violet worked on purpose. I didn't know if she had asked the staff there to call Violet's attention to this baby or if she had taken Violet into her confidence, but at any rate, Violet told me about this adorable, needy baby boy. I could see perfectly well that Hubert wanted this child for some reason, and voilá—we ended up with their baby.

I agonized a great deal over their affair and what I meant to do about it. I did remind myself, in cooler moments, I had "stolen" Hubert away from Dolly in the first place, even if I didn't know I was

doing it. I also reminded myself I was not, always,
the perfect wife.

Huh. Did that mean she was not perfect because she was always at work and not at all domestic, or did it mean, as I suspected, she'd had a fling or two of her own? More mystery, I guess.

I became quite certain, by observing the two of
them and knowing both of them well, that the
affair was no longer being carried on. Dolly had
gotten religion. She attended the Unitarian
Church—where she assured me "you could believe
anything at all"—my response being, "So why don't
you just stay home and believe anything at all?" She
wasn't particularly interested in my opinion but did
laugh at my joke. I always thought Dolly tortured
herself over Jordie, maybe she even believed some
silly thing like his infirmities were a kind of
judgement on her for getting involved with her
sister's husband.

In the end, I finally decided to leave it all alone.
I felt bad, naturally, about Hubert having an affair
with Dolly, but—after all—I was not your run-of-
the-mill wife and, although I loved him dearly, I
did not adore *him. Adoration was not my style.*
Dolly clearly did adore him, and I could under-
stand how attractive that must've been to a man
who was in his middle years with an extremely dis-
tracted wife and a job with ample frustrations.
Dolly, of course, was not such a twit that I would
ever defame her by saying something stupid like "she
couldn't help herself," but, in some ways, she prob-

ably couldn't.

Anyway, they made a mistake. That was that. We all make mistakes, some worse than others, but it's the result of living a life. I decided to do nothing, to let things go along as they were. Jordie was a delight and certainly my own little boy as much as theirs. Hubert and I were not unhappy. I had no doubt Dolly had thoroughly punished herself for her choices.

It might have just been fine if Jordie hadn't died. For Dolly, this was the final blow, the final judgement, I think. She was inconsolable, felt she should have been able to save him, even though he was dead before she reached him that day, was morose and withdrawn for months after his death. I was only peripherally aware of all this because I was dealing with my own grief—and Hubert's.

About a year after Jordie's death, Dolly killed herself. I will spare you the gory details—

Even at nineteen, I kind of wanted those "gory details" but also felt appropriately uncomfortable at my voyeurism.

—sufficient to say it was horrifying for all of us. Your grandmother and I had had a spat, after Jordie's death and her hasty marriage to that odious man, and didn't talk to each other for a while. Consequently, she never knew the details of Dolly's death.

I don't know how Hubert and I held up, both of us grieving our child and now both of us grieving our beloved Dolly. At first, I felt angry toward him,

angry he didn't realize she was so close to hopeless-
ness. He should've known and saved her from her-
self. Eventually, I realized I was angry at myself for
those things. Jordie's and Dolly's deaths left a big
hole in my heart. It took a long time to heal. For
Hubert, too.

We did, finally, talk it all over. He had no idea
I'd known all those years. I had been mostly right in
my conjectures—there had been no husband; Dolly
had been overwhelmed when Jordie was born with
such large problems; they took a risk that I'd be
intrigued enough when I heard about this unfortu-
nate baby to want to take him. No one else ever
knew. In the end, Hubert and I drew closer than
ever.

I wonder, now that I'm so close to death myself,
why I never told you all these details. I wonder how
much conventional thinking made its mark on
me—even though I always thought I'd successfully
avoided it my entire life—that I would keep these
secrets from everyone close to me. Why would I act
as if it were too shameful to tell? The more I think
about it, though, the more I'm convinced my secre-
tiveness was more about avoidance than shame.
Dolly's and Jordie's deaths were the most painful
events of my life, and I have always been loathe to
relive that agony. I don't know that I now think
that was a good decision for my life; it's just the one
I made.

So there you have it, Maddie. You know it all,
now. Not such a big deal, perhaps, fifty-some years
later, but it was a big deal when it happened. As

life always is. It's important, Maddie, that you live
a conscious life, making careful choices and deliber-
ately determining the difference between mysteries
and secrets. One is the spice in one's life, the other is
deadly, in more ways than one.

I love you, Maddie, and remember: death does
nothing to diminish love. It's permanent. Forever.

Love, Gummie

I read and reread this letter many times, tears flowing like a spring river swollen from melting snows, until I finally buried my head in my pillow and howled as I had the day on the street when Gummie died. Even through the sobbing and wailing and wrenching pain and loss, I knew how lucky I was to receive the gifts this remarkable woman had given me: an extraordinary grandmother and mother, the clarity and confidence to know I could be whoever I wanted to be, go wherever I wanted to go, make whatever choices needed to create a happy and productive life. I knew—beyond imaginable measure—how blessed I was to be one of those Jordan girls.

Reader's Guide

Those Jordan Girls
Joan M. Drury

Spinsters
Ink

Questions for Discussion

1. Why did Hester disapprove of her mother? Have you ever disapproved of your own mother? If so, why?

2. Do you believe, as Hester did, that women should refrain from having children without the "benefit of marriage?" Why or why not?

3. Gummie was an uncommon woman. What characteristics do you think make a woman uncommon? Do you consider yourself to be an uncommon woman? If so, how?

4. Gummie states she didn't get an education to use it, but rather because she wanted it. Is there a difference? If you furthered your education after high school, what influenced your decision to do so?

5. Throughout the novel, Gummie shares a number of important "lessons" with Maddie. Which do you feel is the most enlightening or important? And why?

6. Did you have an older relative like Gummie—or some other person—with whom you spent a great deal of time talking and who taught you lessons you didn't learn elsewhere? What did you learn?

7. Gummie felt the word "sin" was problematic because its meaning is so arbitrary. How do you define it?

8. The march in Alabama exposed Maddie to something she'd never have learned in a classroom. Have you ever taken place in such an event? If yes, what did you learn? If you have children or intend to have them, would you take them to similar events?

9. Gummie expressed that Communism and Christianity have a great deal in common. Do you agree or disagree? Explain.

10. Gummie argues that "oppression doesn't just happen to some of us . . . it happens to all of us." What do you think?

A conversation with
Joan M. Drury

Before writing Those Jordan Girls, *you wrote three acclaimed mystery novels*—The Other Side of Silence, Silent Words, *and* Closed in Silence. *Why mysteries? And why did you change genres?*

I wrote mysteries because I love reading mysteries. I enjoy working on the "puzzle" of a mystery and the subsequent orderliness. I believe mysteries are so popular with women because we crave justice that doesn't much exist otherwise for us. And mysteries generally reach a large audience, a readership I want to touch. All good novels have a "mystery" in them so writing *Those Jordan Girls* wasn't that different from writing a mystery novel, except of course, I wasn't constricted at all by a "formula" of any sort. Sometimes, writers get "caught" in a genre and never find their way out (some don't want to, naturally). I didn't want that to happen to me. *I write*—not just mysteries or not just books. I just write. And whatever story comes to me, I have to go with it. The next book I have planned is also not a mystery, but I fully expect to return to mystery-writing eventually.

Those Jordan Girls is a character-rich novel. Did you begin with characters in mind? Do you have any sense where these specific characters came from?

I *always* begin with character. The seed of this novel was the stories I'd heard as a child about my dead grandmother. They tickled my imagination, and I knew—for years—that I would someday have to find a way to write about her. That was the beginning. The other characters just seemed to join me as I began to write Gummie's story. I thought I knew them pretty well before I began writing, but they kept surprising me, all the way through the creation of this book. It was a fabulous experience.

What do you mean when you say they kept surprising you?

I kept finding out new things about them, things I hadn't planned and yet I knew, immediately, were true. I would begin a chapter with a clear idea of what I was going to do, and I would suddenly veer off into a whole new situation, feeling as if I were being led by one or another of my characters. I had no control whatsoever. After a while, as this story just poured out of my fingers into my computer, I felt as if I was merely the scrivener.

So these characters are very real to you?

Oh absolutely! I never thought of them as an extension of me, the way you sometimes do with characters. It was—I don't know how to explain this without sounding like I've gone "around the bend" —like they truly existed and were dictating the story to me. They were so real, I played Scrabble with them! And sometimes one or the other even beat me!

And this hadn't happened to you before?

No, it had. Just not quite as extensively as it did with this book.

Do you have an explanation or theory for why this happens?

Sure. I think that each time you write something and it gets published and is well-received, your confidence level rises. The more confident you become, the more you trust your ability to write. And the more trusting you are, the more you open up to that creative river that runs around and through all of us. Stories begin to flow like they're tumbling over a waterfall.

Some readers may think that Iris Jordan is not likely to have existed in her time. How would you respond to such a criticism?

Independent women who refused to live within the confines of societal expectations have lived in every time throughout history. We have knowledge of women who were running their own businesses and writing books and studying the stars or chemistry or the law or mathematics and refusing marriage thousands of years, B.C. There have always been and always will be women like Iris Jordan. Unfortunately, they are too often not included in the scrutiny of novelists or historians or any of the "gate-keepers"— those individuals who record the so-called truths of human lives. So, did she exist in her time? Absolutely—and thousands of others like her. Was she rare? Probably, but "rare" doesn't mean there were only two or three like her.

Some critics seem to think Iris was portrayed as a little "too perfect." Do you agree?

No, not at all. I think that an individual who finds Iris too perfect may be feeling uncomfortable in comparison to her. I see Gummie as a role model for us, a woman some of us might want to be "when we grow up." Or grow old, at any rate. One reader told me she didn't like Iris because she was "too unfailingly principled." I thought that a remarkable observation. What is our world coming to when unfailing principles are viewed as negative? I also think a reader who finds Gummie "too perfect" is, perhaps, not reading carefully. It seemed clear to me that, although Gummie was a pretty terrific grandmother and great-grandmother, she was not all that a daughter might want in a mother. She was clearly not "there," physically and emotionally, as much as her daughter needed, and she also expected too much of her daughter, wanting her to be just like her. What I do think is that Gummie herself pretty much thought she was perfect. And that, naturally, is a flaw in and of itself.

What do you think is the main theme of your book?

Oh . . . that's hard to answer, isn't it? If I had to choose one dominant theme, I guess it would have to be goodness. Even with her flaws, Gummie embodied integrity, honesty, caring, dedication, ethics. Her education of Maddie was all about morality, a word completely missing in the book but constantly present, nonetheless.

Why did you write this book?

There are so many answers to this question. I wrote it because I believe in goodness and the importance of it and think there's an odd paucity of "morality" in art these days. I wrote it to counteract stereotypes about old women—this ridiculous attitude that they are all doddering, old fools (as opposed to old men who are, usually, our presidents and judges and legislators). I wrote it to remind people that tough, intelligent, capable women didn't just arise in the past decade or two but have always existed. I wrote it to display, to some degree, the progressive politics that have shaped Minnesota politics. I wrote it to also counteract stereotypes about small towns and the people who live in them. There were, in the nineteenth century and the beginning of the twentieth century, many progressive and socialist newspapers scattered across the countryside in small towns in Minnesota and in other states, often run by women, but who knows about this now? And I wrote it because I wanted a venue for the stories I'd heard about my own grandmother (dead before I was born). Although this isn't her life and Gummie is *definitely* not my grandmother, many of the stories I heard have found their way into this book—in some form or other.

Did this book require a lot of research?

Oh yes, more than I've ever done. I had a couple of assistants who tracked down specific pieces of information for me, but I had to read many volumes—of the history of progressive politics, agricultural and labor activism, socialism, rural living—in order to capture Gummie's character accurately but also to reproduce times and places. Most of what I learned never found its way into the book. I might read five books about any given subject, and then in *Those Jordan Girls*, there would be no more than a paragraph or two. Sometimes only a line or two. It was a fascinating task where I learned so much more than I thought I would. And sometimes it was frustrating because I wanted to put more in the book. I had to keep reminding myself that the politics and activism were the backdrops of this book, not the main issues.

What do you want in the books you read?

I want characters I love and care about—and at least one I can relate to. I want a good story, one that makes me keep turning the pages. I want good writing—the kind that is both invisible (so good you just keep reading without thinking about it) and wonderfully visible in its fresh and exciting use of language. I want a balance of "good" and "bad,"—yin and yang, if you will. I have no use for an unrelievedly negative story nor do I appreciate the Pollyanna-approach either. Good and bad things happen to people who are both good and bad—that's real life. I want hope, not necessarily a "happy ending" always, but definitely hope—and growth. I want to learn something new or be prodded toward seeing something from a different perspective.

Does Those Jordan Girls *meet your requirements for an enjoyable book?*

I hope so. I think writers write the books they want to read. At least, I certainly do. And this book proves that in every way.

Photo by Ann K. Marsden

Joan M. Drury

I live in a house perched on unyielding rock overlooking the endless surprises of Lake Superior. I am surrounded by seven acres of dense woods full of mountain ash, spruce, cedar, birch, maple, and other trees as well as a goodly number of wild creatures. A couple of these acres are dedicated to flowers. In this place of astonishing beauty and serenity, I walk from my house teetering on the edge of the limitless horizon of this inland sea through the garden and forest, alongside a creek to a gingerbread-y "summer house"—my writing studio—cozied up to the edge of a pond. Spinsters Ink "North" resides in an office back at my main house. Here the computer and fax and copier and phone machine hum away without disturbing my writing. My days are split between these two places, my fabulous coworkers at the main Spinsters office in Duluth (ninety miles away) making it possible for me to oversee operations from this distance. Norcroft: A Writing Retreat for Women is located next door to my property, where a capable Managing Director maintains the daily operations. I am an activist; all my work—both paid and unpaid—is focussed on feminist social change. I am blessed and fortunate to share this idyllic existence with my sons, daughter, granddaughters, and dearly beloved family of friends, scattered both near and far.

———

Besides writing, Joan Drury is the owner and publisher of Spinsters Ink, executive director of Norcroft: A Writing Retreat for Women, and president of Drury Enterprises. Her Tyler Jones mystery trilogy consists of *The Other Side of Silence* (1993)—a Minnesota Book Award finalist—and *Silent Words* (1996)—a Mystery Writers of America's Edgar Allen Poe Award finalist, a Small Press Book Award finalist, a Midwest Independent Publishers Association's Midwest Book Achievement Award merit winner, a Minnesota Book Award winner, a Northeastern Minnesota Book Award winner, and a Publishers Marketing Association's Benjamin Franklin Award winner—and *Closed in Silence* (1998)—a Minnesota Book Award finalist, a Publishers Marketing Association's Benjamin Franklin Award finalist, and, a Midwest Independent Publishers Association's Midwest Book Achievement Award merit winner. In 1999, she was awarded "The Publisher Service Award" from the Lambda Literary Foundation.

Other Novels Available from Spinsters Ink

The Activist's Daughter, Ellyn Bache. $10.95

Amazon Story Bones, Ellen Frye. $10.95

As You Desire, Madeline Moore. $9.95

Child of Her People, Anne Cameron. $10.95

Dreaming Under a Ton of Lizards, Marian Michener. $12.00

Fat Girl Dances with Rocks, Susan Stinson. $10.95

Finding Grace, Mary Saracino. $12.00

A Gift of the Emperor, Therese Park. $10.95

Give Me Your Good Ear, 2nd ed., Maureen Brady. $9.95

Goodness, Martha Roth. $10.95

The Journey, Anne Cameron. $9.95

Living at Night, Mariana Romo-Carmona. $10.95

Martha Moody, Susan Stinson. $10.95

Modern Daughters and the Outlaw West, Melissa Kwasny. . . .$9.95

No Matter What, Mary Saracino. $9.95

Sugar Land, Joni Rodgers. $12.00

Trees Call for What They Need, Melissa Kwasny. $9.95

Turnip Blues, Helen Campbell. $12.00

Vital Ties, Karen Kringle. $10.95

A Woman Determined, Jean Swallow. $12.00

Spinsters Ink was founded in 1978 to produce vital books for diverse women's communities. In 1986, we merged with Aunt Lute Books to become Spinsters/Aunt Lute. In 1990, the Aunt Lute Foundation became an independent nonprofit publishing program. In 1992, Spinsters moved to Minnesota.

Spinsters Ink publishes novels and nonfiction works that deal with significant issues in women's lives from a feminist perspective: books that not only name these crucial issues, but—more important—encourage change and growth. We are committed to publishing works by women writing from the periphery: fat women, Jewish women, lesbians, old women, poor women, rural women, women examining classism, women of color, women with disabilities, women who are writing books that help make the best in our lives more possible.

Spinsters titles are available from your local bookseller or by mail order through Spinsters Ink. A free catalog is available upon request. Please include $2.00 shipping for the first title ordered and 50¢ for every title thereafter. Visa and Mastercard are accepted.

Spinsters Ink
32 E. First St., #330
Duluth, MN 55802-2002
USA

(phone) 218-727-3222   (fax) 218-727-3119
(e-mail) spinster@spinsters-ink.com
(website) http://www.spinsters-ink.com